Karl
to a good friend
& a fellow legislative
junkie
Tim Hodson

Fair, Balanced... and Dead

A Novel

By Steve Swatt

Order this book online at www.trafford.com
or email orders@trafford.com

Most Trafford titles are also available at major online book retailers.

Cover design: Jeanie Fan

Note for Librarians: A cataloguing record for this book is available from Library and Archives Canada at www.collectionscanada.ca/amicus/index-e.html

Printed in Victoria, BC, Canada.

ISBN: 978-1-4251-8480-3

Trafford rev. 9/9/09

www.trafford.com

North America & international
toll-free: 1 888 232 4444 (USA & Canada)
phone: 250 383 6864 • fax: 812 355 4082

For Susie, who pushed to make this happen

Acknowledgements

Grateful appreciation is offered to friends and colleagues who made helpful suggestions to improve *Fair, Balanced...and Dead.* They include, but are not limited to: Sherri Boone, Scott Bowler, Kent Brudney, Ashley Clarke, Ross Johnson, Barbara O'Connor, Tom Griffin and Dan Walters. Special thanks goes to Susie Swatt, my in-house editor. She kept urging me to continue when I was inclined to throw in the towel and play golf.

Prologue

At first, all he could sense were unfamiliar female voices. It was like he was trying to come out of a deep sleep but wasn't yet ready to wake up. He tried to open his eyelids but failed. He couldn't make out the words being spoken, but within seconds he recognized that unmistakable, antiseptic smell. Of course, he realized. I'm in a hospital.

"He looks different," one voice said. "I can't wait to tell my mom that we saw a real celebrity," another said.

Jack Summerland was slowly coming out of a drug-induced slumber. He gingerly moved his head and saw the early morning sun force its way through a crack in the window shade, casting a slight shadow in the room. Jack's head pounded and whenever he moved, he was aware of bruises and aches throughout his body.

"Good morning, Mr. Summerland. Do you know where you are?"

Jack tried to talk but his throat was terribly dry and nothing came out.

"You're at the UC Davis Medical Center," a pretty 30-ish nurse said as she pushed a straw into his mouth. "You were brought in late yesterday afternoon after a car crash at the Capitol building. Nothing's broken. You're probably going to be back to normal in a couple of days."

The nurse smiled. "You know, you're the second TV guy we've had in here in the past month. That weather guy, what's his name? Oh, yeah, Bernard something, he was in here for some tests a couple of weeks ago."

The nurse realized she was talking too much, so she quickly took the straw out of his mouth and placed the cup of water on a table next to his bed. She waited for her patient to say something.

Instead, Jack closed his eyes, exhaled and leaned back on his pillow.

Slowly, it came back to him. The meeting. The gunshots. The chase. The screeching tires. The crash.

He sat up with a start. "I've got to get out of here," he croaked. "I'm on deadline."

One

Two Weeks Earlier...

It was one of those evenings that threatened yet again to drive Jack Summerland into retirement. Or at least into an active career-changing mode.

In a driving rainstorm, uncharacteristic for Sacramento in early May, Jack stood on the soggy grass outside the California State Capitol. He had worn his new $65 loafers, his first new pair of shoes in six years, and his feet were soaked. Water dripped down his cheeks.

A steady stream of legislative employees trickled past Jack on their way to their cars. "Hey, Jack. Got a big one tonight?" asked a Senate Education Committee consultant. Jack recognized the man but temporarily was at a loss to remember his name.

"Not tonight," Jack said. "Just run-of-the-mill BS."

Jack watched the beginning of KBLT's six o'clock news on a small black-and-white television monitor propped on a box in front of him. In his earphone, he could hear the reporter intone about Northern California's freak rainstorm catching residents by surprise.

"We're on in seven minutes," someone shouted from the large TV truck parked on Tenth Street.

"Terrific," Jack muttered sarcastically to himself. "I get pneumonia in the name of ratings. Just terrific."

Despite the dreadful conditions, a small knot of spectators — obviously with no home life to speak of — gathered outside the garish purple oversized van with the lettering "Action News 4 — We Take You There" printed in lime green on the side panel.

Jack always felt a little uncomfortable doing live reports outside the studio. Spectators made him feel he was on display, and sometimes they would go to extraordinary lengths to get their faces broadcast from Lake Tahoe to the Bay Area.

Once, a college student — on a dare, no doubt — dropped his pants and mooned the camera during one of Jack's live shots.

A middle-aged woman wearing a yellow rain slicker sloshed up to the van and pressed her face to the window in back. "Is Conrad in there?" she asked no one in particular.

For Chrissakes, Jack thought, shaking his head. What people won't do just to get a look at that pompous ass.

Conrad Dalton, the station's lead anchor, was an institution in town, having anchored at the capital city's top-rated news station for 23 years. His colleagues and rival newscasters knew him for what he was — a newsreader who wouldn't know how to report a legitimate news story if it bit him in the butt.

Dalton was, in journalism vernacular, a "pretty face." After earning his Associate of Arts degree at a Texas community college, Dalton headed west and landed a job as a disc jockey playing rock and roll at a small station in Pocatello, Idaho. He quickly became a major celebrity in town. It didn't hurt that Dalton had Hollywood good looks and a smile that could melt an iceberg. After a local television station tripled his salary and made him a weeknight anchorman, Dalton was on his way to stardom. After Pocatello, there was Reno, then Fresno, then Sacramento—a top twenty media market and for many decades a center of serious broadcast journalism.

The station rarely let Dalton out of the studio. He was a reader, not a reporter. Sacramento journalists loved to tell the story – apocryphal, to be sure, but believable – about the time that Channel 4 sent Dalton to San Francisco to interview the vice president. He needed an entourage. Besides Dalton, the station sent a news photographer, a news producer to help write the story, a staff still photographer to take promotional shots of Dalton interviewing the vice president, and – the story went – a news intern to show Dalton how to get home once the interview was over. Rumors had circulated years earlier that Dalton had actually grayed his temples before every newscast so he'd appear older and more authoritative.

And then there was the time the station sent Dalton to Washington, D.C., to cover the inauguration of President George W. Bush. Dalton let his producer do all the work, while he pranced around town in a new $500 trench coat, looking every bit the iconic correspondent. At a news event involving California political and business leaders, a reporter for a rival station noted Dalton's absence and asked the KBLT photographer about the whereabouts of the anchorman. The photographer deadpanned, "He's covering the inaugural from his hotel room."

Jack turned to the aging Dalton groupie. "No ma'am," he volunteered. "Conrad is back at the studio."

Clearly disappointed, the woman shot a glance at Summerland, shrugged, then walked off heading north on Tenth Street.

Jack didn't have the lead story that evening. Rain led the newscast. Rain almost always led the newscast, because viewers told researchers in focus groups they were most interested in the weather. And, of course, the titillating trifecta – celebrities, crime and sex. Politics usually ranked near the bottom, even in a government town like Sacramento.

Two reporters and the station's chief meteorologist exhausted every angle of the rain story, including pretty Doppler pictures of the storm's track and an interview with farmers who worried about their waterlogged crops. "Team coverage," they called it. Actually, a few raindrops gave the TV moguls a chance to show off their expensive hardware. Helicopters? Satellite trucks? That's old news. Everybody has a helicopter and satellite trucks these days. But not everyone has the Whopper Doppler 5000 Extreme, or some such gadget. Jack half expected the station's weatherman one day to blurt on the air, "Watch my forecast because my Doppler is bigger than theirs."

After the weather package, there was a story about a Hollywood actress getting into a fistfight with a heckler during a location shoot in town several hours earlier in the day. The station had actual video of the empty street where the fight had occurred, and an interview with a bystander who saw the actress take a swing. Big deal.

There was something about a bear terrorizing a rural community 60 miles away, complete with interviews with terrified residents. The bear remained at large. Residents were warned not to start shooting.

"Stand by," someone suddenly shouted from the truck.

"While Northern California farmers are bemoaning this late spring storm," Dalton told his viewers, "we're only getting a drizzle out of the governor's office concerning a replacement for the late Senator Bernie Edelstein. Our political reporter Jack Summerland is live with details. And it looks like the wet stuff is still coming down at the Capitol. Jack?"

For a split second, Jack seemed startled. What a blow-dried imbecile, he thought. Dalton had re-written his lead-in again, a half-assed attempt to make it cute. Why does everything have to tie in to the weather?

Jack stared into the camera lens, ignored Dalton's lead-in and updated viewers on the political story that a week earlier had rocked the U.S. Senate like a lightning bolt.

Summerland on camera

Governor Colin Frank today issued a brief statement indicating he is in no hurry to announce a replacement for the late senator. He said he's prepared to take a couple of weeks to fully vet likely candidates.

Video – Senator Edelstein montage

As you'll recall, last week only two hours before he was scheduled to chair a closed Senate Foreign Relations Committee hearing on the Middle East terror threat, veteran U.S. Senator Bernie Edelstein of California suffered a massive stroke and brain hemorrhage. The wily 71-year-old Democrat, who had served more than four terms in the Senate, was found in his plush office in the Russell Senate Office Building, slumped over a stack of classified documents from the Department of Homeland Security.

Video – George Washington University Hospital

Doctors kept Senator Edelstein heavily sedated as they performed three surgeries to relieve bleeding in the brain. After his third operation, surgeons gradually reduced the level of anesthetic, but the senator failed to regain consciousness or open his eyes. He responded to pain stimuli, but made no noticeable progress after that. He died three days later.

Video – U.S. Senate

Senator Edelstein's death has set in motion a seemingly crass, yet critical, set of political maneuverings designed to restore the Senate to its full 100-member complement. A great deal is at stake – control of the Senate, itself, which reflects the nation's political polarization. Fifty senators are Democrats; forty-nine senators are Republicans. Senate Democrats had anointed Edelstein the Foreign Relations chair and he was the nation's foremost political authority on international relations.

Video – Gov. Frank

With Edelstein's passing, the California Constitution gives Governor Frank, a Republican, sole authority to select his successor. No legislative confirmation is required, and the new senator would not have to stand before voters until next year's statewide election.

Summerland on camera

If Frank replaces Democrat Edelstein with a Republican, the Senate will be deadlocked and Republican Vice President Clifford Hollings will cast all tie-breaking votes.

That's why all eyes are on the governor. And he's not ready to show his hand. Back to you in the studio.

"Thanks for that live report," intoned Dalton in his perfect anchorman voice. "Coming up, after the break, Britney Gallagher continues her series on suburban prostitutes. Tonight, how you can tell if your neighbor is a slut."

Jack rolled his eyes and shook his head. He said nothing, concerned that his microphone might still be hot. When he was certain the station had gone to commercial break, Jack unhooked his mike and helped carry the television cables to the live truck.

Jack was at ground zero on the biggest political story in years. It's one thing for an aging senator to die in office, but quite another for his replacement to re-shape the political makeup of the entire Senate and help dictate the nation's political agenda for years to come.

And Jack was keenly aware of the political drama unfolding behind the scenes.

Modern California history suggested that Governor Frank needed to consider carefully all potential political ramifications before making his selection. Both political parties had been burned by unpopular choices.

In August 1964, Pierre Salinger, who had been President Kennedy's press secretary, was appointed by Democratic Governor Pat Brown to fill a Senate seat left vacant by the sudden death of Democrat Clair Engle. Salinger served less than five months and was defeated for election by one-time Hollywood song and dance man George Murphy, a Republican.

In January 1991, Republican Pete Wilson became governor of California and resigned his U.S. Senate seat. He appointed Republican State Senator John Seymour to replace him in the Senate. Like Salinger before him, Seymour flopped at the polls. Twenty-two months after his appointment to the Senate, Seymour was trounced by Democrat Dianne Feinstein.

In Sacramento, even while Senator Edelstein lay in a coma, the guessing game had begun. Who would Frank select? Would he tip the Senate scales to the Republicans? Pressure groups of all political stripes descended on Sacramento to try to influence Governor Frank's decision. Each day, news reporters and columnists speculated on potential candidates. One name stood above all the rest: Republican Assembly Speaker Johnny Callahan.

Two

Jack Summerland tossed the cable into the back seat of his photographer's nondescript white SUV. "Hey Ron, wanna grab some dinner and wait for the rain to let up?"

Before Ron Middleton could answer, Jack felt the familiar vibrating of his cell phone against his right hip. "Okay, I'll be right there," he said into the phone. "Yeah, I'll tell him."

"What's that all about?" Ron asked.

"I'm being summoned back to the station. Something about a breaking story they want me to work on."

"Tonight?" Ron asked.

"Yep. That's what they said."

"What about me?" Ron shot back.

"Sorry," Jack said. "They're freaked about the budget again. No overtime tonight."

The drive to the KBLT studios, straight down Tenth Street,

took less than five minutes. While Ron unloaded the camera gear into the garage, Jack swiped his card key through the security pad, heard the familiar click of the back door unlocking, then walked down a long hallway to the news director's office. He couldn't help but leave mud footprints all over the indoor-outdoor carpet.

"What's this all about?" Jack asked as he took a seat in Jimmy Johnson's cluttered office. Johnson was the station's news director, brought in from a highly successful station in Portland seven years ago to keep the ratings from slipping. For the most part, he had done a decent job.

"Let Monica give you the facts," Johnson said."

Jack braced himself. Production assistant Monica Carruthers, beautiful, blonde and perpetually tan, had all of eighteen months experience in the journalism business — if you consider that experience to be a brief stint as a writer for *Showbiz Weekly*. She had grown up in Beverly Hills with her thrice-divorced mother, who was one of those Paris Hilton-type celebrities. Mom, apparently, was famous but nobody knew why.

"I have a great scoop on Johnny Callahan," Monica said.

Jack seemed incredulous. "You have a scoop on the Assembly speaker?"

"Yeah. One of my Hollywood contacts is the PR guy for the *Starlight.*"

Jack raised his eyebrows and gave a quizzical look to Johnson. "The *Starlight?* You mean that crappy supermarket tabloid?"

"Yeah," Monica said. "I used to date this guy for awhile and it seems they're giving us a story about Callahan that they're going to run in a couple of days. They think the advance publicity we'll give the story will help boost their sales."

Again, Jack turned to Johnson. "Since when do we chase the tabloids?"

"Look, Jack," Johnson said. "It's a good story about a big political figure, and we're in the middle of sweeps month. I want you to do it for tonight's eleven o'clock show."

Monica outlined the story. "It seems the *Starlight* has proof that Callahan visited a prostitute in L.A.," she said.

Jack was pleading now. "Jimmy, this isn't a story for us. We're supposed to be a respectable news organization. And I'm supposed to cover public policy at the Capitol. This is..." Jack stammered, "...this is a bunch of crap. Callahan isn't even married. He's a widower, remember? Besides, he's a leading candidate for the U.S. Senate. He can get his pick of women. It makes no sense to connect him to a prostitute."

There was a second of silence. Johnson seemed to be pondering Jack's point.

"Another thing," Jack blurted. "There are others who hope to be appointed to the Senate. This could be nothing more than a dirty trick."

"The more reason we should follow this story all the way to the end," Johnson said. "I want something on the eleven o'clock show."

Jack had built a reputation as a reporter who did his homework and didn't take cheap shots. As often as possible, he followed the unwritten journalistic code to have two independent sources verify the facts before they are reported, and he felt uncomfortable covering a public figure's private life. But this was the all-important May sweeps when anything goes on television, when every nuance of the ratings is dissected and analyzed, and advertising rates are based on the results. Christ, he thought, my career has come to this?

Summerland hated this kind of story, dubbed a "chaser" in journalism lingo. And he despised reporting on the kinds of stories these supermarket tabloids peddle. But a job is a job, particularly when you have trouble matching income with expenses, thanks to a couple of ex-wives he continued to help support. At least his two children, both daughters from his first marriage, were grown and on their own.

Johnny Callahan had never been associated with even a hint of scandal before. He was the powerful Assembly speaker, a Republican with a golden future in national politics. Only in his mid-forties, Callahan was a shooting star from California's bastion of conservatism, Orange County.

Callahan had never lost an election, first winning a city council seat in fabulously wealthy Newport Beach at the age of 33, after brief but successful stints as an assistant district attorney and corporate lawyer. Six years later, Callahan parlayed his support from gun rights advocates and his tax-cutting fervor to win a seat on the county board of supervisors.

After several years dealing with garbage contracts, potholes and zoning changes, Callahan sought election to the state Assembly and won the Republican nomination in the 70th district against four opponents. Two of his rivals had spent many years in local politics. One, in fact, was the wealthy owner of a string of Southern California restaurants who had served eight years in the state Senate but sought the Assembly seat after being termed out of office.

Callahan easily defeated an inept Democrat with 74 percent of the vote. He had campaigned against tax increases, but that was a no-brainer. California was in the third year of a debilitating recession, and Democrats in Sacramento were trying re-fill the state treasury by ramming through an increase in income taxes on the state's wealthiest citizens, many of whom lived in multi-million dollar mansions in gated enclaves within a three-wood of California's high-rent Orange County beaches.

Johnny Callahan, however, had something the other candidates didn't have. Star quality. He had that all-important name identification, thanks to six years as a prosecutor of some of Orange County's most notorious criminals, a couple of years of high-profile corporate work, nine years of local politics, and four years of headlines in the sports sections of the *Orange County Register* and the *Los Angeles Times.* Johnny had been a three-year starting quarterback on the University of Southern California football team, leading the Trojans to an 11-1 record his junior year, including a 24-19 Rose Bowl victory over Michigan. His football career collapsed late in 1985, his senior season, when he blew out a knee in the UCLA game and never played again.

Johnny went from football hero to USC Law School and marriage to a Pasadena socialite. Little wonder that after Callahan's election to the Assembly, the *Register* selected him as "Orange County's Best and Brightest."

Tall, tan and fit, with just a whisper of gray hair at the temples, Callahan looked like he was sent from central casting to star in the latest Tarzan movie.

Besides being a rising political star, Callahan was one of the state's leading advocates for decency in the media. He had founded Californians for Decency, a conservative organization that raised funds and campaigned for increased scrutiny of radio and television. Starting with the Reagan administration's obsession with de-regulation, the Federal Communications Commission had become a toothless federal bureaucracy. Californians for Decency pressured the FCC and Congress to crack down on what it considered "the foul-mouthed, anti-family mass media."

Callahan was a constant interview subject on the cable talk shows, particularly Fox. After Janet Jackson exposed her right breast during a Super Bowl halftime show, Callahan even made the cover of *Newsweek*, under the headline, "Smut Crusader." Oprah Winfrey helped make him a known commodity nationwide.

Jack walked out of the back door and stood under an awning as the rain continued falling. He needed to decompress and compose himself after the run-in with his boss. He watched the heavy drops hit the parking lot pavement, pulled out his cell phone and hit #6 on his speed dial.

"Office of the Assembly speaker," a voice on the other end said.

"Hey, this is Jack Summerland of KBLT, is…" Before Jack

could finish his sentence, the voice on the line interrupted. "I'm sorry, I'm the only one here right now, and I'm not allowed to talk to the media."

"Can you tell me if the speaker is accessible tonight?"

"Again," she said, "I can't tell you anything."

Jack dialed the cell phone of Callahan's press secretary. No answer. He left a message. Now he was getting desperate. He was about to air a story – generated by a low-life tabloid, of all things – that could threaten a political career, but he had no independent confirmation or denial and no comment whatsoever from the story's subject. Journalism at its best, Jack thought, mockingly.

Jack thought for a few seconds, then dialed Karen Paulson. He knew this would be a tough call.

Jack's semi-girlfriend of two years, Karen, `just happened to work for Johnny Callahan as his scheduling secretary.

Jack knew there was a perception problem if he covered Callahan while he dated Karen. He was concerned that his credibility as a journalist would suffer. That's why the pair tried to keep their relationship quiet. But there are few secrets inside "the building," as everyone called the Capitol. It was common knowledge that the two were dating.

Karen understood Jack's concerns but tried to convince him that entangled relationships were nothing new at the Capitol. Reporters often dated – and at times married – legislative aides and public policy advocates. It came with the territory and no one, other than a few editors in ivory towers, seemed to care.

Outside the Capitol, particularly at Channel 4, their secret seemed safe.

Karen never interfered in Jack's work and never questioned his stories, and Jack never used Karen to get information for a story. Until tonight.

"Karen, I need some help on a story involving your boss."

"What story?" she asked. "Are you working on a story *to-*

night?"

Jack stammered. "Look, I'm not happy about this, but it's a story I've been ordered to do. It's pretty ugly, but you can help me shoot it down."

There was silence on the other end of the line.

"We've been tipped that the speaker has been hanging out with hookers. Specifically, April 28 in a downtown L.A. motel."

Jack knew she'd be angry. He was right. She hit the ceiling.

"Jack, you can't do this story," she fumed. "It could ruin his career, and it's a bunch of crap," she said indignantly. "I don't have my scheduling book with me but I'm sure he wasn't in L.A. that night. This is completely unfair."

"I don't disagree," he said apologetically. "I don't like it any more than you do. But if I turn down the story, someone else will be assigned to it, probably Thackeray. I know you don't want that hack doing a story on Callahan. At least I'll be fair to your boss."

After a three-second pause, Jack heard Karen exhale loudly. She responded, "What do you want from me?"

"I just need Callahan's home number. I've been trying to get something on the record in response but I'm getting blanked."

"You're crazy if you think I'm going to give you the speaker's home number. I'll lose my job. I'll give you Billy Galster's home number. Johnny's press secretary is the closest you're getting to Johnny tonight."

"Look," Jack said. "I feel bad about this, but I'm on deadline. I'll call you later."

Jack dialed the press secretary. "Billy, sorry to bother you at home at this hour but we need a comment on a story we're running tonight at eleven."

"What story?"

"We've been tipped that the speaker has seen some hookers. Specifically, two weeks ago in a downtown L.A. motel."

Galster exploded. "That is goddam ridiculous. You can't run that story. Where'd you get this shit?"

"I'm sorry, Billy, I have no choice in the matter."

Jack coaxed a few on-the-record comments from Galster, most of them peppered with four-letter words. Six minutes after they hung up, the speaker's angry chief of staff, Samuel Cockerill, called Jack to forcefully warn him against running the story.

"Billy just told me what you're up to. Johnny wasn't even in L.A. that night," Cockerill insisted.

"There's nothing I can do," Jack responded. "My boss is directing the coverage. I'll use your strong denial. And I'll be fair. No cheap shots."

Later that evening – leading the 11 p.m. newscast this time – Jack stood in the rain in front of the west steps of the Capitol and gave the *Starlight* the publicity it craved.

"A freak rainstorm hammers Northern California. We'll get to that in a moment, but new tonight at 11, sex and politics at the state Capitol. Our correspondent Jack Summerland has details. Jack?"

Jack finally had a lead story but was thoroughly embarrassed. Nonetheless, he did his job.

"Action News 4 has learned that the *Starlight* tabloid, in its next edition, will run an article accusing Assembly Speaker Johnny Callahan of cavorting with a Los Angeles prostitute."

Summerland detailed all the steamy facts, careful to pin everything on the *Starlight.* He wanted to distance himself as much as possible from the *Starlight* scoop. He commented on how the scandal, if true, could cut short such a promising political career.

Looking directly into the camera, Summerland concluded, "Callahan was unavailable for comment on the charges this evening, but a press spokesman said the charges are false and accused the *Starlight* and Channel 4 of 'gossip-mongering.' He said the speaker's office tomorrow will detail Callahan's activities at the time he is alleged to have been spending time with a prostitute.

"Until this is cleared up, Callahan's once bright political future will be clouded and uncertain. This is Jack Summerland reporting live from the Capitol."

Conrad Dalton shot back a carefully scripted question that Jack had forwarded before airtime. "Jack, Callahan is being mentioned as a possible U. S. Senate appointee. Couldn't this be a political trick by one of his opponents?"

"Well, Conrad, in the rough and tumble world of politics you always have to look at that possibility. A number of capitol observers tonight have speculated that's exactly what is happening here."

"Thanks for that report," beamed Dalton. "Stay dry."

What a bozo, Jack thought to himself. I've gotta get out of this business.

Three

Moments before midnight, Jack Summerland walked into his apartment and draped his drenched overcoat across a chair in the tiny kitchen. He slipped off his sodden shoes and soggy socks, poured himself a J&B on the rocks, flicked on the television and slumped into his soft and ancient sofa.

David Letterman was interviewing some actress, or singer, he had never heard of when his mind started to drift about his future in journalism.

Summerland desperately wanted to change careers, but he felt trapped. Once an investigative reporter for the *Kansas City Star* and *Sacramento Bee*, Jack felt television had more impact on the public than newspapers. He loved the immediacy of broadcast news. Channel 4's news director, at least the one who hired him 18 years ago, gave him a nice salary boost to become the station's star political reporter. Now 53, Summerland looked younger than his years, with wavy brown hair and only a few wisps of gray. At 6-feet-2, 215 pounds, with barely a hint of a middle-age paunch, Jack was an imposing figure at news events, often standing above the crowd and dominating a question- and- answer session. On camera, the first thing viewers noticed were his ice-blue eyes.

Although at the top of his game, Jack was burned out and cynical. He was old school, when reporters simply dealt with facts, not innuendo, when a politician's private life remained private unless it interfered with his job.

Over time, Jack hated what local television news had become — a collection of vacuous stories, endless crime reports and car chases. And, of course, the weather. But he was too old to change careers, he thought. And he needed the money television pays.

Jack recalled one of his favorite newspaper columns, written in the mid-'80s by journalist Hunter S. Thompson. "The TV business is uglier than most things," Thompson wrote. "It is normally perceived as some kind of cruel and shallow money trench through the heart of the journalism industry, a long plastic hallway where thieves and pimps run free and good men die like dogs, for no good reason."

Jack poured himself a second drink, glanced at his watch and thought for a second. He weighed the pros and cons of making his next phone call, then decided to go for it.

"Got a minute?" Jack asked. "I need someone to talk to. Okay?"

"Now might not be a good time," Karen said sternly. "I'm pretty angry at you for that bullshit story." Without giving Jack a chance to start talking, Karen continued. "You and I both know this doesn't pass the smell test. First of all, Johnny is so good looking he doesn't have to pay for sex. And second, it's not as if he's married and cheating on his wife. She died six years ago. Inoperable brain tumor, remember?"

"I know, I know," Jack said. "I'm sorry. It wasn't my choice.

Look, that's what I want to talk about. I just can't stand this business anymore. I need to vent."

Karen's voice rose. "You want to vent after you put that crap story on the air? You should have done your venting a little earlier, don't you think?"

Jack didn't want to do anything to jeopardize his relationship with Karen. After two failed marriages, he was gradually becoming convinced that he wanted to spend the rest of his life with her.

Karen and Jack were on again, after several years of a roller coaster relationship. Because Karen worked in Johnny Callahan's Capitol office, their relationship was strained by Jack's work. Jack had broken it off twice before, but always came back to Karen. There was no denying that she was just what he needed. Whenever he got too full of himself as a hotshot reporter, Karen brought him back down to earth. Whenever he complained about his job and his bosses – as he often did – Karen was a good listener. She seemed to understand what he was going through and always offered good advice, even if it was merely, "Calm down, have a beer and let's talk this through."

Bright and energetic, Karen and her then eight-year-old daughter, now a sophomore at the University of Nevada, had followed Jerry Paulson, her engineer husband, to Sacramento a dozen years earlier when his firm had been awarded a contract to strengthen levees along the Sacramento River.

Karen's marriage fell apart a year later after her husband ran out on her. Needing to find work, Karen landed an entry-level secretarial job with a freshman Republican assemblyman from San Jose. He didn't last long in Sacramento. After two years in office, he narrowly lost re-election when a collection of public employee unions tossed $600,000 into the campaign on behalf of his Democratic opponent.

Karen then held a succession of jobs with three other Assembly members, all the while moving up the legislative staff ladder and learning the ropes at the Capitol. One day, a co-worker introduced her to one of the Legislature's fresh faces, Johnny Callahan. A former football hero and a rising political star from Orange County, Callahan was the closest thing to a rock star at the Capitol. And it just happened that he had an opening in his Sacramento office for a smart, savvy jack-of-all-trades – someone who could write letters to constituents, handle the assemblyman's schedule and accompany him to fundraisers.

In a district where a Republican victory was guaranteed, Callahan captured nearly three-fourths of the vote and seemed invincible.

Karen had met Jack Summerland by chance soon after she began to work for Callahan. While covering a committee hearing on the Capitol's third floor, Jack's cell phone battery died, and he needed to call his office. He walked into the assemblyman's tiny office, used the phone and was floored by the woman standing at the copy machine.

Karen and Jack hit it off immediately. At first, he was attracted to Karen by her looks. Jack thought she looked like Meg Ryan, cute – no, beautiful – with short-cropped blonde hair and a permanent smile. She was thin, but not too thin. Jack loved her smile that revealed just a hint of dimples in her cheeks. He liked the idea that after twelve years toiling at the Capitol, Karen knew more about the inner workings of the Legislature than he did. He marveled at her knowledge of arcane legislative minutiae. As their relationship matured, he realized that her sense of humor and their common interest in politics and policy issues drew them together.

Karen worried about her future. She knew there was no such thing as job security at the Capitol. Politics was a rough business and term limits, enacted by voters in 1990, shortened many careers. Still, she thought Johnny Callahan was a political meteor and hoped there would be a place for her wherever he landed.

Jack's future, on the other hand, lacked clarity. He couldn't help but think of himself as a dinosaur in the broadcast news business. At one time, every major television station in California covered the State Capitol. But in the early 1970s, as audience-measuring technology improved, they became slaves to ratings, and surveys said the public didn't want to be force-fed political news. Broadcast outlets, even local stations, began closing their Capitol bureaus and concentrating on more marketable story subjects. Only two Sacramento-based stations maintained Capitol bureaus, with the others coming and going, depending on which Hollywood star was in town to push favorite legislation.

Every morning the A.C. Nielsen Company sent Channel 4 and other stations in town a printout of the Sacramento media market's ratings for the previous 24 hours. The ratings were broken down into 15-minute increments. Jack's news director could tell at a glance if the ratings went up or down at 6:15 the previous evening. Did the story on the *Starlight* spike the ratings? Did our weather coverage boost the numbers at 6:01? What made the ratings at rival Channel 8 increase at 5:25? Did coverage of the state budget drive viewers away?

Jack swirled the scotch-flavored ice cube in his mouth.

"Karen, you're right about last night's story. But you know how this business works. Every story at 11 has to be 'new,' no matter how important. And it has to be live, because that makes it look important and late-breaking.

"Look," he told her, "I wasn't given enough time to check out the story, and we now operate in a 24-hour news cycle. All they care about is quantity, not quality. I not only had to chase the *Starlight* story, but I had to write a piece for our website even before I had all the facts. And we're in a sweeps month. Ratings have turned television news into a popularity contest, where being best and most responsible isn't as important as being on top."

The higher the ratings, he explained, the more the station could charge for advertising, which meant greater profits. Television ratings were calculated daily, but advertising rates were set three times a year – based on viewership during the months of

February, May and November. During those ratings sweeps months, as they were called, TV stations covered pseudo news stories and pumped up the volume on crime coverage. In fact, one survey showed that over an entire year a major news station in Los Angeles devoted 51 percent of its news coverage to crime, at a time when the state's attorney general was reporting that the crime rate in Southern California had hit a 30-year low.

Another survey of Los Angeles television stations, this one taken during the week before an important gubernatorial primary, illustrated a similar disdain for political coverage. The L.A. stations devoted between 23 and 54 percent of their news time to crime coverage and spent a mere eight and half minutes to the governor's race, cumulatively, the entire week.

"Karen," Jack said, "for the first time in my life I'm thinking about getting out of journalism – at least out of TV. We cover stories we wouldn't dare touch years ago. If a tabloid, or a cable talk show or one of those far-out web sites runs a juicy story, we're chasing it, often without checking the facts."

"Haven't we had this conversation before?" Karen asked. "You've been disillusioned for some time now. Are you saying it was this junk story on Johnny that pushed you over the top?"

"Maybe it was," Jack said. "Management is worried about all those viewers with trigger fingers on the remote. That's why stations are going out of their way to avoid covering government and politics. You can't pay stations to run Capitol stories unless it involves a celebrity, crime or sex."

Jack explained that the pressure to boost ratings is the real reason why the Johnny Callahan story would be a ratings blockbuster. It involved a big name – names make news, of course – crime and sex. Not as smashing as O.J., Monica Lewinsky or Gary Condit, of course, but a nice little scandal during sweeps month.

The station had teased the Callahan story once an hour throughout the evening. "A sex scandal at the Capitol involving one of the most powerful political figures in California," intoned Conrad Dalton between blockbuster game shows. "Exclusive details tonight at 11."

If that didn't attract casual viewers, nothing would.

Karen was incredulous. "Let me get this right. You guys rush to repeat a bogus story from a third-rate tabloid, don't bother to check the facts and blame it all on the public's twisted viewing habits? What kind of responsibility is that? And what about the credibility of your damn TV station if you report an untrue story?"

Jack felt like a school child being lectured for not handing in his homework assignment. He paused a second, then responded. "That's why I was careful to pin everything in the story on the *Starlight.* It covers us in case the story is inaccurate."

Karen said nothing. Jack sensed she was seething.

"You know what bugs me the most?" Jack asked. "Television stations are raking in billions on political television ads. It just about doubles every four years. Christ, in 2004 there were two million political spots – the equivalent of 677 solid days of advertising, and much more in 2008."

"How do you know that?" Karen asked.

"I've been doing some research for a speech in a couple of weeks. Do you know that in many states, viewers of local newscasts see four times as many campaign ads as campaign news stories during a single newscast? And they get almost no government coverage at all."

"Listen, Jack," Karen said, "I appreciate the history lesson, but I've got to get some sleep. I agree with you about the TV industry, and I think maybe it's time that you look at a mid-life career move. And I'm pretty sure you agree with me about that phony story on Johnny. All I'm saying is, think about who would like to embarrass the speaker, check out the facts and get your boss to run a retraction if the story is false. Let's talk more about this tomorrow. Goodnight." She hung up without giving him a chance to respond.

Jack did agree with Karen that the Callahan story didn't make sense. Callahan, the widower, dated plenty of women and was considered one of California's most eligible bachelors. Why would he pay for sex and jeopardize his career? He wouldn't, Jack thought, unless he was incredibly stupid. Which he wasn't.

Four

Truth be told, Johnny Callahan wasn't the rock-ribbed right-winger that many of his supporters thought he was. He considered himself a pragmatic conservative, although his voting record, out of necessity, tilted to the starboard side.

The 70th Assembly district had been Republican forever and would remain that way. Sure, there were a few Democrats, primarily the gay and artist communities in Laguna Beach, but with a two-to-one Republican-to-Democratic registration edge, Johnny represented one of the most conservative Assembly districts in California, "The Untouchable 70th," according to the California Republican Party.

Johnny's only potential political danger would come from what detractors called "wing-nuts," remnants of the old John Birch Society who might challenge him from the right in a primary. Johnny had no choice but to be a solid, card-carrying conservative. Privately, however, Johnny had little use for what he called the "religious phonies" who wanted to impose their moral beliefs on all Californians. They were the self-proclaimed power brokers who thought they ran Orange County, entrepreneurs and religious zealots who controlled the flow of money into political coffers and swayed voters with their American Values slate mailer every election that reached all Republican households.

Johnny supported the American Values agenda — school prayer, a ban on abortions and gun rights — but he chose to champion other issues such as tax cuts and anti-crime legislation.

Once Johnny won his first Assembly contest, however, he was off to the races. He won so convincingly that no prominent politico dared risk embarrassment by challenging him. He faced only token opposition in the next Republican primary and Democrats didn't even run a candidate against him in November.

Six-foot-three, athletically built, with wavy black hair and sparkling eyes as blue as the Pacific, Johnny was the center of attention whether walking down the halls of the Capitol or playing pick-up basketball at the YMCA. He quickly rose to the top of the political pyramid, first as vice chair of the Revenue and Taxation Committee, then as vice chair of the Governmental Organization Committee. Democrats controlled the Assembly in those days. The best a Republican could do is become the committee's second in command.

Around the Capitol, Assembly GO, as it was called, was known as a juice committee, which meant it dealt with legislation affecting some of the richest special interests in the state — gambling, horse racing and liquor — where money flowed freely to committee members in the form of campaign contributions.

The money rolled in to Johnny's campaign fund from racetracks, Indian gaming tribes, beer and wine wholesalers and hundreds of others. Even after California voters approved a campaign finance reform measure, Johnny Callahan remained the top fundraiser in the Assembly, and he knew precisely how to spend his money.

Johnny didn't need the cash for himself. He could win re-election in the 70th district as long as he had a pulse and stayed out of jail. He remembered what former Louisiana Governor Edwin Edwards once said about his re-election chances, "The only way I could lose this election is if I'm caught in bed with a live boy or a dead woman."

Johnny wasn't stupid enough to make such statements in public, but he did feel impervious to political attack, and he knew how to make his money work for him. He had learned from some of the most powerful and successful Assembly leaders of yesteryear — Willie Brown and Jesse Unruh — who understood that the best way to make and keep friends was to help them get elected and re-elected. They raised, and doled out, tens of millions of dollars to political buddies who would never forget the source of the largesse. That's how they rose through the ranks of party politics to secure the votes when they ran for Assembly speaker, long considered the second most powerful political post in California government.

Callahan took advantage of his GO position by holding one fundraiser after another and inviting hundreds of high-priced lobbyists who represented interests that had legislation before the committee. One year, on his birthday, he invited the Third House, as the lobbying corps was called, to his birthday party. For $5,000, invited guests played golf at the venerable La Hacienda Country Club, a Sacramento landmark since the early 20th century, where the rumored average age of club members was 67. The Sacramento joke was that La Hacienda is where golfers go to die.

Four months later, Callahan invited lobbyists to a riverboat cruise down the Sacramento River. Price tag: $4,000. Lobbyists had no choice but to attend on behalf of their clients, because the young, brash Callahan was the key Republican player on the Assembly committee that could put companies out of business or make them wealthy beyond their imagination.

Assembly Republican Leader Hal Vuckovic, a former Modesto police chief, was the GOP's chief fundraiser during the election, but Callahan was the chief strategist and a big draw at fundraising events from San Diego to Eureka.

In a single election cycle as vice chair of the Assembly Governmental Organization Committee, Callahan raised $5.4 million for his campaign fund from thousands of donors and helped raise many millions more while traveling the state on behalf of Republican candidates.

Out of his own campaign fund, he wrote checks to 16 of his Republican colleagues running for re-election, all of whom easily won. Callahan also transferred a couple of million dollars to the California Republican Party, which then funneled money to seven Republicans who found themselves in uphill dogfights against popular and established Democratic incumbents.

"Boy Genius," is how the conservative *Los Angeles Daily News* referred to Johnny Callahan the day after the November election. "In what can only be described as a stunning series of upsets, Republicans recaptured a majority of seats in the state Assembly after the political apparatus of Orange County whiz kid Johnny Callahan engineered four upset GOP victories."

Republicans were euphoric. The Senate remained heavily Democratic, but the Assembly was back in Republican control with 42 of the 80 members. Four veteran Democrats were defeated by Callahan's well-financed opposition campaign. Like a Muhammad Ali roundhouse, the Democrats never saw it coming.

The money had paid for mail pieces and radio commercials the final week of the election. Careful polling had determined the Democrats' vulnerabilities, and Callahan's team pounced. Each Democrat had years of voting records and political activities to attack. Two had voted for a state budget that raised the state sales tax. They even had advocated that Internet sales be taxed. Another had taken so much money from Indian gaming tribes that he was nicknamed – privately, of course – "Chief Hand-is-out."

"Warning: Colleen Ruiz Has Dangerous Friends," screamed the headline on one mailer. Below the headline was the photo of Assemblywoman Ruiz, one of the Assembly's more conservative Democrats, and child molester Clarence Gibbons, the two of them smiling at the camera and shaking hands. Gibbons, a small-town restaurateur, had paid $250 to attend a district fundraiser for Ruiz four years earlier. His contribution entitled him to a couple of beers, some cheese and crackers and a photo op with the candidate. How could she know that Gibbons would turn out to be a political embarrassment after being convicted of fondling a six-year-old girl in the kitchen of his restaurant.

Callahan had hired a crack opposition research team to dig up dirt on Ruiz and the three other targeted Democrats. Usually, op research teams only found small stuff, such as legislative votes they could twist in their favor. Occasionally, they hit the mother lode — a tax lien against their house, a long-forgotten spousal battery complaint, or a campaign contribution from an unsavory character.

Ruiz represented much of Bakersfield and many of the small farming towns that lined Highway 99, which ran north-south through the heart of California's great Central Valley and provided the vivid backdrop for John Steinbeck's epic *Grapes of Wrath.*

Ruiz had been a solid vote for her district, but she committed a cardinal sin in politics — underestimating her opponent and ending her campaign with unspent money in the bank. She was sure of re-election and convinced that her opponent, Tulare water consultant Henry Palacios, was a political lightweight who wouldn't run a strong campaign. With her $50,000 surplus, she had enough for a solid radio buy in Bakersfield, in which 45 percent of the voters lived.

A month after the election, in the Legislature's two-day organizing session, Callahan had only token opposition for speaker. He had engineered the GOP takeover and promised key committee chairmanships to influential Republican members who might have caused him difficulty. "Keep your friends close," the old political adage went, "and your enemies closer."

By rights, Vuckovic should have become speaker, but he was 61 years old, termed out of office in two years, and the Republican delegation wanted a younger, more dynamic leader. Besides, Vuckovic had set his sights on running for the state Senate, and he'd soon be seen as a lame duck with waning power.

The final speakership vote was 42-0. All the Republicans, even Vuckovic, supported Callahan. Democrats sat on their hands and didn't vote. They didn't want their constituents back home to think they had supported a Republican.

After only two years in Sacramento, Johnny Callahan had reached the top. He had proven to be a master at counting votes and engineering political deals. He rewarded his friends, turned enemies into supporters and built a political machine that hadn't been seen in Sacramento for decades.

In the years after the Legislature became a full-time body in 1967, the state had grown into a world economic power and the speaker had life or death control over legislation, hundreds of political appointments and political careers. Once, while boasting of his power, Willie Brown referred to himself as the "Ayatollah of the Assembly."

Of course, being Assembly speaker wasn't what it used to be. Term limits led to a succession of caretakers with diminished political power. Still, Callahan commanded the respect and attention of anyone who wanted to play in the Capitol arena, and recent events had made the speaker a burgeoning national figure.

The sudden death of Democratic U.S. Senator Bernie Edelstein offered California Republican Governor Colin Frank the opportunity to appoint a successor who could become one of the most prominent political figures in the country for decades to come. And it was no secret that Callahan was Frank's political protégé.

If Callahan became a U.S. senator, he would be one of the most quoted and televised Republicans on the national scene. And who knows where that could lead. California, after all, had one-fifth of the electoral votes needed to elect a president. The *Starlight*, which skewered politicians for sport and decried Callahan's self-righteousness, was delighted to get him.

Callahan understood that political fortunes are won or lost in an instant. Only one story in the tabloid media could undermine everything he had worked for. The press would have a feeding frenzy if he didn't stop the bleeding immediately.

As it was, the Action News 4 report at 11 p.m. was picked up by the Associated Press but was too late to land in any morning newspapers. "According to a Sacramento television station, the *Starlight* tabloid is reporting that Assembly Speaker Johnny Callahan had an encounter with a prostitute at a Los Angeles motel. A spokesman for the speaker denied the allegations. Officials at the *Starlight* were unavailable for comment."

The AP had written three paragraphs and moved it on its radio wire in the pre-dawn hours. A few news websites linked to the AP story. Several radio stations picked up the story off the AP wire, but their accounts were a bit more lurid, and morning drive-time disc jockeys had a field day at Callahan's expense.

Five

If there was one thing Governor Colin Frank hated, it was being blind-sided. He always liked to be in control of situations, no matter how delicate or politically risky. His chief of staff, Curtis Lawrence, knew the governor usually went to bed before 11:00 p.m. and awoke religiously at 6 a.m. That's why he waited until 6:10 to place the phone call.

"Governor, this is Curt. Sorry to bother you, sir, but there's some nasty shit — excuse me, sir, I mean information — about Johnny Callahan on the radio this morning. Apparently there was a TV story last night. According to Channel 4, the *Starlight* is about to run a story saying Callahan has been messing around with a hooker."

There was a brief moment of silence on the other end of the line.

"Governor?"

"That's ridiculous," Frank finally offered. "But even if it's true, who's going to believe one of those trashy rags?"

"With all the speculation that you might appoint the speaker to the U.S. Senate, we'll need to do some damage control," Lawrence continued. "The press will be all over this story. I'll put together some talking points for your review when you get in the office."

At 7:45, Frank's driver passed a half-dozen protesters on the N Street sidewalk about 50 yards from the entrance to the Capitol garage. One matronly woman who appeared to be in her 60s angrily shouted, "No more budget cuts for the poor" as the black Ford Crown Victoria edged into the curving driveway that led to the garage. A California Highway Patrol officer, stationed in a kiosk near the entrance, raised the wooden barrier and motioned the car forward.

"Is that the best they can do?" the governor chuckled. "Protests aren't what they used to be, that's for sure."

Governor Frank, along with his bodyguards from the California Highway Patrol, slipped out of the car and walked about five feet to a private elevator — off limits to the public and news media — that carried them to a narrow hallway only a few feet from the governor's inner office. Capitol habitués referred to it as the "corner office," located at an elbow in a large horseshoe-shaped office complex in the Capitol's first floor. Guests visiting the governor, however, had to negotiate a long, 100-foot hallway, walking past the bustling press office and the offices of his chief of staff and deputy chief.

Frank's private office was bedecked with decades of memorabilia — autographed photos of himself with John Wayne, Sylvester Stallone, Ronald Reagan and a dozen other Hollywood and political conservatives.

In one corner was a riding saddle given to him by a king of some Middle Eastern country. On Frank's desk were baseballs autographed by the 1959 and 1988 Los Angeles Dodgers. In a corner bookcase was a football autographed by Mike Garrett, USC's first Heisman Trophy winner back in the '60s.

Frank's best days were behind him. Now 64-years old, Frank remained distinguished-looking, with thick, white sideburns, salt and pepper hair and a friendly smile. Trim and fit at 175 pounds, he had gained only seven pounds since college.

Frank flirted with a presidential run two years into his second term as governor but, like so many California politicos before him, was embarrassed in the Iowa caucuses and New Hampshire primary. What was it about winning the governorship that drove men to believe they could be leader of the free world?

Frank had finished fifth among seven candidates in Iowa. He didn't have a clue about agriculture policy, and it showed during the campaign. It also didn't help that he came from California, derisively called the land of fruits and nuts.

Recalling Governor Jerry Brown, nicknamed Governor Moonbeam by a Chicago journalist, one columnist for the *Des Moines Register* called Frank Moonbeam II, despite the fact that Frank and Brown were polar opposites.

Brown was a free-wheeling, unconventional politician, a bachelor who dated a rock star and eschewed the trappings of political power. He lived in a tiny one-bedroom apartment across the street from the Capitol, walked to work each morning and — when driven to official events — turned down a fancy limo in favor of an old blue Plymouth.

Frank, it seemed, wore his dark gray suit to bed each night. After Iowa, Frank trudged through the January slush in New Hampshire — Manchester, Keane, Nashua and a dozen other forgettable towns. Frank completely embarrassed himself on election day, winning a scant three percent of the primary vote. The morning after the election, Frank dropped out of national contention forever, content to be California's Big Kahuna and consigned to fringe prime-time speeches at Republican conventions.

Frank figured he wouldn't have to fight too many more political battles. He'd serve out his term as governor, ease into retirement, secure a lucrative job with a prestigious Los Angeles law firm and become a rich elder statesman.

Callahan had attended the University of Southern California with Frank's son, Marty. The pair were fraternity brothers, best friends and teammates on the football team.

Once, after an upset victory over Alabama their sophomore year, Marty referred to Callahan as Moses. "Johnny is like Moses leading our team to the promised land," he told a *Los Angeles Times* reporter. The *Time*s ran a feature story on Callahan's heroics – headlining it, "Moses Leads His People" – and the nickname stuck. From time to time, newspaper accounts referred to "Moses delivering his team to victory," or "Moses commands Trojans to upend UCLA." Decades later, *USA Today* headlined a story on Callahan's likely Senate appointment, "Moses to Scale New Heights?"

The "M Boys" – Johnny "Moses" Callahan and Marty Frank – were quite a pair in college. Johnny was the dashing, smart quarterback who took academics seriously and wanted a law career. Marty was the ne'er-do-well wide receiver who rarely went to class. He knew which courses – they called them Mickey Mouse courses – the football players should take. Marty Frank had no trouble bringing down a 2.1 grade point average. He entered the National Football League draft and was selected in the sixth round by Cleveland, but he washed out his first year and went home to Los Angeles.

Against his father's wishes, Marty opted to teach golf and surfing to rich Southern Californians in Huntington Beach.

Johnny Callahan, the son Colin Frank never had, was a different story. After pro scouts made it clear they weren't willing to gamble a high draft pick on a quarterback with a bum knee, Callahan set his sights on a future outside of football. He graduated near the top of his class at USC Law School, was president of the campus Young Republicans, honed his skills as a criminal prosecutor and corporate attorney and then entered the world of politics. Now, nearly a quarter-century later and taking full advantage of his brains, money and connections, Johnny Callahan was scaling political heights that few could reach.

Despite their different paths since college, Johnny and Marty remained close — perfect symmetry, one a hard-working rising star, the other a slothful washout. Colin Frank, disgusted at his son's lack of drive, became Callahan's mentor and friend. He took a personal interest in his success.

Marty went along for the ride. Once Johnny started tapping the public payroll as a successful politician, he kept his old college teammate gainfully employed — as an aide to the city councilman, county supervisor and state legislator. Marty performed odd jobs for Callahan, heading up esoteric research projects. Much of the time, however, he seemed to be doing nothing. Staffers in the speaker's office couldn't figure out why Callahan kept Marty around. But all realized that the former wide receiver who never quite grew up had important connections.

After a few months working inside the speaker's office, Marty decided to get rich. He started a consulting firm and raked in large retainers to give clients access to his powerful benefactor.

"He's here," said an invisible aide, seconds before Johnny Callahan angrily made his way into the governor's office.

"Before you say anything," Callahan told the governor, "it's not true. If they've got pictures, they're phonies. Somebody must be out to embarrass me to keep me from getting the Senate job. I think..."

Frank held up his hand before Callahan could continue.

"Johnny, I've known you for most of your life. I doubt there is even one ounce of truth in that *Starlight* story. What this says to me is that the Senate appointment is going to be nasty."

Callahan opened his mouth to make a point, but Frank cut him off.

"Listen, Johnny. I'm trying to build my legacy. Seven years of relative prosperity, no big earthquakes, no major scandals. I want to send you to Washington, but sometimes circumstances have a way of making the best political plans go awry. You better hope this story doesn't have legs. I need to know if you have any skeletons in your closet. You know you're not the only one who wants the Senate appointment. Barnes has been calling me every day and his friends are all over me."

Harold Barnes was a Northern California state senator who was revered by the right wing. He had more than his share of powerful allies, carefully cultivated during decades of public service. CEOs of tobacco companies and gun manufacturers considered Barnes a friend. A close friend. It was no coincidence that Barnes consistently led the fight in the Legislature against tobacco taxes and anti-gun legislation.

Johnny Callahan may have been a reliable vote, but Barnes led the charge. Ambitious, and convinced he was perfectly suited to carry the conservative banner on the national scene, Barnes felt he had outgrown Sacramento. His friends were determined to pull out all stops to get Barnes to Washington. They lobbied Frank relentlessly for the senator's appointment. A top executive at an east coast gun manufacturing company, who counted both Frank and Barnes close friends, had called the governor three times to press for Barnes.

Barnes, of course, wasn't Callahan's only competition. Three members of the state's congressional delegation and a has-been actor had let it be known they wanted the appointment. Dangle a U.S. Senate seat in public and the wannabes crawled out of the woodwork like ants at Uncle Charlie's 4th of July picnic.

Callahan took off his coat jacket and draped it over a chair. He turned to the governor.

"Colin, you know I'd never do anything to embarrass you. I'm telling you this is a set-up. The night those photos supposedly were taken, I was attending a meeting of my 'Platinum Club' members in San Diego. We met in the upstairs room at the Sea

Shanty. Two dozen of my contributors and advisers will back me up, as will the maitre'd and parking lot attendant."

"Then who do you think is behind this crap?" the governor asked.

"I can only speculate," Callahan responded.

A secretary brought Frank his third cup of black coffee. The governor's press secretary walked into the office, joining the governor and the Assembly speaker.

"Okay, here's what we should do to stop the bleeding," Frank said. "Nobody likes those tabloids. You need to get the mainstream press on your side. Have a press conference and threaten to sue the newspaper. Once the dust clears on this episode I'll be in a better position to make a final decision.

"I have to be careful. Barnes is stirring things up, and the Democrats are demanding that I pick someone with Edelstein's political philosophy. I'm going to wait on this awhile."

Callahan groaned. "Shit, anything can happen while you wait. And if you take too long, you could look indecisive."

Frank turned red-faced. He couldn't conceal his anger, betraying the always cool demeanor he showed the public.

"Look, I'm not jeopardizing my position by being hasty in this. Let's do our due diligence and vet potential candidates before I make any announcement. Besides, you've just been slammed for screwing around with a whore. You need to clear this up. Immediately. Then, I'm calling Shackelford to do some polling before I make the appointment. Any more bad publicity could screw this up for you."

Callahan, surprised at Frank's sudden and uncharacteristic outburst, started for the door. Then he stopped and turned back toward the governor.

"All I'm saying is, don't overlook the obvious. Isn't a rash of bad publicity exactly what my opponents would like?"

Six

Jack Summerland walked into the newsroom and found his way to his cubicle, stopping first at the coffee machine for the first of a half-dozen pre-noon caffeine jolts. As he walked to his desk, he glanced at the large clock on the wall near the assignment desk. Constantly checking the time, often without realizing it, was an old habit. Jack once missed a deadline and was scolded by his news director, "You can have the greatest story in the world, but it doesn't do anybody any good if you don't get it on the air."

"Good story last night, Jack," said Joyce Michelson, the noon show producer. "We're running it again." Jack winced. He had hoped the story would die a quiet death.

Someone handed Jack a copy of the Associated Press story on Callahan. "Oh shit," he said to no one in particular. Under normal circumstances, a reporter would love to have the AP re-write his story and send it out on the state wire. But this story embarrassed Jack. While he hoped it would be forgotten quickly, he knew it would be big news – a story with legs. He scanned the brief article, written for the morning broadcast wire, but he knew the AP would update the story, and it was sure to end up on various political websites.

Jack's tiny work space was a clutter of press releases, notes, reports and videos. After nearly 30 years in the journalism business, Jack's entire career was crammed into a six-foot square cubicle in the middle of the reporters' work area, called "the pen" and a filing cabinet that was so full of papers it couldn't be closed.

Offices were rare in most local TV newsrooms. They usually were reserved for the news director, the executive producer and other executives. Not even the self-styled "Voice of Sacramento" had an office. Conrad Dalton labored with the working class.

Jack turned on his computer and began an electronic search of major California newspaper websites to see if the AP story had been picked up. Jack checked the *Los Angeles Times* first, then the *San Francisco Chronicle*, *San Diego Union-Tribune* and a half-dozen others. Three newspapers had placed the brief story on their websites.

Jack leaned back in his chair and quickly scanned a few other California newspapers. His eye was drawn to a yellowing photograph on one wall of his cubicle. The photo, taken by a *San Francisco Examiner* photographer, showed a University of California football player smashing into a Stanford trombone player during Cal's improbable five-lateral touchdown on the last play of the 1982 "Big Game" with Stanford. That photo always brought a smile to his face. It had been a gift from a journalism professor at Berkeley who Jack had come to know over the years.

Jack Summerland was a transplant. He had grown up in St. Louis and earned two degrees at the University of Missouri, an undergraduate degree in business administration and a masters degree in journalism. He originally thought he wanted to be a lawyer, then changed his mind to avoid a lifetime of country club golf and boredom. He chose a profession that offered new and exciting challenges every day. Besides, hanging out with governors and other political heavyweights had its moments.

Jack was so anxious to see the morning play of the AP story that, at first, he didn't even notice the flashing red light on his phone. He had three voice mail messages. The first two were from his ex-wives. The money was late. Jack took a deep breath and slowly exhaled. He wondered if he'd ever be free of debt.

The third message, received at 8:23 a.m., was from Callahan's chief of staff, Samuel Cockerill. As a capitol reporter, Summerland had cultivated relationships with hundreds of Capitol dwellers – Democrats, Republicans and those in between. Cockerill wasn't a friend but they used to drink beers together on occasion.

"Listen Jack," Cockerill started. "The *Starlight* story is wrong. You shouldn't have run with it. That was bad journalism and it could ruin Johnny's reputation. We've got proof. We're having a news conference at 10 o'clock to set the record straight."

All of a sudden Jack broke into a sweat. His mind raced. Jesus, he thought, did I say the wrong thing last night? Did I blow it? Wait a minute, I pinned the whole story on the *Starligh*t. Tom Blickman, a general assignment reporter, walked by Jack's cubicle. "Nice job," he said as he sauntered toward the assignment desk. Jack didn't respond. He started shaking and quickly slipped into the bathroom off the newsroom. He splashed water on his face and stared into the mirror.

The worst feeling for a reporter is the thought he had been inaccurate. Jack went over his eleven o'clock script, word for word. Then he grabbed a video copy of the 11 p.m. newscast and watched the complete story, including his ad-libbed answers to those inane anchor questions. Whew, he thought. I never accused Callahan of anything, but merely quoted the *Starlight.* Technically, he was safe, although the public might not get the nuance.

He breathed a sign of relief, then became angry. He had argued against running the Callahan story in the first place. Once he was overruled, however, he felt he could write it without resorting to over-the-top innuendo and speculation. Now, his reputation was on the line, inexorably linked to a second-rate tabloid and its phony story. He popped a breath mint, then walked hurriedly back to his desk so he could dial Sam Cockerill and begin damage control.

Cockerill liked Jack. He respected his journalism and ethics, and he knew Summerland would never deliberately air a bad story. Still, he was angry. So angry that he told his secretary to tell Jack that he was busy taking other reporters' phone calls and that there'd be a news conference in the speaker's office at 10 a.m.

In a corner of the sprawling newsroom, during the Channel 4 morning producers meeting, Jimmy Johnson chuckled when the subject of Johnny Callahan was raised. As the station's news director, Johnson was charged with keeping the station ranked Number 1 in the market. And what better way to boost ratings than to force feed the viewing public a daily dose of the hottest political sex scandal.

"Look at what O.J. Simpson and Monica Lewinsky did for the cable stations," he told the assembled producers. "I'm glad we made the Callahan story the lead last night. Let's keep it front and center today, okay?" The producer of the noon news nodded; the assistant news director, a 35-year veteran of print and broadcast journalism, rolled his eyes.

Until the *Starlight* hit the supermarket in two days, Channel 4 would own the Callahan story. Action News 4 had the details and the fuzzy photos. The other stations would try to play catch up, but always would be a step behind. Johnson loved it. He had his May ratings boost and he wanted it hyped. Even the weather would be a second-string news story now.

Johnson ordered his news producers to tease "the latest on the Capitol sex scandal" during network breaks at 10 a.m. and 11 a.m. with crawls on the bottom of the screen to read: "Assembly

Speaker Callahan named in Capitol Sex Scandal…Details during Action News 4 at Noon."

Johnson had sent an e-mail to both his noon news producer and Summerland that he wanted a second-day angle on the Callahan story and that it would lead the newscast. And he wanted new details by noon.

"Cover the shit out of this story, Jack," Johnson wrote. "Get this guy and we'll get a 20 rating and you'll get a few extra bucks in your next paycheck." Johnson didn't know Johnny Callahan from Adam and didn't care about his politics. But he knew a good story, and it wouldn't hurt if KBLT was known as the television station that brought down an Assembly speaker.

Jack walked into the news director's tiny, cluttered office where Johnson was holding court with his producers. "As I feared, we've got a problem," Jack told the group. "Callahan's people not only say the story is false, they're having a news conference to refute it. They're going to say the *Starlight* got duped and that we legitimized the lie. This could be real embarrassing to the station. I'm heading over there now."

"False? What are you talking about," one of the producers responded.

"All I know is that his chief of staff says the story isn't true, and that he has proof that the *Starlight* story was phony. He's pretty pissed."

Everyone in the room went silent for what seemed like half a minute. Instinctively, everyone looked with anticipation at Johnson, who was deep in thought.

"Look, we're okay on this," he said. "Even if the story isn't true, we were just quoting the *Starlight*. This happens all the time. Let's cover this as a breaking story and make both Callahan and the *Starlight* the subjects. Be sure to give Callahan plenty of airtime to respond. Jack, after the noon news, do an updated story for our website. Clay, can you check with the *Starlight* to see what those guys are saying? No matter how this breaks, it's still a ratings bonanza."

"I'll check with them," Clay Bertrand, the assistant news director, responded.

"And, one other thing," Johnson said, turning to Bertrand, "I think we should get Harley on the line and see if we have any potential legal problems. My guess is that we're in the clear. You know how hard it is for a public figure to prove libel. They'd have to prove we acted with willful disregard for the truth. But just in case, let's check, okay?"

Bertrand grabbed a phone, the producers scattered to their cubicles and Jack recruited a cameraman. Ron Middleton, his usual photographer, was on the night shift this day, assigned to helicopter duty, so he yelled across the newsroom, "Antonio, pack up your gear, we're headed out."

Jack looked at his watch and planned the next few hours. He had plenty of time to put a new slant on the Callahan story and air it on the noon news. Jack reviewed his notes as Antonio drove the short distance to the Capitol and parked the news van on Tenth Street. From there, it was a three-minute hike to the Capitol's north entrance, tripod, camera and other gear in tow.

Decades earlier, police let news crews park in the basement of the Capitol building, along with legislators and other VIPs. Over the years, reporters lost their parking privileges and, in fact, were banned from the basement altogether after a San Francisco television reporter tried to make a name for himself by filming the lawmakers' state-leased cars, many of them Cadillacs and other expensive models, in the Capitol garage. Angry legislators convinced the Assembly Rules Committee to permanently ban all cameras and reporters from the basement.

For several years, the committee allowed television vans to park on the north or south lawns of the capitol until a news crew chewed up a chunk of muddy sod after a rainstorm.

Now, just getting into the Capitol building was a chore with heavy equipment to maneuver through X-ray machines. Even longtime Capitol fixtures like Jack Summerland had to endure the new rules. He longed for the day when all he needed to do his job was a notebook and pencil. Yet another reason, he thought, for getting out of this business.

As Jack walked through the rotunda, he glanced up at the 125-foot dome and briefly thought about all the history that had been made in this imposing, classical structure since it opened in late 1869. Ground had been broken in 1860, but construction delays – due to floods, Civil War-caused material shortages, a brick production strike and lack of funds – prompted the Legislature briefly to consider moving the Capitol to Santa Cruz, San Jose, Oakland, Benicia, or San Francisco.

Originally, the Capitol building housed all state government – from the elected officials to the bureaucrats who made government work. Over the years, the Capitol had been remodeled numerous times. In 1973, two years after a major earthquake jolted Southern California, seismic engineers concluded that the unreinforced brick Capitol likely would not withstand a major earthquake.

Legislators thought about tearing the grand old building down, or turning it into a museum. In the end, the Legislature appropriated $68 million for an inch-by-inch restoration. At the time, the project had the distinction of being the most expensive structural restoration in the nation's history.

Jack and Antonio negotiated up the wide, richly carpeted staircase leading to the speaker's office. In the waiting area of Callahan's opulent second-floor suite, a dozen reporters mingled and waited for someone to say something. One reporter, for the *Orange County Register,* couldn't help making a joke at Jack's expense. "Getting your news in the supermarket check-out line?" Jack smiled and shrugged his shoulders, as if to say, "So what's the big deal?"

Billy Galster, Callahan's somewhat nerdy press secretary, personally had phoned key members of the Capitol press corps, urging their attendance. Galster had to be the last living human to wear a bow tie and horn-rimmed glasses. Normally, a news conference announcement would be sent to the Associated Press and the Capitol Morning Digest, which would post the event in their "daybooks." But this event would be one of those "hastily called news conferences" that offered little advanced notice.

Cockerill walked out of his office and into the reception area where reporters and photographers had gathered. Jack thought he looked like he hadn't slept in two nights. Maybe he hadn't. Was that the same wrinkled pinstriped blue suit he wore yesterday? His white dress shirt was open at the collar, and his knotted blue and gray tie hung about three inches below his Adam's apple. Jack noticed that Cockerill was wearing one blue and one black sock and his eyes were the color of cranberry sauce.

Cockerill told reporters that Callahan would be available in a couple of minutes. Cockerill was a former newspaper editor. He knew he had to end this story today, or kiss goodbye his career as a U.S. senator's chief of staff.

A few minutes later, the reporters were led into a private office. Unlike most legislative offices, which were built in 1952, the speaker's suite dated back to 1869 when the Capitol was built. It was impeccably restored, so much so that staffers weren't even allowed to hammer nails in the walls to hang pictures. It was decorated in ornate turn-of-the-century furniture – blue felt chairs and sofa, rich cherry wood cabinets filled with blue-covered law books.

Callahan sat behind a large desk. He looked stern in his crisp blue suit, white shirt and red tie. Standard politician's uniform, Summerland thought.

Callahan's office was completely devoid of clutter. Nothing out of place. Everything was so neat, it reminded Jack of the Oval Office. On Callahan's desk, Summerland noticed only a telephone, a desk pen set and a framed picture of Callahan and his late wife. In a bookcase, prominently displayed, a USC football helmet, and a football autographed by the entire 1985 team.

Jack smiled briefly at the sight of Callahan's neatness and wondered what it would be like working in an environment devoid of clutter. Jack's colleagues back at the station called him "Pack Rat" because he seemed to collect every news release, every government study, every piece of potentially useful video.

Cockerill motioned to Galster, who then set the ground rules. "The speaker has a statement and will only take a couple of questions. He's late for a Republican caucus on the tax bill."

Callahan started to read, looking up frequently at the bank of cameras. Quite clearly Jack saw the speaker clench his teeth, exposing a bluish-purple vein on his left temple. Jack turned quickly to his cameraman and made a circular gesture with his right index finger that told him to start shooting video. Summerland made a note of the time code on the side of the camera, and then started taking notes.

"Those photographs you may have heard about are phony," Callahan said sternly. "The story is wrong and preposterous. The night in question I was attending a private function with 23 of my supporters at a San Diego restaurant."

Callahan reached into a folder, pulled out three sheets of paper and held them up. In an instant there was a cacophony of camera shutters clicking and lights flashing. This was the photo that would appear on the front pages of every newspaper the next morning.

"These letters were faxed to me this morning. The originals will be in my office by mid-afternoon. One letter is from the restaurant's maitre'd. Another letter is from Gordon Wilhelm, a prominent San Diego industrialist, who is one of my most trusted advisers."

Callahan paused a few seconds as the cameras zoomed into the letters he held in his right hand. "The third letter is from Samantha Garragus, Mayor of San Diego. All three state unequivocally that I was at San Diego's Sea Shanty the night in question."

There was an audible gasp from one of the assembled reporters. Amazing, Jack thought. The story is only a few hours old and Johnny Callahan has unearthed what appears to be undeniable proof that the story is a fake. Kudos to his staff.

Despite the journalistic company it kept, the *Starlight* did try to verify important facts before publishing the story, but clearly the tabloid failed basic Journalism 1A and had been sloppy – to say the least – on this one.

"As you know, the *Starlight* was planning to run this false story about me later this week. My lawyers confronted the *Starlight* this morning with incontrovertible evidence that the story is false, and it has agreed not to run it," Callahan said. "For now I'm letting it drop. And I hope my friends in the media will do the same. I'll take a few questions."

Three hands shot up immediately. Jack heard at least four voices, including his own, shout out in unison. "Mr. Speaker? Mr. Speaker?" Summerland wanted to ask Callahan if he thought someone was out to ruin his political career. He wanted to make the *Starlight*, not himself or Channel 4, the focus of the second-day story. He also figured the speaker wouldn't call on him – Callahan's way of teaching Jack a lesson, reminding him that it was he who was the Assembly speaker and that Jack had been too quick to run a story that was nothing more than tabloid crap.

Actually, Galster once told Jack that Callahan liked his reporting. "A straight-shooter," Callahan was quoted as saying. The speaker had benefited from many of his stories in recent years, but on this day he had a point to make.

Callahan pointed to Carl Williams, a Capitol reporter for the *Sacramento Bee*. "Carl?"

"Mr. Speaker, who do you think is behind this story? And what was the motive?" Williams asked.

Jack smiled. Great minds think alike, he thought.

"I can't tell you who Governor Frank is going to appoint to

fill the vacancy left by Senator Edelstein's death, but it is no secret that I am being considered. It is apparent that someone wants to keep me out of the U.S. Senate," Callahan responded. "As for who is behind this cowardly hit piece, I won't speculate, but my staff will get to the truth. I will tell you this: if our nation is to be the beacon of truth and freedom for the rest of the world, we must put an end to the insidious politics of personal destruction here at home."

"One more," Galster blurted. This time, five voices rose in unison. Four of the questions were unintelligible. The booming voice of a *San Francisco Chronicle* columnist was heard over the rest. "Are you worried that this episode might cause Governor Frank to name someone else to the Senate?"

"You'll have to speak to the governor about that. Right now I am only concerned about doing my job as Assembly speaker, and ensuring that the governor's agenda – particularly his tax cut – is sent to his desk by the Legislature. Thank you."

Speaker Callahan hurried out of his office and left Galster to herd the gaggle. "Nice job," whispered Cockerill as Callahan rushed to the elevator and a Republican caucus that was waiting for its leader.

Summerland tied up the story nice and neat for the noon newscast. He had video of Callahan and his denial, that grainy *Starlight* photograph of an unidentified man and woman in the L.A. motel room, plus file video of Governor Frank taken at an elementary school two days earlier. He had an interview with a Republican member of the Assembly who chided the press for its irresponsibility. He'd add one more interview with a Senate Democrat after lunch, then re-work the piece for the 6 p.m. newscast. End of story. No ruined political career. No sex scandal. No ratings.

Between newscasts, Jack wrote an updated story for the station's website. Once an afterthought and considered a passing fad, station websites had become major sources for millions of news consumers and a growing revenue producer for newspapers and television stations, which were steadily losing their audience.

In fact, a recent report by the Pew Internet and American Life Project showed that 50 million Americans turn to the Internet as their daily source of news and information. Indeed, another study indicated that the Internet had surpassed television as the dominant news medium between 9 a.m. and 5 p.m. A far cry from September 11, 2001, when only three percent of the American public turned to the Internet as their primary source for breaking news on the New York Twin Towers terrorist attacks.

Jack proofread his web report on the Callahan news conference and sent it to the station's webmaster. The station supplemented his story with a full ten minutes of unedited footage from the Callahan news conference, including the speaker's entire statement and question-and-answer session with reporters. Jack's noon report on Channel 4 timed out at a little more than two-and-a-half minutes. But on the web, the possibilities were limitless.

Jack sat back in his chair and took a deep breath. He was glad this story was ending, embarrassed that he was even associated with the tabloid trash story. From the beginning, Jack felt this story stunk like so many rotting fish. But once the brains at Channel 4 decided to go with it, he was glad he had the assignment. He shuddered at the thought of nightside reporter Gary Thackeray covering this story. Newsroom colleagues referred to Thackeray as "Geraldo." He could over-hype a city council meeting and breathlessly make it sound like the scandal of the year.

Jack still thought of himself as a serious journalist. He had won numerous awards for his political coverage and was considered one of the best reporters in California. His work had been cited in a number of journalism and political books and he was constantly fending off speaking requests. He knew he could pin the blame for this fiasco on the *Starlight* and its shoddy, sensational yellow journalism. "What the hell," he said to himself. "This is television, after all – not brain surgery."

Seven

Seven

Jack Summerland wrapped up his evening story at 6:04. As usual, he had delivered his story live just off the west steps of the Capitol building, always a risky proposition. Sacramento's busy Tenth street was only a few feet from his camera position. A live shot so close to the street made Jack vulnerable to obnoxious motorists who'd love nothing more than to disrupt a live TV report. Sometimes they'd drive by and honk their horns; on a few occasions, particularly rowdy kids would yell obscenities.

A small knot of tourists had worked its way into the camera frame until a news producer waved them off.

Again, he was the lead story. The story may have turned out to be a dud – the Capitol scandal that wasn't – but it still was the lead story. Not coincidentally, Jack thought to himself, there was no rain this evening.

His photographer and engineer were rewinding cables and packing up the live truck when Jack's cell phone rang. It was Jimmy Johnson. "How about a drink tonight, Jack? I'll buy. I'll meet you at Sally's Place right after the newscast, okay?"

Jack wondered why his news director would want to buy him a beer. Jimmy Johnson never socialized with his reporters after work. What does he want? Jack thought.

Sally's Place was one of those Capitol watering holes frequented by legislators and staffers after work. It was notorious for a late-night incident years earlier.

"Assemblyman Herman Smart (D-Riverside) and two female lobbyists were arrested Thursday night at a downtown watering hole in what a police spokesman termed 'an after hours sex party,'" wrote the *Sacramento Union.*

As it turned out, the trio was engaged in three-way sex on the pool table in the back room. A freshman Republican, who had been dressed down by Smart earlier in the day during a budget debate in the Ways and Means Committee, had caught a peek of the action through the back door and anonymously alerted the cops. He thought it would be fun to watch Smart wriggle out of the publicity. In a testament to Smart's stamina, the legislator and his two companions were still intertwined in "political discussion" when the cops burst through the door and made the arrests.

Smart's lawyers got the charges dropped, but the damage had been done. Mail pieces featuring the *Union's* account of the incident made their way into every voter's mailbox during Smart's re-election bid later that year. He was toast. A Democrat hadn't represented the district since then, and it took years before the Capitol's growing and competent cadre of female lobbyists lived down the embarrassment.

After nearly two decades of prowling the Capitol hallways, Jack had covered roughly 4,000 legislative hearings, news conferences, rallies and other assorted political stories. He was as much a fixture at the Capitol as the statue of Spain's Queen Isabella in the rotunda. He was on a first name basis with nearly 200 lobbyists, and considered many of the no-nonsense, take-no-prisoners women lobbyists to be the brightest and most capable.

Sally's Place handled the publicity much better than Herman Smart. Despite receiving a citation for serving alcohol after closing hours, Sally's Place became the bar of choice at the Capitol – partly because the beer was the coldest in town (helpful during Sacramento's 100 degree summers), partly because of its location across the street from the Capitol, and partly because it wasn't typecast as either a Democratic or Republican hang-out. The pretzels and Budweiser were bi-partisan.

"Let's keep this story going," Johnson told Summerland as he ordered a second beer. "It's a grabber. Everyone's talking about it, so let's go with the flow. Maybe we can turn this into a running feud between Callahan and the tabloids. I know this story isn't as sexy as we once thought, but the public still will eat it up. We need to keep the ratings going, you know."

Goddamn ratings, Jack thought to himself.

Jack knew it was an argument he couldn't win. He often told Johnson, "Do what you want with the newscast, but let me have two-and-a-half minutes for solid Capitol news." Usually, Jack wasn't pushed.

"I'll check it out some more, but it seems like this story is going nowhere," he told Johnson. "If I can't come up with any proof, I think we'll just have to drop it. Our credibility is at stake."

Johnson lowered his voice and quickly looked left, then right. "Jack, can I be straight with you?"

"Of course," Jack said.

"Just between you and me – and please don't repeat this – I'm in some trouble at the station. The brass in New York want a bigger return on their investment. They've been pretty direct that they need higher numbers for our news programs. My contract is up in six months, and I'm not really sure where I stand."

"I'm sorry, Jimmy," Jack said. "You've always been straight with me. But, with all due respect, you've changed the past few years. I can see where the corporate pressure has affected your news judgment. I don't agree with it, but I understand it. I hate seeing news being sold like a bar of soap."

"So do I," Johnson said, "but times change. Local television is no longer in the news gathering business; it's in the audience gathering business, and I can't stand it. Now that you know where I'm coming from, do me a favor. There are ways to keep this story going without sacrificing too many principles." He suggested Jack do a sidebar on tabloid journalism and its effect on political careers.

"You know, how the tabloids helped derail Gary Hart's presidential campaign in 1988 and ruined Congressman Gary Condit but didn't kill Bill Clinton," he said.

Jack felt guilty. He had jumped on a dubious story because he felt he could mitigate the fall-out, but he was concerned that people might think he was just another sleazy reporter who took cheap shots and didn't care for the truth.

After meeting with his news director, Jack walked across the street to the Capitol, figuring Billy Galster would still be at work. The press secretary, hunched over his computer, was putting the finishing touches on a draft press release.

"Billy, sorry to bother you, but I didn't have time to talk to you today, and I just wanted to apologize for that story last night. I didn't want to run with it, but I had no choice. I argued with my news director. But we're in sweeps. You know how it is."

Actually, Galster did know how it is. He was a former reporter for the *Los Angeles Times* and understood what makes news. "I've been there," he said.

Galster also knew that even though many people probably believed the original story tying Johnny Callahan with a hooker, his boss eventually could come out this episode smelling like a rose. Callahan would be the aggrieved public servant who stood up to the grimy tabloids and won.

"Look, Jack. We've always had a good relationship. I'll admit you gave us a few headaches, but we're surviving. Your mea culpa on the air tonight was first-rate. Let's have lunch in a couple of days."

Jack was a political eunuch, registered Decline-to-State, and didn't have strong feelings for Democrats or Republicans, but he always wanted to be considered a fair reporter. If Galster – and by extension, Callahan – thought Jack had handled himself professionally, then there'd be no long-term damage.

"How do you think this thing started?" Summerland asked, fishing for a new lead on the story. "Who set you up?"

"Hell if I know," Galster responded. "It came out of nowhere. The only thing I can think of is that someone wants to prevent Johnny from going to the Senate and will do anything to stop him."

Summerland could sense an air of relief in Galster's voice. There's nothing like being a martyr, he thought, and Johnny Callahan is playing it perfectly.

"I've already heard from three newspapers," Galster told Jack. "They plan to run editorials trashing negative and personal politics. We took some grief last night, but we're in even better shape today."

As Jack left the speaker's office, he detoured to the back of the office suite. Karen, working late and writing a letter on her computer, didn't see Jack approaching. He leaned over and whispered in her ear. "Everything okay?" he said.

Karen whirled in her chair and smiled broadly. "As a matter of fact, things are going great today, no thanks to you," she said in mock disdain. "The *Starlight* overreached and we're going to benefit."

Callahan's appointment wasn't in the bag yet, but few would bet against it.

Eight

It was a typical May in Tucson. Hot and dry, no hint of clouds. Carl Jansen sat at the dinette table in his small, spartan apartment as the whirring sound of a portable fan broke the silence and stirred the stale air. He lit his first cigarette of the day. Spread out on the coffee table next to the sofa was a copy of *USA Today* opened to a page on state briefs.

> **Los Angeles** — The tabloid *Starlight* newspaper today apologized to California Assembly Speaker Johnny Callahan for suggesting that Callahan, a widower, spent time with a prostitute. The newspaper pulled the Callahan story before publication but acknowledged that it leaked details to the news media. Callahan is considered Gov. Colin Frank's likely choice to replace the late Bernie Edelstein in the U.S. Senate.

Jansen read and re-read the article. No one knew that he was behind the botched story.

Jansen had set-up the *Starlight* and almost pulled it off. He found a hooker on Sunset Boulevard and paid her $1,000 to pose for some photos. Using sophisticated software, he doctored a couple of photographs to make it look like Callahan and the hooker were interested in more than tax policy. One photo showed Callahan and the woman, a tall brunette wearing nothing but high heels and a diamond necklace, in what appeared to be a passionate lip lock.

Jansen then located a slug named Richard Blattman in the personal ads of an alternative Los Angeles newspaper, gave him the photos and told him to feed the phony Callahan story to the *Starlight.* Blattman provided one of its reporters with all sorts of bogus facts – including the hooker's cell phone number — to back up the accusation.

Deep down Jansen wasn't sure the *Starlig*ht would run the story. Even a rookie reporter, he thought, would question the legitimacy of the allegations. But Jansen seemed to hit the mother lode. The *Starlight* took the bait and was preparing a major expose of the powerful Assembly speaker. With a little advance publicity, thanks to KBLT, the *Starlight* story would be the latest to cross the diaphanous line to become a mainstream news source.

Jansen had been pleased with his handiwork when Blattman reported that the *Starlight* had accepted the photos and appeared to be interested in the story. From a distance, he'd be able to monitor the post-publication chaos on the Internet in follow-up stories from California's major newspapers. He was stunned, however, to read subsequent accounts that made Johnny Callahan look like the victim of a vicious smear. Not only did the *Starlight* fail to run the story, but the entire episode seemed to make the speaker's political stock rise.

Jansen's eyes darted from the coffee table to a small desk in the corner of his apartment, cluttered with a computer, printer and papers piled about two inches high. He walked to the desk and thumbed through the pile of papers and pulled out a checkbook. He carefully wrote a $3,900 check and made it payable to the "Johnny Callahan Speaker's Committee." He scribbled "Harvey Pittman" on the bottom. "Okay, so it's on to Plan B," he mumbled to himself.

He stuffed the check in an envelope with a return address that said Reliance Security, Irvine, CA. He typed a mailing label on his computer: Assembly Speaker Johnny Callahan, Room 219, State Capitol, Sacramento, CA 95814. Personal and Confidential.

It was a trap, with $3,900 in bait. "This is for you, Toni," he whispered.

Jansen was a consultant for Desert Security, Inc., a small but successful outfit based in Tucson and serving various Arizona cities. It wasn't always this way. At one time, Carl Jansen was a rising star with the FBI.

Thirty years earlier, Jansen was the golden boy in the Houston FBI office. He had made headlines by playing an important role in tracking down the bomber of three abortion clinics outside Houston.

With his career ascending, Jansen talked his superiors into letting him take a one-year sabbatical so he could accept a research and teaching post at the University of California in the Criminology Department. Teaching in Berkeley at one of the nation's most prestigious universities was a dream come true.

Jansen taught a course on forensics for seniors and graduate students during the spring semester, 1985. In the summer and fall, he taught Criminology 101 and spent much of his time in the university's vast library system researching serial killers for a book he was writing. He contacted his office frequently with research updates. The Bureau's brass in Washington liked the potential publicity that an agent-author could bring.

Jansen's wife of 12 years, Samantha, had split time between suburban Houston and the Bay Area. Often, they spent their free time hiking at Mt. Tamalpais and exploring Muir Woods in Marin County north of San Francisco. They took weekend jaunts to

Mendocino, Monterey, Napa and Sonoma, and even rafted down the American River in Sacramento. Often they'd hang out in Jansen's tiny off-campus apartment and explore the offerings of the university – an exhibit of early San Francisco relics at the Phoebe Hearst Museum of Anthropology, or a visit to the Lawrence Hall of Science in the hills above Memorial Stadium.

Jansen's life changed after a routine lecture in Criminology 101. Toni was a senior sociology major, and one of most beautiful women he had ever seen. She reminded him of one of those supermodels, although not as rail-thin – hazel eyes, flowing auburn hair, long legs and a smile that could melt the coldest heart.

Carl Jansen had cut a dashing figure himself – well over six feet tall. He had a strong jaw, a perpetually tanned face, wavy brown hair and bulging biceps from years of lifting weights. Little did he realize, at first, that the wide-eyed beauty in the first row of his class was madly in love with the professor.

It started with innocent flirting during office hours. Toni would come in before class, her perfume dancing in his head. Together, they'd review reading assignments; she was the most inquisitive student in the class. Jansen tried to maintain a professional distance, but he longed for her visits. At first, he purposely left his office door open during each office call. He didn't want any other faculty or students to sense his feelings.

By the time the semester ended, their relationship had progressed into something more serious. They called each other daily; their meetings for coffee became romantic. The physical relationship that followed was inevitable. When his wife was back in Texas, he would take Toni to San Francisco on weekends, and they'd picnic in Tilden Park in the Berkeley hills.

In November, however, Jansen's behavior seemed to change. He never said anything, but faculty colleagues noticed that he seemed distant and unresponsive. He missed a few lectures and once was called into the department chair's office and lectured about his responsibilities as a visiting instructor. Jansen had few friends at Berkeley — certainly, no one close. Many wondered if he was using drugs or having difficulty making his long-distance marriage work. By mid-December, the day after he administered the final in his criminology class, Jansen was gone.

Inexplicably, his career nose-dived after his stint at Berkeley. He returned to Houston and seemed to lose interest in his book. He was assigned to a team probing corruption at the state house in Austin. The Houston field office covered 41 Texas cities, including Austin, and Jansen jumped at the chance to nail some dirty politicians.

It all came crashing down when Jansen masterminded a bungled sting of six Texas legislators. He had posed as a wealthy owner of a chain of private schools seeking narrowly drawn legislation to give his company a huge tax break. The scheme had blown up in his face when he was recognized in an Austin restaurant as he was passing a check to one of the lawmakers.

The publicity was horrendous. "FBI Runs Amok," screamed one headline in the *Austin American-Statesman.* The FBI had no choice but to make Jansen the fall guy. The office's special agent in charge seemed to be near tears when he told Jansen he was being fired. "We had such high hopes for you. You were going places," he told Jansen. The FBI's rising star had flamed out. Jansen contemplated what his life had become. No job, no pension, and no prospects.

For the next several years, Jansen and Samantha bounced around the Southwest, depending on his employment prospects. He spent a few years in Dallas as a private investigator, then started a small investigative firm in Santa Fe. He had several technology companies on his client list until the tech crash in 2000. The pair picked up stakes again and headed for Tucson, where Samantha's brother knew the president of Desert Security, Inc. Jansen felt like a charity case, but he accepted a job offer at DSI.

Jansen's blank stare at the *USA Today* article from Los Angeles masked the fact that he held inside a blockbuster secret that he dared tell no one. Years ago, his life had briefly intersected with the man who later would become California's powerful Assembly speaker. Now, three months after Samantha's passing from liver cancer, revenge was all he cared about. He had a score to settle and a story no one would believe. He'd get Johnny Callahan and punish him for ruining his life.

Jansen knew taking on Callahan was playing with fire, but he didn't care. He had lost his wife, his lover and his career. He had nothing left to lose.

Plan B actually had begun two months before the *Starlight* fiasco. It was a back-up plan, designed to do more than merely embarrass the Assembly speaker. But it needed time to develop. Jansen posed as the owner of Reliance Security of Irvine, using the name Harvey Pittman. He had numerous phone conversations with a Callahan staffer who convinced the speaker to carry legislation that would offer tax credits to small companies that manufactured specified high-tech alarms. In the post September 11 environment, anti-crime legislation was a slam dunk.

Callahan introduced Assembly Bill 613 with little fanfare. On occasion, newspapers would include a one- or two-sentence synopsis of the bill in their legislation round-up stories. Of course, many reporters didn't read the bill, so they didn't know that the legislation was written to benefit a single company, the one represented by Pittman.

Callahan thought he was doing a good deed; instead, he unknowingly walked into a sting that threatened his career and could lead to serious prison time at Club Fed – Boron's desolate federal penitentiary in the middle of the Mojave Desert.

Assembly Bill 613 moved quickly through the Legislature. It was approved easily by the Criminal Justice and Revenue and Taxation committees and won passage on the Assembly floor on a 61-4 vote. Three of the "no" votes came from Democrats angry with Callahan over all the political hay the speaker received from pushing his tax bill. A Republican, Assemblywoman Patricia Craig from Mendocino, who actually read the bill, cast the other dissenting vote. Instead of blindly voting for the measure, as her Republican caucus chair had suggested, she noticed that the legislation seemed too narrowly drawn for her liking. She didn't make a big deal about it, and didn't speak against it on the Assembly floor, but quietly voted against it.

Jansen, pretending to be Harvey Pittman, understood how politics worked. He had withdrawn $12,000 from his life savings and spread it around to legislators in the form of campaign contributions. He created a phony company, had some stationery made and represented himself as an honest small businessman who was doing his country a favor.

Jansen's boldest move, however, was coming next. He typed a brief note on bogus Reliance Security letterhead.

"Speaker Callahan — Thanks for Assembly Bill 613. I hope this helps in your next campaign. Harvey Pittman."

He printed a second copy of the note for his files and slipped the original into the envelope with the money.

Accepting money as a quid pro quo for legislation is a federal offense, punishable by significant prison time. Jansen figured Callahan, whose thirst for campaign dollars was legendary at the Capitol, would accept the contribution and finally get what he deserved. Ironically, it was one of Callahan's predecessors, the late Assembly Speaker Jesse Unruh, who once said, "Money is the mother's milk of politics."

Jansen had collected newspaper accounts of a successful sting in Sacramento in the late 1980s that ended up netting legislators, staffers and lobbyists. An FBI agent, posing as a wealthy southern shrimp farmer, sought legislation that would make it easier to establish a west coast operation in West Sacramento. The agent spread money around and there was a late evening raid of legislative offices at the Capitol.

Agents swooped into the Capitol, searched files in a half dozen legislative offices and actually walked onto the Senate floor during an evening session – grabbing a senator by the lapels and taking him out to the balcony to try to get him to rat on his colleagues. Eventually, a federal grand jury indicted a number of legislators on bribery and racketeering charges. They were convicted in highly publicized trials and sent to prison. An assemblyman pleaded guilty and spent four years becoming a born-again Christian while serving time in a federal prison. The FBI had video of one senator accepting a $3,000 check at a downtown restaurant. A female agent had placed a small camera in her purse and recorded the evidence.

The media had a field day with "Shrimpscam," as they dubbed it. Newspaper editorials called for an overhaul of California's campaign finance laws. The chastened Legislature placed on the ballot – and the voters approved – a measure that prevented lawmakers from accepting honoraria, or speaking fees, and limiting gifts they can receive. Voters also approved the nation's first term limits initiative, limiting Assembly members to six years in office, and Senators and statewide elected officials to eight years.

Jansen put the envelope in a briefcase, surveyed his small apartment and wondered where his life had gone awry. Successful career, up and down marriage – then Toni. He couldn't take his eyes off her that year in Berkeley. He couldn't stop thinking about her now. Or Johnny Callahan.

Jansen grabbed his briefcase, threw it in the backseat of his aging Toyota Corolla and headed for the airport and a trip to Southern California.

Nine

The *Starlight* controversy and the ensuing fallout turned out to be the perfect career-booster for Johnny Callahan. Just about every daily newspaper in California editorialized against tabloid journalism and complimented Callahan on his handling of the story.

"The lines between tabloid and mainstream journalism are becoming more blurred every day," wrote the *Sacramento Bee*, "and it is our job to doggedly pursue the truth and not fall victim to sensational innuendo and half-truths. Although we don't see eye-to-eye with Speaker Callahan on many issues, we do respect the way in which he has conducted himself in office since his initial election to the Assembly. And as Governor Frank weighs the pros and cons of likely successors to Senator Edelstein, he could do a lot worse than naming Speaker Callahan for the job."

Not exactly a ringing endorsement, but this was – after all –

the *Sacramento Bee*, which historically never met too many Republicans it liked. The traditionally conservative *San Diego Union-Tribune* was more effusive.

"Johnny Callahan has demonstrated the leadership and courage it takes to be a great U.S. Senator," the newspaper said in its lead editorial. "Governor Frank should send him to Washington as soon as possible."

Johnny Callahan had turned a public relations nightmare into a golden opportunity. The *Starlight* had been discredited and was forced to pull the bogus hooker story from publication and issue a public apology to the leader of the state Assembly.

Once the flap over the *Starlight* fiasco evaporated from the news, Jack Summerland was back covering mundane legislation and the usual pre-summer budget two-step.

The brass at Channel 4 hated to see Jack covering the Assembly Ways and Means or Senate Budget committees. What could offer more boring video than a bunch of men in dark suits – and a few women – sitting in committee meetings arguing over the complexities of a state budget.

Management would rather have Jack get into the spirit of sweeps month by reporting stories that involved those time-honored ratings staples of sex and crime, perhaps combining both into a series on paroled sexual predators and the government's efforts to keep tabs on them for life. But after much debate, they saw the wisdom of assigning the sexual predator series, heavily promoted on the air and the station's website, to another reporter.

Finally disentangled from the phony Callahan sex scandal, Jack returned to covering real news – legislators actually doing the people's business by writing laws that affected his viewers.

As Jack walked into the Capitol's spacious fourth-floor hearing room with a cup of coffee in one hand and a cinnamon raisin bagel in the other, he noticed that the Assembly Revenue and Taxation Committee was just getting started. He quickly surveyed the scene. Jack's burly and baby-faced photographer, Ron Middleton, had claimed his four square feet of floor space for himself and his tripod and camera. He had a perfect unencumbered view of the witness table.

No other television crews had arrived. An exclusive? Jack pondered. He anticipated another tedious hearing. Only five of the 13 committee members were in their seats on the raised platform. Two others had popped in for a minute and had their names recorded so the committee could function with a quorum.

The hearing room, adorned with a giant portrait of California's legendary former speaker, Jesse Unruh, was one-tenth full. A handful of lobbyists, mostly representing business interests, mingled in the back of the hearing room. Jack recognized lobbyists from Microsoft, the California Chamber of Commerce and the California Taxpayers Association seated in the second row, just behind the row reserved for legislators. A couple of print reporters sat at a desk behind a railing separating the committee from the two-dozen rows of spectator chairs.

Everyone looked like they had hangovers. In fact, many did. The lobbyist for one of California's largest savings and loan institutions slumped in his second-row seat and snored periodically in a foggy half-sleep.

Another lobbyist – they preferred to be called legislative advocates – stood in the back of the cavernous chamber and pulled out of his coat pocket an electric razor. As he began to remove a night's worth of stubble, a muscular sergeant-at-arms, impeccably dressed in a dark blue suit, craned his neck, scoped the buzzing offender and started to walk up the aisle to give him the heave-ho. The lobbyist quickly ran out the back door of the hearing room to finish his grooming in the hallway.

The night before, no fewer than six Assembly members and three senators had fundraisers, and it was still a year away from the next election. Senator Carl Fitchberg had a 50th birthday party at Sally's Place. Cocktail weenies and drinks for $1,000. Assemblywoman Virginia Ames had a summer beach party poolside in a donor's backyard. Pizza and daiquiris for $750. Senator Al Ross, termed out and facing no more elections, held a $1,000 per person fundraiser to help retire his past campaign debts. His invitation to lobbyists said his event would "bring back the magic at the Capitol." Beer, wine, cheese puffs and A-La-Shazam, who performed card tricks for thirty minutes before falling off a stool and breaking an ankle.

As the morning wore on, the crowd in hearing room 4202 grew, anticipating a show. By 11:15, the non-controversial legislation had been approved with little debate. Next came the main attraction. Assembly Bill 1002, Speaker Callahan's tax cut.

The bill lowered tax rates for the wealthiest Californians, bringing them to pre-2003 levels. During one of California's chronic budget crunches, Democratic legislators had muscled through a tax hike for individuals earning more than $150,000 per year and couples earning more than $300,000.

Now that the Republicans were in charge, it was time to undo the damage.

As a 21st century Assembly speaker, Callahan didn't have the absolute power some of his predecessors enjoyed, but he certainly was first among equals in the lower house. In the 1960s, Jesse "Big Daddy" Unruh ruled the Assembly with an iron fist. Members crossed Unruh at their peril and paid the price. Unruh stripped his political opponents of choice committee assignments. They were unceremoniously evicted from their prime office space and banished to the Capitol's sixth floor near the cafeteria.

Between 1980 and 1995, Willie Brown also wielded power with audacity and flamboyance.

A series of reforms, including term limits, enacted during Brown's waning years as speaker, diluted the power of the office for all future speakers. The Assembly speaker no longer had life or death control over legislation but still had plenty of firepower, most prominently the ability to raise huge sums of campaign contributions for friends and the authority to appoint each member of every committee.

Johnny Callahan stacked the deck in the Revenue and Taxation Committee. Eight of the 13 members were Republicans. If everyone attended the hearing, the final vote would be 8-5. No suspense. The tougher job would be getting a two-thirds vote on the Assembly floor.

But first things first. Callahan received word that morning that Clint Blocker, a Republican from Fresno, had a family emergency and would not attend the hearing. That meant he needed all of the other Republican votes to move his tax bill. Callahan had the power to appoint another member to fill-in for Blocker, but that was a maneuver that would be attacked bitterly by Democratic members and end up being a huge news story. No, Callahan figured he could maneuver his bill through committee with or without Blocker.

One by one, TV camera crews filed into the hearing room and set up their tripods behind the curved dais near the front of the chamber. "So much for having this story to ourselves," Jack whispered to Middleton.

In walked Johnny Callahan, looking like a man on a mission. He was flanked by Billy Galster and two other aides. Obviously, Galster hadn't gotten the word from Callahan's choreographer, because Callahan and the other aides looked like triplets, all wearing dark blue suits, white shirts and red ties. "Look, it's Huey, Dewey and Louie," sniffed one photographer. Galster wore a green sports jacket and a black bow tie.

"Mr. Speaker," the committee chair announced, "the floor is yours."

Within seconds, absent members of the committee sauntered into the hearing room, alerted to the vote in their offices by a live feed of committee proceedings.

Callahan spelled out the provisions of AB 1002. Two handpicked witnesses, a business professor from Stanford and a tax expert from the conservative California Foundation, testified that the tax cut would stimulate job growth by encouraging business owners to invest in their companies.

In brief debate on the measure, Callahan invoked the memories of Ronald Reagan and economist Milton Friedman as he argued that tax cuts would benefit employers who would use the added revenue to hire more workers.

Democrats argued Callahan wanted to help his rich friends – who just happened to be the governor's friends as well. They argued that "trickle down" economics was a fraud and that California's already fragile budget would take a multi-billion dollar hit.

One of the Capitol's dirty little secrets was the notion that lawmakers actually debated issues and thoughtfully considered legislation before casting votes. In fact, the debate was just for show. The inside players knew exactly how the charade would play out. Each side presented arguments as the committee members nodded and asked questions as if they were actually deliberating. In fact, there was no suspense.

The vote broke along party lines, except for one apparent holdout. San Diego Republican Assemblywoman Corinne Jackson wavered. Not on principles, mind you, but she wanted concessions from Callahan before she'd vote aye.

A moderate maverick who often fought the Assembly leadership, Jackson came to Sacramento after eight years in Congress. She had been upset in the Republican primary by a local pro football hero who painted her as a Democrat in GOP clothing. Two years later, she rehabilitated her career by winning a seat in the Assembly. She knew how to barter for votes, and as the committee chair announced a five-minute recess, she pursed her lips and waited for Callahan to approach her seat, not five feet from Jack Summerland's camera.

Callahan warily shot a glance at Summerland as he approached Jackson. He held a hand over the microphone in front of the assemblywoman and whispered in her ear. "Let's go outside into the hallway," he said.

"No," she responded in a barely audible whisper. "Let's talk here."

Summerland couldn't hear the whispered conversation, and his microphone only picked up a few words. He thought he heard Jackson ask for a financial commitment to help her in the coming year's election. He definitely heard Callahan say, "Okay, you've got it." He wasn't sure what she got, but in a matter of minutes, he expected, she would announce she was voting for AB 1002.

Summerland couldn't wait for the vote. It was 11:43 and he was on deadline, assigned to do a live report from the Capitol steps for Channel 4's noon news. He had the lead story — not because the noon news producer thought it was the most important story of the day, but because it was fresh. He whispered to Jackson, "You going to vote aye?" Jackson nodded affirmatively.

Jack grabbed the video disc from Middleton and started sprinting for the door. As he worked his way down four flights of stairs to the ground level, Middleton remained in the committee room to capture the vote and any last-minute video.

A Channel 4 live truck, with an engineer and editor, waited for Jack at the usual spot on the Capitol's west steps. He'd barely have time to feed a sound bite from the hearing before going on the air. Once he had reported the story, he'd have to trudge back upstairs to the hearing room for follow up interviews, first seeking Assemblywoman Jackson, then various combatants on both sides of the legislation. It was a hell of a way to earn a living.

At 11:59, Summerland fastened the top button on his shirt, tightened the knot on his tie and shoved it into his throat. He scribbled a few words and word segments into his note pad: "victory...7–5...Jackson...centerpiece...Callahan...Appropriations." Gibberish to most people, but a tight roadmap enabling Jack to meander through his story without missing any key ingredients.

"Hold it," snapped Ray Edwards, a muscular photographer sent by the station to shoot his live shot. "They didn't get a clean feed. We have to feed it again. Hold on."

For reasons Jack didn't understand, the video broke up as it was being sent by microwave seven blocks from the Capitol to the studio. The engineer re-racked the video and fed it again. Meantime, Jack could hear music in his earpiece signifying the beginning of the broadcast. It was going to be tight. Jack's heart pounded a little harder.

As noon anchor Chandra Kramer started to introduce the story, Edwards flashed a thumbs up sign with his right hand. Seconds later, Summerland — glancing occasionally at his notepad scribblings — told the world, or at least a portion of Northern California, about Johnny Callahan's handiwork.

Summerland on camera

Momentarily, a big victory for Speaker Johnny Callahan. In what likely will be a 7-to-5 party line vote, the Assembly Revenue and Taxation Committee is expected to approve his huge tax cut proposal.

Video – Committee hearing

The committee is still debating the measure at this hour. It lowers personal income tax rates for individuals earning more than $150,000 a year and couples earning more than $300,000 a year.

Republicans say the measure will undo the harmful tax increases approved by the Democratic-controlled Legislature several years ago.

The key vote is expected to be cast by Republican Corinne Jackson of San Diego, but only after some negotiations with the powerful speaker. This tax cut is the centerpiece of the speaker's legislative agenda.

Video/Audio – Callahan

> "We are just starting to rebound from a devastating recession. Now is not the time to restrict job creation by taking more money from our citizens. Government already overburdens our taxpayers. This legislation will bring some sanity back to our tax policy."

Summerland on camera

> After today's vote, the measure goes to the Assembly Appropriations Committee, which is expected to follow suit. Reporting live from the state Capitol, this is Jack Summerland, Action 4 News.

Jack had no time to savor another job well done. He had to get back to the committee and wrap up the story. He unhooked his microphone and walked hurriedly back into the Capitol. Sprinting up the stairs two at a time, Jack turned a corner in the stairwell and smacked into Karen.

"No time to talk. Gotta run," Jack panted as he resumed his climb.

"Hold on, Jack," Karen said. "If you're going back to Rev and Tax, it's over. After Johnny got his bill out, the room cleared. I saw Ron tearing down his camera."

"Shit," Jack muttered. "They want me to cover the news but they make me do a damn live report before it's over. And then I miss the vote. What a bunch of crap."

Catching his breath, Jack slowly trudged up to the fourth floor to meet up with Middleton. He'd knock out a couple of quick interviews, then head back to the station to put his story package together for the evening news.

As he opened the door connecting the stairwell to the fourth floor, he saw Callahan, Galster and another member of the speaker's staff talking in a little alcove off the hearing room. Callahan flailed his arms and jabbed a finger in the staffer's chest. Summerland thought he heard Callahan say, "Don't touch it. It might have fingerprints."

Jack made a mental note to call Galster and ask him about that strange hallway conversation.

Ten

For the second time in a week, the powerful speaker of the California Assembly had been the target of a malicious smear.

A secretary had opened an envelope containing a $3,900 check. She read the note from Harvey Pittman at Reliance Security and recognized immediately that something was wrong. She was smart enough to know that the law prohibited government officials from accepting contributions in return for official government acts.

Callahan's chief of staff called the FBI and turned the check and accompanying note over to an agent who came to the speaker's office for the pickup. It took only moments to determine that Harvey Pittman didn't exist, that Reliance Security was a non-existent company at a non-existent address in Irvine.

Callahan didn't know who had planted the phony story in the

Starlight. He had no idea who sent him a political contribution. But he guessed it was another effort to discredit him. His press secretary, always thinking, smelled a public relations coup. He'd make Callahan the innocent victim, which he was, and boost his approval ratings by ten percent – if he could generate the proper media coverage.

The FBI's special agent in charge of the Sacramento area suggested that Callahan's office hold off revealing the bribery attempt, but politics came first. Ron Galster knew he had a chastened Jack Summerland by the balls. The reporter had broadcast a trash story that turned out to be false, and he felt guilty about it. Now, Galster would leak enough of the bribery attempt to give Summerland a huge scoop. Summerland, still embarrassed from the *Starlight* story, would bend over backwards to give Callahan a positive story.

The following morning, during a 45-minute meeting on a bench in Capitol Park, Galster told Summerland about the contribution and how the speaker had turned the check over to the FBI. He insisted that the entire conversation had to be off the record and that no one from Callahan's office would comment publicly.

Jack thought, so that's what I overheard Callahan whispering about yesterday.

"Don't overlook the obvious," Galster said. "After all, there's been plenty of talk mentioning the speaker as a potential U.S. senator, and in politics you make plenty of enemies."

"I just don't know about this," Jack said. "I've already been burned on the *Starlight* story. I need someone to go on the record with this."

Galster recognized that he wasn't giving Summerland much to work with and felt the reporter was balking at taking the bait. "Don't you have sources at the FBI who can back me up on this?"

Summerland nodded, but he didn't say a word.

Then, Galster played his trump card. "Okay," he said. "I'll

give you two hours to decide if you want to run with this. After that, I'm giving it to Tollefson."

That did the trick. Lawrence Tollefson was a veteran Sacramento reporter for the *Los Angeles Times.* Summerland would love nothing more than to scoop California journalism's 800-pound gorilla.

"Hold on," Summerland snapped. "You don't have to do that. But I'd like to talk to Speaker Callahan — off the record, of course. Just give me five minutes."

Galster refused, but offered Chief of Staff Sam Cockerill, instead, who gave Summerland the same story without much embellishment, except to wonder out loud if someone was trying to frame the popular and fast-rising California Assembly speaker who seemed destined for the U.S. Senate and national stardom.

Summerland phoned Clay Bertrand at the station and told him he didn't want to cover Governor Frank's appearance before the League of California Cities conference. He knew exactly what the governor would say, anyway. Frank would pander to the mayors and city council members by vowing not to raid local tax revenues to help balance the state budget.

"Give it to Blickman, or someone else. I'm working on an exclusive that could be explosive."

Summerland called his mole in the FBI office who confirmed everything. Off the record, of course. Then he started putting his story together. He had to be careful not to burn any of his sources, and he needed some video to spice up his story. He developed a theme that Callahan — on two occasions, now — had been the victim of botched attempts to blunt his U. S. Senate selection.

Some television reporters write their stories first, before figuring out what video to use. Summerland assessed his video possibilities first, and then fit the narration to the pictures. This ensured a flowing story where video and audio matched — making it easier for the viewer to understand. It also ensured that even a print-only story, with no discernible picture possibilities, could be interesting to watch.

He jotted down his video possibilities – the front page logo of the *Starlight* newspaper, which had accused Callahan of sleeping with a prostitute; a shot of Callahan and an aide walking down a corridor; a quick sound bite from Callahan's news conference, in which the speaker said, tersely: "It's not true. It didn't happen. Someone is out to embarrass me." For perspective, he located footage in the news archives from the 1988 FBI sting, including a snippet of video showing a legislative office – with papers strewn about and file cabinets open – moments after agents had rifled through it. He then found black and white hidden camera video, introduced as evidence during one of the Capitol corruption trials, of a state senator accepting a check from an undercover FBI agent.

He looked under his desk and retrieved a video disc labeled "Governor at Sheraton" which included footage taken several months earlier of Callahan and Governor Frank together at a political fundraiser at a hotel a few blocks from the Capitol. He asked his photographer, Middleton, to get a few generic shots of the federal building that housed the FBI, and a few shots outside the entrance to Callahan's office. Then, he briefed Jimmy Johnson.

Johnson could smell a good story, and corruption at the Capitol was another ratings bonanza. Besides, it hadn't rained in several days, as mid-May showers had turned into a heat wave in the low 90s.

Johnson asked several times about Summerland's sources and offered only one suggestion. "We need some sound with this story. Who can you interview?"

"No one will talk to us on the record, but I do have a bite of Callahan at his news conference last week questioning why someone is trying to nail him."

Johnson shot back. "Okay, get an MOS at the Capitol.

That'll round out the story."

MOS, or man-on-the-street interview, was a news technique that Summerland hated. If you ask enough people you could find opinions on anything you wanted. Stand in the parking lot outside a shopping center for five minutes and you'd find people who want to impeach the president, and others who want to put his face on Mt. Rushmore. MOS interviews were a waste of time, Jack knew. But the brass loved it. "Viewers would rather see real, everyday people talking about issues than stodgy legislators," Johnson reminded Summerland.

When Middleton returned from the FBI shoot, the news team drove to the Capitol, parked on Tenth street and started asking questions of people milling around the Capitol building. "We've learned that Speaker Callahan refused a $3,900 bribe and immediately notified the FBI. What do you think about this?"

It wouldn't take a Phi Beta Kappa to anticipate the answers. One tourist from Fresno suggested that bribery was a way of life in Sacramento. "Corruption is everywhere," she said. Most, however, said they were shocked and admired the speaker for blowing the whistle. Several, recalling the recent *Starlight* flap, seemed to echo Callahan's plaintive cry: "Why is someone trying to get Johnny Callahan?"

It was 2:03 p.m. when Middleton and Summerland returned from the Capitol and started putting their story together. The story wrote itself. As he always did, Summerland asked Middleton, "What's the first video?" He had his own idea of how to start the story, but he always wanted input from the man responsible for the video images.

Middleton and Summerland had worked together for several years. They traveled to Washington, D.C., and covered the national political conventions, presidential and gubernatorial campaigns together, and spent just about every other day meandering the halls of the State Capitol looking for stories. Each knew how the other thought.

"Let's start with that shot of Callahan walking down the hallway. It's a perfect set-up shot," Middleton suggested.

Jack shouted across the newsroom to the 5 p.m. producer, Ginny Hollingsworth. "How much time do I have?"

"How much do you need?" she responded. Usually, Jack's stories were limited to no more than a minute, forty seconds. It felt great to have some latitude.

"I don't have much in the way of sound, but let's go with two minutes, max."

With Middleton looking over his shoulder, Jack started typing into his computer.

Anchor lead

Action News 4 has learned that Assembly Speaker Johnny Callahan was the subject of a crude bribery attempt yesterday. Reporter Jack Summerland has live, exclusive details from the State Capitol. Jack?

Summerland on camera

Someone purporting to be a Southern California businessman sent the speaker a $3,900 check in return for Callahan authoring a piece of anti-crime legislation. A source with direct knowledge of the incident told us Callahan's office immediately notified the FBI, which is not commenting on the case. Callahan's office is not offering any public comment, either.

Video — Callahan walking the hallway

Yesterday's bribery attempt represents the second time in a week that someone has tried to discredit the powerful Assembly speaker...

Video – Frank and Callahan

who is a leading candidate to be Governor Frank's choice for the U.S. Senate.

Video – Outside speaker's office

Apparently, the check was received by the speaker's Capitol office…

Video – Outside Federal Building

and immediately was turned over to the FBI without Callahan ever seeing it. It is illegal for lawmakers to trade votes for contributions.

Video – *Starlight* front page

Just last week, in a bizarre occurrence, the tabloid *Starlight* was prepared to run a front-page story implicating Callahan with a prostitute. But it backed down in the face of evidence that the story was false.

Video/Audio – Callahan

"It's not true. It didn't happen. Someone is out to embarrass me."

Video/Audio – Woman

"I think it's terrible that someone is trying to set him up. He's a great leader."

Video/Audio – Man

"I'll bet it's a Democrat who doesn't like the speaker's politics. It's disgusting."

Video/Audio – Woman

"Nothing surprises me about what goes on here. But I do feel sorry for Callahan. He's a good man."

Video – Capitol

Veterans at the Capitol recall 1988 – the last time a bribery scandal rocked the Legislature. FBI agents established a dummy company and offered campaign cash in return for favorable votes on legislation.

Video – Assembly office

Agents swept into the Capitol and searched the files of numerous legislators.

Black/White Video – Senator receiving payment

Eventually...several legislators and other officials either pleaded guilty or were convicted of federal racketeering charges and each spent several years in federal prison.

Summerland on camera

No one involved in this current incident – the FBI or Callahan's office – will confirm or deny the bribery attempt on the record. But there is plenty of speculation at the Capitol as to the motive behind this incident.

Jack looked at Middleton, one of those station employees who both photographed and edited video. "What do you think?"

"It's a winner," Middleton shot back. "Start laying your track and I'll grab an edit booth."

Jack re-read the script silently, then read it out loud to himself so he could hear how the story would sound to viewers.

When he delivered the story live from the Capitol at the top of the newscast, he attracted a small crowd of tourists and passersby. After airing his story, he unclipped the microphone from the lapel of his suit, turned to face the grand, domed pantheon of politics and noticed Johnny Callahan's chief of staff and press secretary looking down on him through a second floor window in the office of the Assembly speaker.

Once the story broke, Galster was free to issue a statement, which was sent to members of the Capitol Press Corps.

"The speaker's office had been in contact with a purported constituent who said he owns a business that makes anti-home invasion security systems. We agreed to carry common sense legislation that we thought would benefit the people of California. But when a $3,900 campaign contribution from this 'constituent' arrived with a note linking the contribution to Assembly Bill 613, Chief of Staff Sam Cockerill immediately notified the FBI and state authorities. The speaker will not move AB 613 through the Legislature and is cooperating fully with law enforcement."

Back in Tucson, Carl Jansen lit a cigarette and stared in disbelief at his computer screen. Under the headline, "Breaking News," KBLT had placed a lengthy story on the ill-fated sting attempt on its website. The story included Cockerill's complete statement and some background information attributed to reporter Jack Summerland, including a still photo of the reporter standing in front of the Capitol building.

He sighed heavily. His life had spiraled out of control, and now he couldn't even successfully bribe a politician. He scanned the KBLT website and clicked on "Contact Us." He found Jack

Summerland's name and a phone number — one, a direct line into Jack's desk in the newsroom and the other a cell phone number. Jansen closed his laptop and started dialing.

Eleven

Eleven

William Talone sat in the back seat of a taxi heading north on the San Diego Freeway out of LAX. It was unseasonably warm this close to the ocean – no hint of the usual thick fog rolling in from the sea, and the driver had both front windows rolled down. Talone tried to keep his hair in place as a steady stream of warm air buffeted against him.

Talone paid little attention to the afternoon business report on an all-news station, and he seemed oblivious to the typical freeway crawl that had become as intrinsic to Los Angeles as the self-indulgent Hollywood community. He reached into the inside pocket of his suit jacket and read, then re-read, a lengthy memo concerning Governor Colin Frank's choice for the U.S. Senate.

As executive director of the U.S. Commerce Association, Talone's primary job was to fill Congress and the Senate with as many pro-business members as possible. Senator Bernie Edelstein had been an enemy, pushing products liability legislation and higher taxes. Johnny Callahan, if elevated to the Senate, would be a friend – perhaps the deciding vote on dozens of critical issues important to the USCA. Talone had flown all the way from Washington, D.C., to meet with a disparate group of Californians who shared the belief that the Senate needed Callahan.

The taxi turned off the freeway and headed west on Sunset Boulevard toward Pacific Palisades. He looked out the window just as the taxi passed Rockingham Avenue, the street where O.J. Simpson once lived. He remembered the name from all the publicity during Simpson's sensational murder trial.

As instructed by Talone, the cab driver turned up a winding canyon road, where the rich and famous owned large homes on acres of hillside property.

Gladstone F. Dreiser, a large imposing figure with a thick salt and pepper beard, lived at the top of the canyon in a sprawling ranch-style home with a breath-taking view of Los Angeles. Dreiser made more money in a year than Talone would see in a lifetime. He was one of Hollywood's most successful movie producers.

Once a brilliant Yale-educated historian, Dreiser wrote two highly acclaimed books on the Civil War, but during the filming of his epic *Last Man Standing* in 1986, Dreiser caught the bug. He chucked his academic career, moved to Los Angeles and tried his hand at movie producing. By the mid-1990s, he was turning out one hit after another, most notably *Stonewall*, an Oscar-winning bio-pic about Confederate General Stonewall Jackson that made Dreiser the toast of Hollywood.

Dreiser used his celebrity status to raise millions of dollars for California Republicans. "Somebody's got to take on the unions, Barbra Streisand and Warren Beatty," he told his friends.

Dreiser was important. That's why the meeting was on his turf. Everyone else had to fight the late afternoon L.A. traffic to get to the meeting. Talone was the last to arrive. Dreiser greeted him at the front door and led him into the entertainment room, dominated by an HD television that was the biggest Talone had ever seen. Along one wall, a huge floor-to-ceiling bookcase was stuffed with classics of American history – tales of bygone wars and biographies of Washington, Adams, Jefferson, Madison, Polk, Lincoln, Theodore Roosevelt and, of course, Ronald Reagan. Talone noticed the distinctive green and gold bindings of the Harvard Classics, as well as a 1931 edition of the World Book encyclopedia. Talone surveyed the players as they sat around a huge glass coffee table.

There was Herman Peterson, owner of Peterson-Pacific, a timber company and one of the largest landowners in California.

Next to Peterson, sipping an iced tea, sat Culver Amundson, Executive Director of the California Tax Reduction League.

Next to Amundson sat Dr. Henry Culbertson, the owner of a string of medical clinics in Southern California that catered to low-income patients. Talone, a frequent visitor to California, recognized Dr. Culbertson from his commercials on late-night television. "You don't have to be rich to get the best healthcare money can buy," Dr. Culbertson would tell his audience, smiling broadly.

"Gentlemen," Dreiser said. "Thanks to all of you for coming today. Has everyone been introduced?" Everyone nodded affirmatively.

"I'm not being overly dramatic when I say the future of our country depends on Governor Frank's upcoming U.S. Senate selection. I've asked you here today because you recognize, as I do, that Johnny Callahan must be that selection. He's a sensible, ethical conservative. He's a winner and he's young enough to make it to the top – the White House – to carry forward an agenda we all believe in. Herman, what do you like about Johnny Callahan?"

"Well, Gladstone, I like his tax cuts and his sensible approach to logging. He respects property rights but isn't anti-environment."

Amundson and Talone said they wanted more business-friendly legislation sent to President Vernon.

Dr. Culbertson said he wanted Callahan to help enact a national system of medical liability based on California's landmark 1975 law, which limits medical malpractice "pain and suffering" court damages to $250,000.

Dreiser produced copies of a two-page memo outlining a strategy for securing Callahan's appointment. It was titled: *Callahan – The Only Choice.* The author was Marty Frank, the well-connected son of the governor who had parlayed his long-time friendship with Callahan into high-paying government jobs and now a lucrative political consulting business. Friends said the two were so close, they referred to Callahan as Don Quixote and Frank as his trusty squire, Sancho Panza.

The document outlined Callahan's voting record over the years, particularly his votes on medical liability reform, taxes, social issues and business. The memo devoted a paragraph to other potential appointees but was particularly critical of Harold Barnes.

"Harold Barnes is a conservative ideologue who could never win a statewide race in California. He is widely considered the most conservative member of the California Legislature," the memo said. "He has sponsored legislation on behalf of the gun and tobacco manufacturers, knowing full well that these measures had no chance of success. Thus, he forced moderate Republicans to take difficult political positions that Democrats have used against them in subsequent political campaigns."

Dreiser lit a cigar, blew foul-smelling smoke in Talone's direction, then continued.

"I hired Marty Frank to advise us on this matter for some rather obvious reasons. But his political instincts are good, and he knows the right people.

"Notwithstanding his relationship with Callahan, he knows what he is talking about. He's convinced the real problem with Harold Barnes is his over-the-top conservatism. If Barnes gets the appointment, he'd still have to run for election next year and have no chance of winning a statewide election. He's such a 'winger' just about any Democrat would have him for lunch and all our efforts would be wasted.

"What did the philosopher George Santayana once say? 'Those who cannot remember the past are condemned to repeat it.' California history is replete with examples of ideologues who couldn't appeal to a broad cross-section of voters. Hell, I'm old enough to remember Max Rafferty back in '68. He was way out there. He knocked off a moderate-conservative Republican senator in the primary, and then got pasted in the general election. And remember Pierre Salinger, Kennedy's press secretary? He was appointed to the Senate by Governor Pat Brown but was too liberal to win a statewide election.

"We need someone who can win with the voters. With Johnny Callahan, we have a conservative but not a crazy. We have someone who the voters will return to office and could stay in the Senate for life, if that's what he wants to do. And, who knows, he could be just the guy who could go all the way to the top."

"You're right," blurted Peterson, the timber mogul. "We can't let Barnes ruin this golden opportunity for us."

"Besides," Dr. Culbertson added, "Barnes may be a conservative but his wife is a trial lawyer. I don't trust anybody with a trial lawyer in the family."

"I'm working on the governor," Dreiser said. "Obviously, he's going to appoint a Republican, but we have to make sure it's not Barnes. I've talked to him twice, most recently about four hours ago, and he's assured me that Callahan remains on his short list."

Talone, appearing a bit tentative, took a gulp of water and cleared his throat. "Uh, may I ask a question?" Without waiting for a reply, he continued. "I agree that Speaker Callahan is right on all the issues. But you know the old saying, 'Where there's smoke, there's fire.' Even 3,000 miles away in Washington we've been hearing all this negative stuff about him – supposedly shacking up with a prostitute and being the target of a bribery sting. I know all the allegations have been discredited, but…"

Dreiser didn't give Talone time to finish his sentence. Quickly, as if he anticipated Talone's concern, he reached into a small tote bag and retrieved a folded newspaper. He tossed it onto the large glass coffee table. It landed with a thud.

"Did you see this?" he said. "It's from today's *L.A. Times* and it rips both the *Starlight*, which started this whole prostitute crap, and the feeble attempt to bribe him. When was the last time the *L.A. Times* said anything good about a Republican? Whoever is behind that trashy article – and whoever sent that money to him in Sacramento — screwed up royally. He — or they — thought Callahan would be crippled, but every newspaper in California is now portraying Callahan as an innocent victim. We can ride this PR wave all the way to the Senate."

"So, Gladstone, explain to me again why we're here," Peterson asked. "From what you tell us, it looks like the governor thinks highly of Speaker Callahan. It seems he has the Senate appointment in the bag."

"Here's the problem," Dreiser answered. "As much as we're winning the PR battle, there's no doubt that someone is out to get Callahan. Someone planted that story and someone tried to entrap him with a bribe. We can't sit back and wait for the next shoe to drop."

"What do you want us to do?" Peterson asked.

Dreiser laid out a campaign plan.

"Marty is working this behind the scenes. But here's what you can do. Get your members to phone and write the governor urging Callahan's appointment. Bill, get one of your major members, someone Frank will recognize, to call the governor and tell him that Barnes couldn't withstand a statewide election."

He paused a few seconds. "And, uh, what else?" asked Peterson.

"I need you to write me a check – today, if possible. We need to run a high-profile PR campaign, and I've hired a private investigator who will help make sure that Callahan goes to Washington.

"If someone is gunning for Callahan and planting these stories, he'll find out. Most of the money, though, will go toward advocacy. We don't have much time, and I want to create and air a commercial in Sacramento, Fresno, San Diego and Los Angeles that pressures Frank into appointing Callahan and urges viewers to write to the governor. I'll make it simple and positive, but we have to buy airtime right away."

Amundson asked, "This won't be cheap. How much do you figure this will cost?"

Dreiser thumbed through the pages of the Frank memo, his eyes stopping at the budget on the last page. "You know how expensive it is to run a statewide campaign in California. We're not even bothering with San Francisco and many of the liberal coastal counties. But a two-week saturation campaign will probably cost 750 a week – a million and a half bucks total."

Dreiser pulled a checkbook out of his tote bag. "Here's my ante: $250,000."

Peterson did the same, writing a personal check for $250,000.

Dr. Culbertson wrote a check for $100,000 and said he'd come up with more in a day or two. Amundson and Talone pledged $100,000 each and promised to work their members for more.

As dark settled on the Pacific Coast, Gladstone Dreiser's guests filed out of the house and headed down the canyon. Dreiser sat at the coffee table and re-read the *Times* editorial. Behind him, a door slowly opened. In walked an overweight and balding 40-ish man who looked like a typical heavy in the movies. He wore a blue blazer, a blue shirt open at the collar and gray pants that looked like they hadn't been pressed in months. On his left cheek, there was a slightly reddened three-inch long scar. He had piercing eyes and acne scars on his face.

Dreiser didn't hear the door open, but he could hear heavy

breathing and the faint wheezing every time Terrence Burke inhaled.

"I got you some money," Dreiser said. "You know what's at stake."

Burke grunted.

"Look, Johnny's the goose that laid the golden egg. If he gets this appointment, I can see him as president someday."

Burke grunted again.

"And he owes me. I've helped to channel millions of dollars into his various campaigns and causes. When he gets to the White House, I'll have more political clout than his vice president."

Burke said nothing.

"Find out who planted that story. Find out who sent Callahan that money. Then I want you to have a little heart-to-heart with whoever did that."

Twelve

Karen Paulson nuzzled up against Jack's bare chest as they watched a DVD about Walter Cronkite's life in journalism.

Jack had been awfully lonely in the months after he and Karen had their last fight and broke up. He was glad they were back together. Watching old black and white footage of Cronkite anchoring CBS coverage of the 1952 Republican National Convention, Jack's mind returned to his career dilemma. He loved journalism, but he was thinking of leaving. He could make better money in public relations and wouldn't have to worry about all those ethics problems that haunt journalists. And no more worthless stories under the guise of journalism.

Jack gulped the last of his Bud Light just as his cell phone rang. Jack was startled. He thought he had turned off the phone. He paused the DVD during Cronkite's recollections of the Eisenhower-Stevenson presidential contest, and Karen jumped to her feet. "Want me to get it?" she asked.

"Sure, you're closer."

"This is Jack Summerland's phone," she said. "What? You're breaking up a little. You want Jack? Just a minute," she said. "Who could be calling at this hour?" she asked.

Before talking, Jack tried to identify the caller by glancing at the digital read-out on the phone. The return phone number was blocked. Slightly annoyed, he confirmed for the caller that he was the news reporter, then listened for what seemed to be one or two minutes.

"What's that?" he asked. "I think we have a bad connection. You on a cell phone?" Another pause. The caller must have moved, because the phone connection improved.

Karen walked into the kitchen to put the finishing touches on the dinner dishes.

"Tucson?" Jack said into the phone. Then, in a hushed tone, because he didn't want Karen to hear, he repeated what he thought he heard. "Callahan? Speaker Callahan? Who is this?"

Karen did hear and was puzzled why someone would call in the middle of the night and talk about her boss. She had no idea what was happening, but when she heard Callahan's name whispered – did she hear correctly? – she craned her neck and from a room away, concentrated on the part of the phone conversation she could pick up.

"I want to go off the record," the caller told Jack.

"Why? I don't even know who you are."

"Let me go off the record and everything will make sense. I can give you the story of a lifetime."

Jack paused for five seconds, thinking. "Okay, what's all this about?"

"I'm not going to give you my name right now, but I'm a former agent for the FBI," said the voice on the other end of the phone.

"You're kidding!" Jack blurted.

"I'm deadly serious," the voice shot back. "We're off the record, alright?"

A bit annoyed, but eager at the same time, Jack responded, "Yeah, okay."

Without identifying himself, the caller started to tell his story. "I'm the one who tried to plant that item in the *Starlight* about Callahan. When that backfired, I foolishly tried to nail Callahan in a bribery scheme. That backfired, too."

Jack was incredulous. "Is this a joke? No FBI agent could be that stupid."

The man continued, "That's not important right now. What is important is the fact that we've got to do something to stop Callahan from getting to the Senate."

"Why would you want to do that?" Summerland asked.

"I know something about Callahan that could become the biggest scandal in California political history. It will end his political career, but I'm not sure I can prove it. That's why I tried to nail that sonofabitch any way I could."

Summerland glanced quickly at the kitchen to see if Karen was eavesdropping. "What are you talking about?"

"Not over the phone," the man said. "I want to come to Sacramento to meet with you. I'll give you the whole story. It'll be your exclusive – if you want it. If you don't, I'll shop it elsewhere."

"Okay," Jack said. He scribbled down a few words in his reporter's notebook, then hung up. Is this guy for real? What if this is a practical joke? He thought for a second. But what if this guy's legit? What's the harm, he concluded, in seeing where this leads.

"What was that all about?" Karen asked, as if she heard nothing.

Jack revealed little. "Oh, it was some guy who said he has a story for me."

"What about?" she probed.

"I'm not really sure. He was on a cell phone that was breaking up. I think it has to do with some bill at the Capitol. I think he's pulling my leg. He sounded goofy to me, maybe even drunk, but I told him I'd at least listen."

Karen was miffed at Jack's evasive answer.

Later that evening, as Jack snored his way through a deep sleep, Karen gently slipped out of bed and tiptoed to Jack's study. She heard him mention Johnny Callahan's name to the mystery caller. She had 12 years invested in legislative employment and needed the job security and future state pension. Or, perhaps, she'd score a job with a rising star in the U.S. Senate. If her boss was in some trouble, she needed to know.

Jack was a reporter with integrity, but she'd try to convince him not to report a story if it affected her personally. She flipped open his notebook. She furrowed her brow and seemed puzzled at the barely legible words scribbled on the ruled paper: "Tues...Christy's...11..."

Thirteen

Across town, in a fashionable section of East Sacramento, Governor Frank took a sip of 12-year-old single malt scotch. He swirled the ice cubes, waiting for the scotch to dilute ever so slightly. The television was tuned to the final minutes of a professional basketball playoff game that attracted Frank's attention every minute or so.

Frank was dressed in tan slacks, a blue pin-striped shirt and a black Christian Dior sweater. This was as casual as it got for Frank. He paced the well-appointed den in the governor's residence in suburban Carmichael. He picked up a baseball autographed by Willie Mays, stared at it for a second, then turned to Johnny Callahan, casually adorned in jeans, a red polo shirt and expensive Gucci loafers.

"So, what have you got?" Frank asked.

"We're using Capitol Research, and they've come up with some minor stuff so far."

Callahan had tried to shorten the odds on his Senate appointment by doing opposition research on Harold Barnes. Just to see if there were any skeletons in his closet.

For $10,000, Capitol Research spent a week looking into Barnes's background. Most of it was squeaky clean. Barnes was a graduate of Sacramento State University. He had a wife of 32 years and two grown kids. During his 13 years in the Legislature, his Democratic opponents constantly looked into his background for dirt, but none had ever surfaced during his many campaigns. Sure, there were plenty of votes that could be attacked, but nothing that stood out as a deal-breaker.

Capitol Research came up with a minor beef Barnes had with the county assessor, but nothing very useful.

Frank thought for a moment, then put his arm on Callahan's right shoulder, like a father to a son.

"Look, Johnny, I'm going to appoint you to the Senate. You've handled the *Starlight* and bribery situations well, your poll numbers are high, and you have the press on your side. But I can't do it just yet. I want to wait until all this junk about you simmers down."

"But, you know it's all a sham," Callahan blurted.

"I know," Frank responded. "But let's give it just a little more time, okay? You're on a roll. This Senate thing is going to happen, but I want it to look like I'm doing my job of analyzing all the potential candidates and not playing favorites. Within a few weeks, you'll be the toast of Washington. And, who knows where that might lead."

"You'd tell me if there was a problem, wouldn't you?" Callahan asked.

"Don't worry," Frank shot back. "I've got big plans for you. I may have bombed out when I ran for the White House, but I can help you make it. I can get you millions from California donors – friends who have helped me throughout my career."

Callahan thought for a second. "You know, Colin, even a couple of days can be an eternity in politics. A lot can happen."

The governor swallowed another gulp of scotch. "Don't worry, nothing will happen."

"But I'll need as much time as possible," Callahan argued. "I'm going to have to stand for election next year, which means I need to start fundraising, and I'll have little time in the Senate to build a track record to run on. Remember John Seymour?"

John Seymour was a fairly obscure Republican legislator from Orange County when he was tabbed by then-Governor Pete Wilson – himself a former senator who resigned his office to run for governor – to fill Wilson's vacant U. S. Senate seat in 1991. After an undistinguished two years in office, and undeniably hurt by President George H.W. Bush's re-election free fall, Seymour was trounced by Democrat Dianne Feinstein. Callahan didn't want to see history repeat itself.

"Look, Johnny," Frank said, "this is not the same. Seymour didn't have the charisma or smarts that you do. Plus, he was a little too moderate for some of the party's big moneybags. You can afford to wait a couple of weeks. In the meantime, let me put my people on the Barnes research, too."

Callahan headed for the door, frustrated that his big appointment was still on hold. "Look, I've got to get home. Got an early start tomorrow." As he slipped out of the governor's den and neared the front door, he saw Marty munching some peanuts from a jar in the family room.

"Hey Moses, what's up?" Marty asked.

"Don't call me that," he said sternly. "Those days are over, okay?"

"Yeah, sure. Whatever," Marty said.

Johnny explained his conversation with Marty's father, then gently grabbed him by the arm and nudged him into a corner of the room. He lowered his voice, barely above a whisper.

"When I'm in the Senate, there'll be a place for you. And remember, I've got even bigger plans than that. I won't forget what you did for me."

"I know you won't," Marty replied, equally hushed, with just a hint of a smirk on his face. "We both know you'd have no career without me."

Fourteen

The alarm woke Jack with a start. It was one of those obnoxious car commercials with the screaming announcer. Groggily, he stared at the red digital face of his clock alarm. It said 8:15, but he knew it was only 7:55. Whenever Karen spent the night at Jack's apartment, she always set the clock 20 minutes ahead. It was her way, apparently, of buying extra time in the morning. Jack didn't understand the rationale, but long ago gave up questioning it.

Jack stumbled out of the bed, threw on a pair of jeans and a rumpled T-shirt that had been left to fester on the floor, and opened the front door. He reached for the newspaper, but his hand caught nothing but air. Then he remembered. It's Tuesday. Karen always got to the office by 7:45 on Tuesdays. She would have brought in the paper before heading for work. He started to close the front door and noticed the clear blue sky. No hint of rain. Another blown forecast. Last night's Doppler Dandies had predicted a 60 percent chance of rain before noon. I should be playing golf today.

Jack noticed a boxed three-paragraph brief on the front page, near the bottom: "Veep in Town to Raise Campaign Cash."

Vice President Clifford Hollings was making two stops in Northern California to raise campaign funds for the California Republican Party. Hollings wouldn't make any real news, but his mere presence in Sacramento guaranteed a lead place on the evening newscast. Unless, of course, his lofty news position was displaced by an axe murder, a scandal at the city animal shelter, or the arrest of a county supervisor for soliciting prostitution. After all, ratings came first in a sweeps month.

A few minutes after nine o'clock, Jack parked his eight-year-old Camry in the fenced parking lot at Channel 4. He hurried into the station, jogged down a long hallway, lined with photographs of the station's news personalities, and lurched for the news director's office. He was late for the morning producers meeting. Normally, Jack didn't participate in this daily ritual, because he hung out at his office across the street from the Capitol. But an appearance by Vice President Hollings trumped anything he could unearth at the Capitol. The news chieftains invited him to the producers meeting so he could describe how he planned to cover the story.

Jack explained that he and his photographer would drive to Travis Air Force Base — midway between Sacramento and San Francisco — where the vice president would deplane in mid-afternoon, say a few words and have a photo opportunity with Air Force personnel.

Then, the vice president was scheduled to fly by helicopter to Sacramento and motorcade to the 12,000-foot mansion of developer Herman Kling for an evening cocktail fundraiser.

Kling was an aging, wealthy soldier in the Republican Party. A college drop-out, he made his first million at the age of 23, buying dilapidated, fixer-up buildings in San Francisco and re-selling them for three times what he paid for them. Kling moved to Sacramento in 1963 where rich farmland was being converted into housing for the burgeoning military and state government workforce. Now 78, Kling was the toast of the GOP, which loved his money and groveled at the man to get it.

Until campaign contributions to individual candidates were restricted by California voters, Kling routinely had funneled tens of thousands of dollars to favored conservatives. Those contributions now were capped, but the new law turned out to be a full employment act for Sacramento's highly paid political lawyers who found numerous loopholes. Since the new contribution limits did not apply to donations to so-called independent expenditure committees, Kling still wrote the big checks and influenced elections; he merely changed the name of the payee. Everybody did it — from big business, unions and nurses to teachers, developers and Indian tribes.

"According to the Hollings press office," Jack told the producers, "the vice president is supposed to have an hour of private downtime at Travis before flying to Sacramento. That will give me plenty of time to drive back without missing anything.

"Kling is supposed to round up the 200 guests around six-thirty and pack them into what he calls his 'great room.' I've been in this guy's house before for a Frank fundraiser. This room is gigantic, a cathedral just off the kitchen. Hollings will say a few words about how the Vernon Administration has restored integrity to the White House and made America safer. Blah, blah, blah. It'll be the usual BS. They'll let us in the house to take a few pictures of the guests and to record the vice president's comments. That's it."

"Okay, Jack, you're the lead tonight at five and six," Jimmy Johnson ordered. "Play up the Travis photo op for the early shows and play up the vice president's comments at Kling's fundraiser for the 11. You're live all the way."

"Uh, I can't do the 11 live," Jack shot back, remembering that he was meeting his mysterious caller at 11. " I'll do a package for the late show."

Johnson didn't even pause to think about it. "For Chrissakes, Jack. We're in a sweeps month. This is the biggest story of the day. You know the drill. It's got to be live."

Yeah, right, Jack thought. It's got to be live. He could never figure out what was so special about airing live reports about an event that happened hours earlier. He knew, however, that it all came down to market research and surveys indicated that viewers considered live reports more exciting and spontaneous than prepackaged news reports.

Twenty minutes later, as Jack reviewed year-old video of Hollings delivering a speech to the National Rifle Association, someone shouted from behind the assignment desk. "Jack, you've got a call on line three."

The last time Jack received a phone call, a mystery man had promised to give him the scoop of his career. This time, he immediately recognized the voice.

"Jack? Billy Galster. Say, uh, do you have time to come by the office this morning?"

"What's up? You guys gonna step on the vice president's appearance and make news, or something?" Jack fished.

"No, nothing like that. It's personal, and I'd rather not discuss it over the phone. We'd like to talk to you for a few minutes. Can you come on over?"

Jack hesitated, then glanced at the large clock on the wall in the newsroom. It read 9:45. He wouldn't have to leave for Travis until about one o'clock — or a half hour earlier if he and his photographer stopped at a roadside fast food burger joint for lunch.

"Sure, what the hell. I'll be right over."

Jack tracked down Middleton, his cameraman on the Hollings story, and told him he'd return in about an hour. He had no hint that his life was about to become a lot more complicated.

Jack wondered why he was being summoned to the speaker's office. And why now? A social call didn't make sense. Could it be connected to the mystery call he received? Galster couldn't know about the meeting at Christy's, could he?

Jack disdained the parking lot across the street from the Capitol and searched for a space along L Street. He found a spot near Ninth Street and walked the block to the Capitol building.

Ever since the terrorist attack at the New York Twin Towers, Capitol security had been tightened considerably. Jack walked through the automatic door on the L Street entrance to the Capitol, emptied his pockets of keys and loose change, walked through the metal detector and headed for Speaker Callahan's office. He nodded to a security guard.

He rode the elevator to the second floor, stopping to chat briefly with two lobbyists for the state's business community. He announced himself to the speaker's receptionist and waited all of 30 seconds before Galster walked into the office reception area and motioned for Jack to follow him into the speaker's private office.

Shit, Jack thought. He hoped he wasn't in the doghouse with Callahan's people. Jack didn't mind upsetting politicians, but he tried to cultivate professional working relationships so as not to adversely affect his access to key government leaders.

Speaker Callahan, wearing a perfectly tailored charcoal gray Armani suit with an electric blue and gray tie, greeted Jack warmly and offered him some coffee.

So far, so good, Jack thought.

Then, Callahan sat down in the plush leather chair behind his oversized desk, with Jack and Galster sitting in chairs on the other side. Callahan did the talking.

"Jack, ever since I've been here in Sacramento I've watched your reports on TV. I think you're fair and honest. I think you're a great writer, and I appreciate how you weren't afraid to admit that *Starlight* story was a phony."

"Just doing my job, Mr. Speaker," Jack responded.

"I like the way you do your job, and I have a proposition for you," Callahan said. "Can we talk off the record?"

"Sure," Jack answered.

"I mean, *completely* off the record."

"Okay."

"Jack, in a week or two, I expect the governor will appoint me to the U.S. Senate to fill the Edelstein seat. I have big plans for the Senate and beyond. I need to start building my staff and I, we, want you to be my press secretary in Washington. Billy will be my overall communications director; you'd report to him. But I want you to be my primary spokesman and help me develop a media outreach plan as I move my Senate agenda forward."

Jack was stunned.

"This is quite surprising," he said. "Why me?"

"Again, I think you're a good reporter, you know TV and you are respected by California political reporters," Galster offered. "And the best part, you're going to make more money and be in D. C. What's your salary over at 4?"

"Well, it was $102,000 until last year's recession. We had to let some folks go and everyone took a salary hit. I'm now making 96."

Galster replied, "As a Senate press secretary, you'll start in the $125,000 range. But there's a lot more potential out there." Galster shot a quick look at Callahan.

"Are you absolutely sure we're off the record. What I am about to tell you can't get out," Callahan said.

"Off the record. Completely," Jack said.

"Completely?" Galster asked.

"Yes," Jack repeated. "This information won't see the light of day."

"Look," Callahan continued. "If everything falls into place, I am going to be a senator at a pretty young age. I'm a Republican who has received endorsements from some of the most liberal newspapers in California. They like my style, if not my entire agenda. Sure, I'm conservative, but I don't wear it on my sleeve. I don't tackle divisive wedge issues that polarize the electorate, and my legislation is common sense. I know what I want and how to get there. What I'm saying is that if I should get this appointment, I plan to run for election to the Senate when my partial term expires in a year, then I'll run for re-election six years after that. In the middle of my second term, I plan on running for the presidency. It's a long shot, perhaps, but I'll have several opportunities to build up my credentials."

"You've got your life all figured out, don't you," Jack replied.

"Jack, I've never lost an election. I have many friends in high places, a fundraising base and California's electoral votes in my hip pocket. That's one-fifth of all the votes it takes to win election. Everything I do from this day forward will be designed to get me elected to the White House. And when I get there, I want you there with me. What do you say?"

Jack exhaled. His mind raced. This was something out of left field. He shot a quick glance at Galster, then back at Callahan. His right hand tugged at his chin as he thought a second, then said: "Quite frankly, I'm overwhelmed. I don't know what to say right now. Of course, this would be a major career change for me, which isn't necessarily a bad thing. Off the record, I do think you're a good legislator and, of course, I'm flattered that you'd ask. I really have to think it over. How much time do I have to make up my mind?"

"I won't have to make a public announcement until after the governor appoints me to the Senate, but I want to hit the ground running in Washington. I'll need someone in place soon after the announcement is made."

Jack shook hands with the two men, turned to walk away and saw Karen out of the corner of his eye in the neighboring reception room. He continued walking and kept silent but slightly arched his eyebrows as if to tell her he had news to report.

As Jack walked down the staircase to the Capitol's first floor, it suddenly hit him. He had just been offered the job of a lifetime, ensuring prestige, money and excitement – only hours before he was to meet a man who promised to ruin his benefactor's career.

Jack passed a newspaper reporter in the hallway. "Hey, Jack. What's up?" he asked. As if in a trance, Jack didn't acknowledge. His mind was racing a mile a minute.

Fifteen

"Hey, Jen," Marty Frank offered to his secretary as he walked into his small suite on the third floor of the 10th and L office building across the street from the Capitol. Old-timers still called it the Boxcar Building, even though Boxcar's bottom floor restaurant went belly up decades earlier.

Frank's small but thriving political consulting business mostly shared the third floor with lobbyists and news organizations. Frank was riding high these days. His father was the governor and his best friend was the Assembly speaker. Corporations and entire industries hired him ostensibly to provide political advice. In reality, they wanted him for his access to the two most powerful politicians in the state.

No one confused Marty Frank with Einstein, but he knew his way around the Capitol environment. Over the years, he gradually improved his political acumen. Many political observers, however, saw him as a lazy parasite who just happened to have good connections. The joke around the Capitol was that Frank must have incriminating photos of Johnny Callahan and was using them for blackmail. Why else, they wondered, would the smart, savvy Assembly speaker have taken care of him so many times over the years?

Marty settled into his neatly appointed office and turned on the computer. He started reading a website devoted to California politics when Jennifer's voice pierced the quiet. "Sam Cockerill is calling," she said. "You want to take it?"

"Sure," he responded."

"Sam, what's up? Is this about the Hollings visit tonight?"

"No, Marty" the chief of staff said. "I just wanted to brief you on the meeting this morning with Jack Summerland."

"Great," Marty said. "How'd it go?"

"Billy said it went pretty well," Cockerill said. "Summerland didn't commit and we gave him some time to think it over. But I don't know how he could turn it down."

Marty logged off the website and entered his e-mail access password.

"He'll take it," Marty said. "He doesn't have a lot of ties to Sacramento, and I think he's sick of TV news. If we take Karen with us to D.C., that should seal the deal, I'd think."

"Probably," said Cockerill.

Suddenly, staring at the computer, Marty cut off the conversation. "Gotta run. I'll talk to you later."

Marty highlighted an unread e-mail. Normally, he didn't open unsolicited e-mails unless he recognized the sender, and he didn't recognize this sender, "657xyq." But a sudden, deep fear enveloped him as he read the e-mail's headline – "I saw what you did."

Marty opened the e-mail and stared at its contents for a minute. Stunned, and turning ashen, he quietly closed the connecting door between his office and Jennifer's desk. He returned to the computer and re-read the e-mail. He scanned to the last line. "I want $200,000 in cash. Put the money in a plain envelope and send it to 1006 Tenth Street, #3546, Sacramento, CA 95814."

The note went on to say: "Notify me immediately if you agree."

Marty's mind raced. Who sent this? It must be the same person who tried to plant that story in the *Starlight* and send the cash to Callahan's Capitol office. First, this guy tries to ruin Johnny – and me – and now he wants money to keep his mouth shut?

Should he tell Johnny? No, he thought, Johnny would freak out. What about Gladstone Dreiser?

As he sat pondering his next move, Jennifer knocked on the door. "Sorry, Marty, but Karen Paulson is on the line. She says it's very important."

Marty picked up the phone. "I'm kinda busy now. What's going on?"

"Marty," Karen said, "I don't know where to turn but you've always looked out for Johnny so I thought I'd start with you."

"Go on," Marty said.

"Well, I think I might know who's trying to get Johnny. Actually, I don't know who it is, but I think you can find out."

Marty exhaled deeply. This could be the break he was looking for. "And?…" he said, prompting Karen to continue.

"Last night, Jack got a strange call on his cell phone. It was pretty late and I only heard part of his end of the conversation." She paused.

"And?…"

"It was about Johnny. Jack agreed to meet this guy tonight at Christy's. At 11."

"Thanks, Karen," Marty said. "Don't worry about it. I'm sure it's nothing."

So that's the story, Marty thought. If I don't agree to give him the money, he goes to the media.

Marty read the e-mail for the third time. He decided not to reply. He looked at the grandfather clock on the far wall of his office. It was 10:58. Twelve hours, Marty said to himself. Twelve hours to flush this guy out and put an end to it.

Sixteen

Jack Summerland had a lot on his mind. Like a bolt of lightning, he had been given a chance to get out of the TV news rat race and shift his career to where the action really was, Washington, D.C. Jack went through the motions as he covered the vice president's abbreviated trip to Northern California. He had covered stories like this many times before. He could report it almost by formula.

He'd get footage of Hollings arriving aboard Air Force Two at Travis Air Force Base, then shaking hands with the troops lined up on the tarmac and making brief remarks. Then, he'd interview a few servicemen about the psychological lift the vice presidential visit generated. He'd high-tail it back to Sacramento in time to get video of the vice president's helicopter arriving in Sacramento, then record his brief remarks at the Kling estate and interview a few Republican donors about the successes of the Vernon-

Hollings team and its high re-election hopes.

To add a little spice and conflict to his story, Jack decided to air an interview he shot three days earlier with Mark Gonzalez, the state Democratic party spokesman, who bombastically listed a litany of administration failures. Gonzalez always was good copy – and better TV. "These guys make Herbert Hoover look good," Gonzalez said. And, finally, Jack asked the station's art department to produce a state-by-state graphic recreating the electoral map, showing how the Vernon-Hollings team racked up 323 electoral votes in the last election.

As Jack and Ron Middleton drove to Travis, the photographer suddenly slipped off the freeway in Dixon. It was burger time. Middleton was addicted to beef and needed a daily fix. Jack ordered black coffee and watched Middleton wolf down a triple-decker and fries. He calculated the calories and fat grams in his head. Middleton was one of the best photographers he had ever worked with, but Jack never could understand his meat fetish.

As Middleton inhaled his lunch, Jack thought about the job offer and decided to confide in his photographer, perhaps searching for the right answer. There's a special bond between reporter and photographer, particularly if they spend a lot of time together on the road covering news stories. Each knew the other's quirks and dislikes. Middleton always had up-to-date dope on Jack's love life.

"I've got a real dilemma," Jack told him. "Can we talk a few minutes?"

Middleton wiped ketchup from his cheek. "Of course. You and Karen on the outs again?"

"No, nothing like that. And you can't say anything for reasons that'll become obvious, okay?"

"Sure," Middleton responded. "What's up?"

Instinctively, Jack lowered his voice so only Middleton could hear him.

"You know how journalism is in my blood," he started,

"going back to my college days. You know, I was the editor of my school paper at Missouri. I'll never forget the thrill of my first byline at the *Kansas City Star*, a story about a local city councilman who was caught by police with his pants down in his car and in the company of a hooker."

Middleton took a large gulp of Coke. "You've come a long way, baby, haven't you?" he said.

Jack explained the job offer and his quandary.

"I just don't know if I'd be happy giving up journalism for a career as a politician's press secretary – a PR flack."

"What are you afraid of?" Middleton asked. "Reporters go to the 'dark side' every day."

Reporters often referred to the public relations business as the "dark side." Journalism's bastard cousin. There was a little jealously in that, because PR people tended to make more money than reporters. But for many reporters, money was a secondary perk. Reporters are addicted to the thrill of the story chase, scooping their rivals, witnessing the first draft of history. And they love to see their byline. TV wasn't much different, except that the pay is higher and the possibilities for ego stroking are greater.

Still, television had changed dramatically over the years and Jack was bothered by the transformation. In the mid-1960s, California voters elected Ronald Reagan governor and created a full-time Legislature. In the process, big cities were given significant new clout in the Assembly and Senate. Legislative districts had been re-drawn to reflect the U.S. Supreme Court's "one man, one vote" doctrine, enabling Los Angeles, San Francisco and other urban centers to dramatically increase their representation in the Legislature. Los Angeles, which had a single senator in 1966, found itself with 13 senators the next year. Big city television stations sent crews to Sacramento to cover the glamorous actor-turned-politician and to keep an eye on their legislators. Out-of-town stations established full-time bureaus at the Capitol and staffed them with some of the best and brightest reporters.

Thanks to such visual news events as the space program, the war in Vietnam, urban unrest, political assassinations, plus technological innovations in the industry, television news soared in popularity. Stations expanded their news programs from one-half hour to an hour and two hours. Unfortunately, television news became a victim of its own success. With stations devoting more and more broadcast time to news, the pressure became greater for them to turn news programming into popular shows that added to their bottom lines.

News departments hired media consultants, or "news doctors" to survey communities about what they liked and didn't like about news shows. The results were stunning. Respondents said they didn't want political or government news because it was boring and involved coverage of a bunch of crooks. Gradually, stations started pulling out of the Capitol and substituted substantive coverage of government with what some journalists called "flash and trash." In order to jack up the ratings, stories about mayhem, crime, sex and celebrities dominated television news.

"You know what bothers me the most?" Jack said to Middleton. "TV stations don't care about news anymore. We're just pushing a product in order to attract viewers. You know," Jack continued, "this whole business is starting to embarrass me. Maybe I've outlived my usefulness working in TV."

"Look, Jack. We've had this talk before. Remember when you almost called Johnson from that bar in Bakersfield? After a few beers you were ready to quit that night." Middleton ambled to the counter for a parfait dessert.

Jack continued the conversation in his mind, like he had done so many times before. He knew that it had been decades since television had passed newspapers as the public's information source of choice, but he was concerned about losing his reputation because he felt the industry he worked for was slowly abdicating its responsibility to cover important public policy issues that people need to know. Working for Callahan could be his exit strategy. When Middleton returned with his dessert, Jack picked up the discussion.

"What do you think?" he asked.

Middleton didn't hesitate. "Unbelievable. I think you should take it and bring me with you. I can be the senator's TV consultant. I could document his work as a senator. You know, that stuff will come in handy if he runs for president. You're ready for a bigger theater," he said. "This is really exciting."

"I'm just not sure" Jack responded. " Plus, you know, I'm not a Republican."

Ever since becoming a political reporter, Jack thought it best to be an independent so critics couldn't accuse him of obvious political bias. He had read the stories of how 89 percent of Washington political reporters voted for Bill Clinton over Bob Dole in 1996. That led to continued cries of liberal bias in the press. Jack acknowledged that most reporters tended to be activists and, thus, usually sided with the Democrats, the more progressive of the two major parties. But he didn't know any reporter who deliberately slanted the news.

In addition, he often told critics, how do you reconcile the conservative slant of newspaper ownership? Between 1932 and the turn of the century, the majority of newspapers had endorsed Republican presidential candidates — with the exception of 1964 and 1992. If anything, the real bias in news gathering was not the coverage, itself, but the type of stories that journalists decided to cover.

Years earlier, Jack produced a five-part series on gun control for Channel 4. He was careful to interview advocates on both sides of the issue and even concluded that gun control might not be very effective against criminals bent on killing.

Even before his first piece aired, he received several complaints and even one death threat from gun owners who alleged that the mere suggestion of gun control illustrated Jack's and the station's deep-seated anti-gun bias.

Jack was daydreaming now, thinking about a possible life in Washington, D.C., with Karen by his side – embassy parties, history in the making, meeting and working with important people who could change the lives of every American. He also wondered if Johnny Callahan really could be hiding something in his past. And finally, he thought, am I being played for a fool? Does an unknown someone with a hidden, personal agenda want me to do his dirty work for him?

"Come on, let's go," he said to his photographer. "We've got work to do. I'll think about this later."

Channel 4's coverage of the Hollings visit to Northern California went off without a hitch. Standing on the street two houses from the Kling mansion, Jack did live reports for the five and six o'clock newscasts. The six o'clock story also included a brief live interview with the vice president's press secretary and an interview with a 32-year-old social worker who criticized the vice president's views on abortion. About 50 demonstrators had protested the event, but they were confined to the sidewalk and kept a full block from the Kling estate. Neighbors, returning home from work, had to gingerly maneuver their luxury cars past the protesters and the gaggle of reporters to get to their homes. A few were amused; most were annoyed.

Hollings departed Sacramento as quickly as he had arrived. He ended up spending about three hours in the capital city before being flown by chopper to San Francisco where he'd spend the night before a breakfast fundraiser at the Hilton.

"Let's see. Two-hundred-fifty paying guests at $2,000 each. That's, uh, $50,000 – no, $500,000," Summerland calculated to himself. "Not bad for three hours of his time."

Jack reached into his briefcase and pulled out his cell phone. He dialed Karen's apartment. He wanted to talk to her about the job offer. No answer. He decided against leaving a message. He walked back to the live truck, gathered his notes and slammed the door shut, telling his engineer he'd be back after dinner to re-edit the piece for the late news. To save on overtime, Middleton had been told to go home. The station would send a nightside editor to meet Jack at the truck later that evening.

Jack ate a hurried dinner alone at Godfrey's, a favorite political hang-out a few blocks from the Capitol. Godfrey's was famous for its margaritas, but Jack never drank while on the clock – not even a beer. He chatted with a couple of legislators and staffers, mostly about sports, before he returned to Kling's house to meet the live truck that had been parked there since 3 p.m. It was equipped with the latest editing gear and made editing in the truck an easy chore.

Jack looked at his watch. It was 8:45. Plenty of time to review all the video that had been shot during the day, re-write and edit a fresh piece for the 11 p.m. newscast.

This was part of the job he hated. The story essentially ended when the vice president left Sacramento hours earlier, but Jack would be stuck outside the Kling house until past eleven o'clock.

As he edited his story in the cramped truck, Jack hoped his mystery caller would still be at Christy's when he arrived, perhaps 15 minutes late. He told his photographer and engineer that he'd be unable to help tear down the equipment because he was meeting a potential news source downtown.

"Yeah, I'm sure," offered Claudio, the engineer, sarcastically. "You got a hot date, don't you?"

"I wish," Jack said. "I'm meeting some guy at Christy's. He says he has a story for me."

The re-cut version of the vice president's trip was edited in plenty of time for the late news. Jack had re-written his narration track, recorded it in the truck and fed the entire package back to the station by 10:30.

As before, the late edition of the Hollings story was flawless, if not exciting. The scene outside the host mansion on Glenbrook Court, however, resembled a street party. Four live news vans were parked in front of the house. All but a handful of the protesters had long since headed for home, but neighbors stood on the sidewalk, some in bathrobes, to watch the media circus. They had lined the street hours earlier to catch a glimpse of the vice president as he exited the Kling estate and entered his limousine. Four television news reporters lined the sidewalk five feet from each other.

It was quite a show. One by one, the reporters introduced their stories.

"That's right Ginny," said one. "Vice President Hollings is now in San Francisco, but earlier this evening, he attended a fund-raising event in a posh section of Sacramento."

Channel 4's prime news competitor, ABC affiliate KNZS, Channel 8, had some technical difficulties getting its story on the air at the top of the show. Jack wondered if the station's Capitol reporter was late feeding her story. Unable to lead the newscast with the Hollings story, the station began with its only other fresh story since the early evening newscasts, an accident on Interstate 5 involving two cars that tied up traffic for about an hour.

Channel 11, the CBS affiliate, also led with the accident, including an interview with a police spokesman who said the problem was magnified by all the drivers who slowed down to see the wreckage.

Jack was extremely competitive. He always worried about how other reporters covered stories. Did they have an interview he didn't have? Did they have a different, better angle? He wasn't worried about Channel 5. The station didn't even have a Capitol correspondent. A night general assignment reporter, who covered a light plane crash the day before and an outbreak of Sudden Oak Death the day before that, was assigned the Hollings story. The reporter was all of 25 years old. Veterans called him, and others like him, a "half-and-half." Half the salary, half the experience.

"Stand by, Jack," Claudio yelled from inside the truck. Jack cruised through the report, noting that the Hollings campaign had just banked a cool half-million dollars for California Republicans. As soon as the report concluded, he yanked the microphone off his lapel, unhooked his earpiece and bolted for his car.

Jack jumped into his Camry and turned onto Arden Way, heading to midtown as quickly as possible. He glanced at his watch. 11:05. He was late for his meeting with the mystery caller and was still a good 10 minutes from Christy's. He fumbled for his cell phone so he could call the bar. Shit, he realized. I must have left it in the live truck.

Christy's was not one of those haunts where the famous and near famous hung out and traded political stories. Christy's was an old neighborhood bar on J Street that had seen better days. It still attracted enough patrons to keep its owners out of the poor house, but the always upwardly mobile political crowd had a dozen other favorite spots.

Jack pulled up to the front of Christy's. He slowly opened the creaky front door of the bar and surveyed the scene. It was dark. Jimmy Buffett's "Margaritaville" played on the jukebox in the corner. There were six tables, one of which was occupied by a middle-aged couple. At the bar, Jack saw three men, all sitting apart from each other. Two were drinking draught beer. The other – is this my guy? – was sitting at the end of the bar under a wall sconce. There was enough light from the fixture to tell Jack that the man was slightly rumpled, about 50-ish with light wisps of gray at his temples and drinking whiskey or scotch on the rocks.

Jack didn't know who he was looking for, but he figured there was a good chance his mystery caller would recognize him from his picture on the KBLT website.

Jack sidled up to one of the beer drinkers at the bar. "How'ya doing," he said.

"Hey, aren't you, uh, that TV guy?" the man asked?

"Sure am. Nice to see you." Jack got that a lot. People saw him on the tube and felt they knew him, even if they couldn't remember his name. The man made small talk about TV news and mentioned that news anchor Christine Valero was "a real fox." After a few minutes of meandering conversation, Jack crossed him off the list.

Jack thought this was stupid, like something out of a Humphrey Bogart movie. Here it is 11:20 p.m., and he's cruising a semi-seedy Sacramento bar looking for someone he doesn't know who might or might not have information for a story that might or might not be a hoax.

Jack identified himself to the bartender, a 300-pound gorilla with a shaved head who was wearing a tee-shirt that was one size too small. It had a Harley-Davidson logo covering much of his gut. "Hey, what's up?" Jack asked.

"What'll be?"

"How about a Bud. Look, my name is Jack Summerland, and I'm supposed to meet a guy in here. Anybody been asking for me?

The bartender shook his head. "Naw."

Jack looked around the bar. "Is everyone in here a regular?"

"We had two guys I'd never seen before in here about 20 minutes ago. They just had a couple of beers and left. I think they were looking for girls, as if any ever come in here."

Jack looked at his watch and decided to park himself at a table, nurse his beer and wait until midnight for the mystery caller to identify himself.

At 11:55, Jack had had enough. By then, he was alone in the bar. The bartender had turned on the TV and was watching sports highlights on ESPN. The lead story dealt with a professional basketball player who had been arrested in a shooting incident in Washington, D.C.

Jack was never certain the mysterious phone call would amount to anything. Reporters get crank calls all the time. And truth be told, part of him was relieved that his caller was a no-show. He had just been offered a job for an up-and-coming national political figure. He thought about the possibility of hitching his wagon to Johnny Callahan's rising star and knew he couldn't consider the job offer while looking into the man who could end up being his boss.

Jack flipped a dollar tip on the bar and walked into the warm evening, convinced he had been the victim of another elaborate practical joke.

Seventeen

Seventeen

The three men sat in the dark. A thin cloud of cigarette smoke wafted through the air. The only light was the red-hot tip of the cigarette and the constant flickering from the television screen.

Harold Barnes fingered the remote control.

"Here's Channel 8," he said.

"Topping our news tonight...a huge pile-up on Interstate 5."

Click. "Let's try Channel 11."

"Traffic was snarled for more than an hour on one of Sacramento's busiest freeways tonight..."

Click. "Here's Channel 5."

"The vice president whirled into town primarily to tap local Republicans for campaign cash. And he's trying to convince California voters that the Vernon-Hollings ticket has a good chance to capture California next time around — an optimistic pitch embraced by veteran Sacramento Senator Harold Barnes."

"Quiet," blurted Roger Nicholson, the senator's campaign adviser. "You're on."

"I have never seen the party as energized as it is now. We have our best chance in decades to deliver California's electoral votes to the Vernon-Hollings ticket."

Click. "Let's see if Channel 4 got a shot of us," Barnes said as he hit 04 on the remote control.

Barnes, Nicholson and Jim Postelwhite, who worked for Nicholson's campaign consulting firm, stared at the screen a few more seconds. Once they saw the two-second shot of Barnes shaking hands with the vice president during Jack Summerland's live report, Barnes flipped back to Channel 8 but had missed most of the story. He then tried Channel 11 and saw only the last 15 seconds of the report on the vice president. Then, he hit the mute button and turned up the lights.

"Not bad for one night's work — a sound bite and a quick cameo," Nicholson offered. "You got more airtime than Callahan. Plus, you might have been on the other two, as well. You should get a TiVo."

"Too bad I'm not running for re-election," Barnes said.

Barnes had just returned from the fundraiser, where he mingled with the vice president and wealthy Republicans. As a special guest, of course, he didn't have to pay. His goal merely was to schmooze with Hollings and try to get his mug on television.

To his conservative constituents, Harold Barnes was the perfect state senator — principled and resolute. He could be as ruthless as the next politician, and he always stood his ground, rarely compromising.

Barnes was smart. A Business Administration graduate from Cal State University, Sacramento, Barnes built up a small publishing business after college, then went to law school and the Sacramento County District Attorney's office before being appointed a superior court judge. Eventually, Barnes tired of the judicial routine. He hired Roger Nicholson, at that time a fairly obscure Republican consultant, to run his campaign for a vacant seat in the Assembly. Nicholson masterminded the candidate's image during that first campaign and had been at his side ever since.

First in the Assembly, then in the Senate, Barnes represented a large portion of Sacramento County that at one time was solidly Democratic. But in the early 1980s, the Democrats lost hold of the region as moderates and conservatives in the city of Sacramento migrated to the suburbs of Citrus Heights, Folsom and Granite Bay and started electing Republicans.

The middle class settled in Citrus Heights, north and east of the capital city, while Folsom attracted many young, upwardly mobile Republicans, many of whom worked in the region's burgeoning high tech industry. Intel had established a large satellite complex in Folsom and other high tech companies had followed. Granite Bay, a relatively new community near Roseville and the western shore of Folsom Lake, mostly was reserved for the privileged. The super rich, who didn't mind the choking 45-minute commute to downtown Sacramento and merely sniffed at high gas prices, owned huge multi-acre, multi-million dollar estates. Several members of the Sacramento Kings basketball team lived in Granite Bay.

Barnes was an institution in the Sacramento area. He was serving his 13th year in the Legislature — seven in the Senate, six in the Assembly. He was so popular that he had no opposition, not even Democratic sacrificial lambs, during four of his elections. Now, however, everything had changed. Voter-approved term limits forced him to look for a new job. He considered a statewide run for treasurer or controller, but the untimely death of Bernie Edelstein offered Barnes a new opportunity. He wanted the Senate appointment and was ready to fight Johnny Callahan for it.

As the trio sipped Diet Cokes and chewed on a late snack of cheese and crackers, they tried to figure out a way to get Governor Frank to appoint Barnes to the U.S. Senate.

"Can't you find something on Callahan?" Barnes asked Nicholson. "There's got to be some dirt somewhere."

Nicholson reached into his briefcase and produced a couple of old newspaper articles. "I did find this," Nicholson said. "It's a blurb in the *L.A. Times* eleven years ago about how Callahan's late wife once called 911 and accused him of slapping her. The charges were dropped, and I can't see any value in using it. And that crap in the *Starlight* certainly wasn't helpful. Shit, the rag ended up not running the story, and it even apologized."

Barnes put down his drink and leaned back in his favorite easy chair. Out of the corner of his eye he saw a picture of Johnny Callahan on television. He grabbed the remote and turned up the sound, catching the last ten seconds of the political spot.

"Write or call Governor Frank right away and urge him to appoint Assembly Speaker Johnny Callahan to the U.S. Senate. Our future is at stake. Paid for by the 21st Century California Committee."

Barnes exhaled deeply. "Geez," he said. "What the hell is the 21st Century California Committee? How can we compete against that?" He then turned back to Nicholson.

"Look, someone obviously is trying to bring him down but is doing a lousy job. First the *Starlight*, then the planted money. Find out who's behind it. There's got to be a real good reason why someone is taking on the all-powerful Assembly speaker. We need to know what this guy knows. Find this guy and coax the information out of him, and then we'll use it. Unlike this clown, we'll do it the right way. Callahan has been winning the PR battles, but if we can find something — anything — that sticks, we can turn this around. We don't have much time. Frank could make his announcement any day now."

Nicholson, with Postelwhite in tow, started out the front door of the senator's Arden Vista home. "What if — and this is a big if — what if we find this guy and he won't cooperate?"

"Use your imagination. Find — or buy — someone who can be, shall we say, very persuasive."

Eighteen

The clock radio roused Jack from a deep sleep. The network news had just concluded and the mellifluous tones of the anchorman started reading the local news when he caused Jack, groggy and still half asleep, to bolt up in his bed.

> "Sacramento police say they discovered a body early this morning floating in the Sacramento River, near Discovery Park.
>
> "He has been identified as Carl Jansen, currently of Tucson, a former FBI agent and private security executive. A police spokesman said Jansen had been stabbed several times and possessed no identification when he was found. The spokesman said a fingerprint analysis confirmed Jansen's identity.
>
> "The spokesman said it appeared Jansen died late last

> night. It is not known why the former agent was in Sacramento. Anybody with any information on Jansen's murder is asked to call the Sacramento Police Department hotline. Callers can remain anonymous.
>
> "In other news…City Councilman Juan Mendoza…"

Tucson? Former FBI Agent? wondered Jack. Is this the guy I was supposed to meet last night?

Quickly, he called the Channel 4 assignment desk. "Hey, Shana. This is Jack. What do you have on that guy who the cops found in the Sacramento River?"

"Not much, Jack," she said. "Just what the police put in their bulletin that came in early this morning. Some guy from Tucson. He was in private security, I think, but apparently was an FBI agent in Texas before that. He was stabbed several times and left for dead in the river. Some couple looking for a place to have a good time found him washed up on the riverbank. One of our stringers got some footage. We aired it on the 5 a.m. show. It's just routine, why the interest?"

"I think I was supposed to meet this guy last night. He may have had information for a story. I thought it was a hoax. Thanks for the info. I'll see you at the office."

Jack showered and dressed in a hurry. He was preoccupied with this mystery man from Tucson. What the hell was happening?

He had wanted to discuss with Karen his job offer from Speaker Callahan after he had returned from covering the vice president. But after his wild goose chase at Christy's, he didn't get home until well after midnight.

As Jack cinched up his tie and grabbed his jacket, he abandoned his usual routine of heading first to his office near the Capitol. This time, he drove straight to the station so he could review the police report on Carl Jansen. He'd have plenty of time to make it to the Capitol and cover the budget conference committee.

Walking first to his cubicle, he noticed the flashing red light on his phone. He quickly punched in his personal code and listened to the messages. The first was from a PR flack for home health care workers who were holding a rally later that day to protest proposed budget cuts. The second message was from a network producer who wanted some background information about Johnny Callahan for an upcoming profile on the political rising star from California.

Jack listened to the voice message and saw his cell phone sitting on his desk, with a note attached, signed by Claudio, the night live truck operator. "Jack, is this yours? I found it on the floor of the live truck after work last night."

Jack exulted at finding his cell phone and checked his messages.

"Hi, Jack, this Andrea. Give me a call. I've got some budget numbers for you." Jack erased the message and listened to the next one.

"Mr. Summerland, my name is Dylan Carpenter." The caller, a graduating student at Chico State, wanted to talk about getting into the news business. Jack saved the message and moved on.

"Jack, this is Carl Jansen…" The message was breaking up badly. "Arrived…airport…Tucson…to Christy's…information about…Cal…minutes…" Then, the message ended. It was timed out at 10:37 p.m.

Jack tried to reconstruct the message and fill in the blanks: "Jack, this is Carl Jansen. I have just arrived at the airport from Tucson and I'm on my way to Christy's. I have some important information about Johnny Callahan. I'll be at the bar in a few minutes."

Jack turned on his computer and hit the web browser icon. He then checked the flight schedules between Tucson and Sacramento. "Bingo," he said out loud. West Coast Airlines, Flight 395, left Tucson at 6:10 p.m., stopped in Los Angeles and arrived in Sacramento at 10:15 p.m. The timing was perfect.

Jack sat back in his chair, took a deep breath, and typed "Carl Jansen" on a Google search. He found a two-year-old article in the *Tucson Citizen.*

> An investigator with a Tucson security firm Tuesday foiled a robbery attempt at Dryden's Department Store by disarming the suspect and holding him until police arrived.
>
> Witnesses say Carl Jansen, employed by Desert Security, Inc., walked in on the robbery attempt while shopping during his lunch hour.
>
> Jansen apparently approached the suspect from behind, knocked a pistol out of his hand and held him in a choke-hold until he was taken into custody.
>
> The suspect is identified as Robert Collier of Phoenix, who has a lengthy police record spanning 13 years.

Jack needed to talk to Jimmy Johnson about all this. His mind raced. Should he call the police? If he did, he'd have to reveal his investigation. He thought it best not to go public yet. He only had suspicions, nothing concrete. Jack also was conflicted between following a good story – perhaps a great, career-changing story involving political intrigue and murder – and taking a job in Washington, D.C., with a senator who someday might be president.

Jack had been to Washington several times to cover the California Congressional delegation. He loved that town, with its intellectual curiosity, dynamite restaurants and political elite. Jack always cherished the idea that he was witnessing history. Washington was the place to be.

Still, his journalistic instincts told him he couldn't just let this story go. Who knows, maybe it's nothing. But what if it's legit? He decided to put his personal dilemma out of his mind for the time being.

Jack knocked on Johnson's door. The news director was looking at videos of general assignment reporters who had applied for jobs at Channel 4. More than 50 DVDs were stacked against one wall. The station had lost two reporters in the past two months. One quit the business entirely and opened a small boutique in Old Sacramento, a mix of restaurants, nightclubs and tourist traps in the historic part of town near the Sacramento River. The other had been raided by a Los Angeles television station that nearly doubled her salary.

Jack filled in Johnson about the recent events — the phone call, the missed meeting at Christy's, the body and the voice message from the mystery man from Tucson.

"I don't want to go to the cops," he said. "At least not yet. We don't know if there's a connection, and you know damn well that the police will try to force us to reveal everything we know. Bye-bye exclusive."

Johnson thought for a moment, then agreed. He wasn't going to pour heavy resources into this story, but he wanted to preserve a potential scoop.

"I think this could be a huge story," Jack told his boss. "But it's not a story that jumps out at you. It's going to take some digging. I'd like to follow it. And I think putting a producer on this will help, too."

Johnson got up and closed the door to his office.

"Look, Jack. I can't do that. We're short staffed as it is and you know how we have to continually feed the beast."

Reporters and producers at Channel 4 were always referring to the morning, noon, evening and late night newscasts as "the beast." Each newscast had to be fresh from the one preceding it, so as to keep viewers from switching stations. To "feed the beast," reporters were expected to file at least one story each day, often re-packaging it for a later newscast. That left little time for investigative digging or research. Television news was into covering events — news conferences, rallies and crime — because they were simple and didn't take much time.

"But if we don't uncover this story, someone else will," Jack pleaded.

"Jack, not now," Johnson shot back. "I have money in my budget to hire two more reporters and I'm working on it as fast as I can." Johnson looked at the demo discs stacked against the wall. "Once that happens and they get up and running, we might be able to give you some time."

"Yeah, but…" Johnson cut off Jack in mid-sentence.

"You don't even know if you have a story here. I can't cut you loose during sweeps to spend time doing research when we're so short-handed. How will I fill the news hole? We're going to need you to have something on the air every day."

Jack argued a few more minutes but realized he couldn't win. His options were limited. He could work on the story on his own time after hours, or he could secretly give the information to a newspaper reporter in town and let the newspaper get the scoop. Or he could drop the whole thing, take the Callahan job and pretend the story never existed.

"What if I work on this story on my own time?" he asked. "I'd just need help with expenses. I think the story leads to Tucson."

"Look, we can't — oh, shit. Okay. Here's what I'll do. I can't give you a blank check. And I can't give you time off, but I'll split expenses with you, up to, say 300 bucks. If you get a story out of it, I'll let you expense the other half. That's the best I can do."

Jack needed someone to talk to. As he drove to the Capitol to cover yet another budget conference committee, he thought about one confidant who might help him with the answer — journalism professor Ed Stewart in Berkeley.

Nineteen

The makeup artist applied a last round of powder on Colin Frank's forehead. She neatly trimmed his eyebrows, then stepped back a few feet. "Looks good, governor," she said with a deferential smile.

Frank ignored the woman, staring into the mirror and cinching his tie. The producer led the governor into a small studio, which seemed to symbolize everything television had become — lights, television monitors and an interview set that included fake books in a cabinet in the background. The governor sat in an ordinary straight-backed chair and squinted into the lights until his eyes became accustomed to the glare.

A technician affixed a small microphone to the left lapel of the governor's suit coat and handed him a small earphone to put in his ear.

"Can you hear okay?" a voice asked him through the earpiece.

"Yes I can, very clearly," Frank responded to the faceless voice.

"Can you give us an audio check?"

"Testing, one, two, three, four, five. This is Governor Colin Frank in Sacramento, California. Testing, one, two, three."

The voice told him to stand by. He said network anchor Thomas Alford would be talking to him in about two minutes.

When Senator Edelstein passed away, Frank knew he'd become one of those instant national news items as he pondered who to appoint to complete the remainder of Edelstein's term. He was right. For only the second time in his political career, if you didn't count his aborted run at the presidency, he was a newsmaker outside California — interviews with *Time* and *Newsweek*, articles in the *Washington Post* and *New York Times*, interviews on national network news broadcasts and, of course, cable television. The balance of power in the U.S. Senate was at stake and Frank was the key player.

Thomas Alford hosted "The Alford Report," a popular nightly political discussion program on cable TV. Frank had appeared on a few network news programs years before, but he always felt a little uncomfortable in front of a camera. He was telegenic with distinguished good looks. But he didn't trust television — or, more appropriately, he didn't trust himself. He constantly worried about his body language or embarrassing himself with awkward pauses between sentences. Frank much preferred dealing with newspaper reporters, but he understood the importance of television.

Frank particularly disliked doing live interviews with someone he couldn't see 3,000 miles away in Washington. He couldn't read the interviewer's facial expressions and body language or tell if an argument was registering, but it wasn't worth a 6,000-mile roundtrip for a short interview. Besides, that's why satellites were invented.

Settling into his chair at Sat-News, a Sacramento-based communications company, Frank waited for Alford to announce his presence. Two minutes later, the wait ended.

> *Thomas Alford*: Next up on the "Alford Report" is Governor Colin Frank of California, speaking to us live from Sacramento. Governor, welcome.
>
> *Colin Frank*: Glad to be here, Thomas.
>
> *Alford*: Governor, you are Chair of the Republican Governors Association, which is meeting next month in New Orleans. We're expecting a quiet affair, but we've heard that one of your Republican colleagues, Governor Guthman of Oregon, plans to introduce a resolution that calls on the Vernon administration to increase federal spending for embryonic stem cell research. He suggests the administration is preventing research on cures of numerous devastating illnesses, such as juvenile diabetes, Alzheimer's and heart disease. This could be quite embarrassing to the administration. Will you try to head off Guthman's move?
>
> *Frank*: I won't, Thomas. We've been telling the American people for some time now that the Republican party is a big tent, that it wants people of all political persuasions to join our effort to reduce taxes and maintain a strong national defense, particularly in the face of global terrorism. It'll be up to the governors to deal with this issue.
>
> *Alford*: On another subject, are you ready to fill Senator Edelstein's U.S. Senate seat? Your party is anxious to get that additional vote in the upper house.
>
> *Frank*: I am very close to announcing Senator Edelstein's successor. As you know, I've been tied up here in Sacramento trying to negotiate a new state budget. I'm considering a number of very qualified candidates. I think you'll be hearing an announcement shortly.

Alford: We're hearing that you're going to appoint a Republican, even though Senator Edelstein was a Democrat. Would you expect some criticism if you did that?

Frank: I have made no decision yet. But the California Constitution gives me the authority to make that appointment, regardless of political party. Let me emphasize that Bernie Edelstein represented this state extremely well in the U.S. Senate. His family has my sincere condolences.

Alford: Here inside the D.C. beltway, we're getting word that Assembly Speaker Johnny Callahan is the leading candidate.

Frank: Johnny Callahan would make a great U.S. Senator. He is principled, articulate, a great leader. But I'm considering several candidates. We're blessed here in California to have a number of very capable and qualified individuals. When I make my decision, Thomas, you'll be the first to know.

Alford: Hasn't he been the subject of a smear campaign?

Frank: He has. First a phony story was planted in a tabloid magazine. Then, someone tried to bribe him. Johnny did the right thing. He called the FBI.

Alford: Any idea who is behind this?

Frank: I have absolutely no idea, but I'll tell you this: I've been impressed by the way he has handled these despicable events.

Alford: Aren't you and Speaker Callahan family friends?

Frank: Yes we are. Johnny and our son, Marty, went to college together and remain close friends today.

Alford: Governor, we look forward to your decision and expect to see you in New Orleans. Thanks for spending time with us.

Frank: Thank you.

Johnny Callahan switched off the television in his Capitol office and turned to Sam Cockerill.

"Well, what do you think?" he asked.

"I don't know what you're talking about, *Senator* Callahan," Cockerill joked, overly emphasizing the word "Senator." "I think it was great for you. He left very little doubt and had some nice things to say about you."

Callahan smiled. "I'll bet Barnes is pissed."

Twenty

Jack Summerland worked his Camry west on Interstate 80 toward the San Francisco Bay Area. For a Saturday morning, traffic was a little heavier than he expected but, then again, it seemed like traffic always was heavy in the Bay Area. Jack had arranged to visit his old friend, Berkeley journalism professor Ed Stewart, before catching a mid-afternoon flight to Tucson out of Oakland.

It was a glorious spring day. Warm, no hint of a breeze and not a cloud in the sky. As he turned off the freeway onto University Avenue, he couldn't help but think of Simon and Garfunkel's '60s hit *Cloudy:*

> *My thoughts are scattered and they're cloudy,*
> *They have no borders, no boundaries.*
> *They echo and they swell.*

From Tolstoy to Tinkerbell.
Down from Berkeley to Carmel.

Nothing against the University of Missouri in Columbia, his alma mater, but Berkeley was something special – the rolling campus on more than 1,200 acres overlooking San Francisco Bay, the groves of oak, eucalyptus and redwood blending with neo-classical architecture and the academic reputation of what long has been considered one of the premier universities in the world.

The University of California's flagship Berkeley campus counted 24 former students and 20 current or former faculty members as Nobel laureates, with Ernest O. Lawrence, inventor of the cyclotron, capturing the university's first Nobel Prize, for Physics, in 1939. Many scientists considered the cyclotron to be as important to nuclear science as Galileo's telescope was to astronomy. During the next three decades, 11 more faculty members would win the prize in either Physics or Chemistry as Berkeley researchers successfully isolated the human polio virus and discovered all of the artificial elements heavier than uranium.

As Jack pondered the university's weighty history, he made his way to Euclid Avenue on the hilly, wooded north side of campus. There, tucked in a comfortable suburban enclave about a mile north of campus, lived journalism professor Ed Stewart.

Jack and the professor first met years earlier when both served on a Society of Professional Journalists panel analyzing the media's coverage of the presidential elections. Jack had just come off the presidential campaign trail and Stewart, a former reporter, was a journalism professor. The two remained friends ever since, often sharing July 4th holidays and backpacking trips to Lake Tahoe. These days Stewart taught various journalism courses for undergraduates and investigative reporting for graduate students. At least once a semester, Jack would guest lecture in Stewart's classes, discussing trends in political reporting, showing videos and sharing war stories from past campaigns. He liked interacting with bright, inquisitive students.

Stewart was older than Jack. He had attended Berkeley in the mid-1960s. He watched the legendary Free Speech Movement unfold, protested against the war in Vietnam and watched the football team struggle each year to win as many games as it lost.

Stewart majored in American history but fell in love with journalism as a reporter for the student newspaper, the *Daily Californian.* Mostly, it seemed, he covered protests and rallies, but he thought it was the most exciting profession he could imagine. After earning a master's degree in journalism, he was hired as a rookie reporter by the Associated Press in San Francisco. A series of reports on political corruption in California caught the eye of an editor at the *Washington Post.* After two years at the AP, Stewart packed his bags for Washington, D.C., returning to California 18 years later to teach journalism. After more than two decades at Berkeley, the professor was well-respected, popular and tenured. Jack considered Stewart a mentor, of sorts. Whenever he found himself facing personal conflict, he sought Ed Stewart for advice. This was one of those occasions.

After some small talk and a couple of cups of coffee, the pair set out on foot toward the north side of campus.

"Here's why I called you," Jack said. "I've got a problem, and I don't know what to do about it."

Jack explained everything — how Johnny Callahan was in line to become a senator, how Jack was duped into reporting a phony story on Callahan, and how someone tried to entrap the powerful politician. He explained that he had been offered a terrific job working for Callahan in Washington, and that someday he could end up working in the White House. He told Stewart how he and Karen had fought when he started to follow an admittedly flimsy lead that might impact Callahan. And he talked about Carl Jansen's murder and Jimmy Johnson's refusal to let him pursue the story on company time.

"I'm in a quandary," Jack said. "I have no idea what to do.

You've been my therapist before. Any thoughts?"

The two had walked the mile to the north side of campus, past a one-block section of restaurants and stores that catered to students. At the northern boundary of campus, they crossed Hearst Avenue, named for the legendary publishing family that donated much of its newspaper profits to the rapidly growing campus around the turn of the century. The Hearst largesse was impossible to miss — Hearst Memorial Mining Building, Hearst Museum of Anthropology, Hearst Women's Gym, Hearst Greek Theater.

Stewart spied a small newspaper rack near the north entrance to campus and picked up a day-old *Daily Californian.* He and Jack sat on a bench, Stewart the shrink and Summerland his patient.

"Look, Jack, I'm not going to tell you what to do with your career," Stewart said. "That's got to be your decision."

"Here's my dilemma," Jack responded. "In my head, I know I should probably take this job. Karen and I could move to Washington, although we're having some problems right now."

"What's going on?" Stewart asked.

"Well, we argued over Johnny Callahan. Karen wanted to know if I was investigating her boss. She said she had seen the note I had written after I received that phone tip. I told her I was just playing the good reporter, following all leads and that I hadn't come up with anything."

"I'm sure you'll work things out," Stewart said.

Jack sighed. "Part of me wants to drop the whole story because it's so flimsy. My brain says 'take the job and move on.' You know how exciting D.C. is. And who knows where I might end up if I follow Callahan there. Journalism is a young person's game and TV is turning into a bunch of crap. I haven't saved any money, and at times I'm embarrassed to see the product our station puts on the air."

Stewart interrupted. "It sounds like you want the job."

"I'm not sure," Jack said. "I'm really torn. Sure, I complain about journalism every day, about how television news is more interested in ratings and audience building than gathering legitimate news. I hate the fact that the station's media consultant is constantly after management to shit-can political news in favor of more crime stories that people want to watch. I hate the fact that I have to air at least one story a day — sometimes with little preparation time – and pass it off as real news. I can't stand taking orders from producers who were in diapers when I was covering Ronald Reagan. They don't know crap about the news business. And yet…"

"And yet, what?"

"Yet, there is nothing like that adrenalin rush when I get a hold of a good story and beat the competition. You remember what that felt like. I'm just not sure if I'm ready to be anybody's flack. And…" Jack paused.

"What?" Ed asked.

"What if this tip I received is for real? I can't explain away Carl Jansen's murder. You know what we always say in journalism: 'There's no such thing as a coincidence.'"

Jack's friend paused a moment, then said, "You may have just answered your own question. Follow your heart."

"But I'm hamstrung at work," Jack said. "This Callahan story could be huge, but they won't give me any time to develop it. Hell, I'm even on my way to Tucson — on my own time for Chrissakes — to see if I can find out anything about this story. If my station doesn't let me work on this, I'm even thinking about leaking it to the *Sacramento Bee* or maybe the *L.A. Times.* At least then the story will become public. Don't tell me to change stations. The others are worse."

Stewart heard the chimes emanating from the Campanile, a 307-foot campus landmark modeled after the famed Venice tower. The pair headed a half-block to an Italian restaurant for an early lunch.

"If it's following up on this Callahan story that has you in a bind, I might be able to help."

Stewart outlined his proposal. "You know I'm teaching Journalism 250 this semester. Investigative journalism for grad students. It's a small class, just eight students. Throughout the semester they've been conducting their own investigative research. Their projects – a series of news articles – are due on Monday. After that, they have nothing to do but attend my lectures and study for a final. What if I scrap the final this semester and turn them loose on your Johnny Callahan story?"

"You can do that?" Jack asked.

"Shit, I'm a tenured professor," Stewart replied. "I can do anything I want. Besides, a real world investigation will teach them a lot more than studying for a final. These are real smart kids. They're from places like Princeton, Columbia, Stanford, the University of Washington and Cal. Most of them graduated college with honors and they've worked for their school papers. Some have experience working on metropolitan dailies. In the two weeks before classes let out, maybe they can find something."

"That's a tempting offer," Jack said. "I've always done my own research. I think I'd like to get this done myself. But I'm not sure the station will let me spend time on a wild goose chase. If I get nowhere, I'll take you up on it, okay?"

"Whatever you need," the professor said. "I'm sure my students would love the opportunity to help break a big story."

Twenty-One

Jack Summerland squinted into the afternoon sun as he walked out of Tucson International Airport. It was 91 degrees, and Jack started sweating immediately. The flight from Oakland, with a layover and change of planes in San Diego, had taken nearly four hours. He had given himself a short weekend to pursue the Carl Jansen story, hoping he'd find enough information to take to Jimmy Johnson on Monday morning.

Jack knew the odds were long that he'd be allowed to work the story unless he had tangible evidence of a scandal involving the Assembly speaker. Unlike the heyday of network news, where some correspondents might work on a story for weeks, local TV reporters didn't have the luxury of spending even a few days investigating a story. With five hours of news to fill every day, Channel 4 expected every reporter to be on the air at least five times a week, not including re-packaged stories for subsequent newscasts.

Jack set his carry-on bag on the curb and looked at his watch. It was 5:45 p.m. Where the hell was Porter?

Just then, Michael Porter pulled up in a five-year-old blue Mazda. Still trim in his mid-50s, with slightly balding salt and pepper hair and gray stubble from day-old beard growth, Porter swerved to the curb and honked twice. He was wearing tan shorts and a green polo shirt. He had just gotten off the golf course.

Jack tossed his overnight bag and blue blazer in the back seat. "Mike, I can't tell you how much I appreciate this."

"Don't worry about it. How the hell are you? I couldn't believe your call last night. What's going on?"

Jack Summerland and Michael Porter had met in 2000 when Jack spent four days in Arizona covering the presidential campaign of John McCain. Porter was a political reporter for the *Arizona Daily Star*. They became fast friends and even took a golfing vacation together in Monterey.

Over beers and enchiladas at Jose's Adobe Cantina, Jack explained everything that had happened the past few days – the bum tip about Johnny Callahan and the prostitute, the botched sting, Carl Jansen's cryptic phone call, then his mysterious death. He left out the part about being offered a job in Washington.

"This has got to be off the record for now," Jack said. "But once I put all the pieces together, I'll give you everything. Okay?"

"Sure, Jack. I won't step on your story. I went through our computer files, but I found only one posting that had any pertinent information," Porter explained. He handed Jack a computer print-out of a two-year-old story.

> Tucson police detectives on Tuesday arrested three employees of Pima Community College on charges of embezzling more than $120,000 from the school.
>
> Police said the three suspects, all members of the administrative staff, were taken into custody during their lunch breaks at the college.

> Sgt. Harold Peters, a police spokesman, said much of the information leading to the arrests came from private security consultant Carl Jansen, who is employed by Desert Security, Inc.
>
> Reached by phone, Jansen declined to offer specifics of the embezzlement accusations, only to say that Pima CC is a Desert Security client.
>
> Jansen said he had investigated an almost identical case several years ago while he was an FBI agent in Houston. "We learned a lot about how criminals use computers to commit their crimes," Jansen told the *Daily Star*. "That knowledge helped us track the stolen money at Pima."

Jack furrowed his brow. "Houston?" he said. "That's the second time I've run across a reference to this guy Jansen coming from Houston. I can't figure out the connection. An FBI agent leaves the government in Houston, becomes a private security dick in Tucson and then is killed on his way to give me information about California's Assembly speaker. I just don't get it."

Porter turned onto South Palo Verde Road and spotted the familiar Days Inn neon sign. "Sorry I can't help you more," he said, as Jack grabbed his bag and jacket and started edging out of the passenger seat, "but Connie and I are taking the kids to Tombstone tomorrow. You know, the O.K. Corral and the fake shootouts."

"Hey, no problem. You've already been helpful. Have a great time. We should play golf sometime, maybe meeting half way in Vegas."

The next morning, a cab dropped Jack off in a quiet light industrial section of town where every one-story building seemed to look like the other. There was little traffic at ten o'clock on a Sunday morning. He tried the front door of Desert Security, Inc. It was locked. He waited for about five minutes, then a black Lexus with the license plate DS 1 pulled up and parked in front of the building.

Jack was apologetic. "Thanks for meeting me on a Sunday

morning, Mr. Truman. I appreciate it."

"Anything to get me out of church. Plus, Carl was a good guy. I hope you can make some sense out of his death. We're really broken up about this."

The two exchanged business cards. Jack had scribbled his home phone number and home e-mail address on his KBLT card. Mark Truman entered five numbers on a keypad on the wall, and then unlocked the glass door leading into Desert Security, Inc. Jack followed Truman into his office. As Truman fired up the Mr. Coffee, Jack scanned the well-appointed office – plush tan leather chairs facing a large wooden desk. Behind the desk was Truman's ego wall – signed photos of professional baseball and football players and an occasional politician.

Truman placed two cups of coffee on coasters on his desk.

"Tell me, again, what happened to Carl?"

"We know what happened, but we don't know who did it, or why," Summerland said. He decided not to explain the bizarre sequence of events.

"What do you want from me?" Truman asked.

"Actually, I'm not sure. Did he ever mention Johnny Callahan to you? Or the California Legislature? Or Sacramento?"

"No," Truman replied. "Here at work he was all business."

"Any enemies that you are aware of?"

"Well, we're in the security business, and he was an ex-federal agent, so I suppose anything is possible. But I can't recall anything. Carl was kind of a loner, particularly after his wife died. He never talked about anything outside of work."

"And he never talked about going to Sacramento?"

"Not to me," Truman answered. "He did take a few days off recently, but he had them coming, so I didn't think anything of it. Are you doing a story on Carl?"

Jack responded, "Quite frankly, I don't know where this is heading – if anywhere. What do you know of Mr. Jansen's stint in Texas with the FBI?"

"Look, I'd rather not get involved with hearsay. I will tell you he was fired from the FBI. He took the fall for a botched sting operation. I had a hunch and hired him anyway. Carl was a good employee."

"Mind if I look around his office for a few minutes?" Jack asked. "I'm trying to find clues to his murder."

"I suppose it's alright. I've removed all his case files. Only a few personal items remain that I haven't had time to box up."

Jack searched for anything that linked Jansen to Callahan or Sacramento. As Truman returned to the break room for another cup of coffee, Jack fingered Jansen's rolodex that occupied a corner of Jansen's uncluttered desk. A-1 Patio Doors, Arizona Meat Co., Capitol Wholesalers. Obviously clients, Jack thought. He paused when he saw a blank card with a handwritten inscription, "Jack Summerland, KBLT reporter." The card listed his office and cell phone numbers and the notation "Christy's in Sac – 11." Jack took the card and slipped it into his pocket. Who knows who else might be snooping around Jansen's office.

The next card caught his eye. It was one of those fancy, embossed cards that said, simply, "Cameron Towne, Esq. Houston, Texas." Houston. Jack looked up briefly to confirm he was alone. He quickly lifted the card out of its holder and placed it in his pocket.

After Truman dropped him off at the airport, Jack totaled the results of the weekend. He learned precious little about Carl Jansen or why he wanted to talk to Jack. He returned on the 1:00 p.m. flight back to Oakland, still convinced there was more to this intriguing story. He also knew Jimmy Johnson would never let him pursue it.

Twenty-Two

The rented blue Ford Taurus had been parked in the dark for 45 minutes. The flick of a Zippo lighter pierced the darkness. The man in the driver's seat inhaled a huge puff and slowly exhaled. He looked at his watch. It was nearly midnight. He took one last look out the rear view mirror, glanced furtively out the front window, and inhaled a second time.

Convinced he was alone in a desolate commercial part of town, the heavy-set man with the scar on his left cheek opened the car door, crushed his cigarette out on the curb with his right foot and walked slowly to Desert Security, Inc. The building was poorly lit. For Terrence Burke, this would be a cakewalk.

The CIA had taught Burke everything he knew. Demolition, breaking and entering, all aspects of covert operations. Burke had spent two years at Langley, then four years in Colombia, ostensibly attached to a non-profit human aid organization. He had a new employer now. Theodore Dreiser, the wealthy academic-turned-movie producer, was paying him handsomely to run errands and do some dirty work for a secretive group that was determined, with a little luck, to own a president.

Burke neatly picked the lock at the building's main entrance, then made short order of the security system. Once inside the suite of offices, Burke turned on his flashlight and looked for Carl Jansen's office. A cat, or maybe a stray dog, nudged against a trash can outside the building, startling Burke for a second and causing him instinctively to reach inside his right-hand coat pocket for his nine millimeter Beretta.

He walked into a small, neat office. On the wall he saw a photograph of four men posing on the first hole of a golf tournament, each with a driver in hand. The photo didn't help. Burke had no idea what Jansen looked like. Then, he noticed on one wall a framed front page of the *Houston Chronicle*. The headline read, "FBI Nabs Bank Gang." Burke's eye was drawn to the third paragraph. "Special agent in charge Barney Wheedon praised agent Carl Jansen for tracking down the robbery gang."

Satisfied he had the right office, Burke methodically covered every square inch of Jansen's work place, leaving behind no trace of disturbance. He had been told to look for anything that connected Jansen with Johnny Callahan.

Burke rifled through a shelf of books and Jansen's desk drawers. Nothing. He looked under the blotter on Jansen's desk. Nothing. He spotted the rolodex on the desk and started reading the entries. Nothing there, either. Burke dropped to his hands and knees and swept the bottom of Jansen's desk. People often taped valuable papers to the bottom of a desk drawer. Again, nothing. He sat for a second in Jansen's desk chair. He looked around the office one more time, even peering behind the photo and framed newspaper article. The digital read-out on his watch said 12:18 a.m.

With only the light from his flashlight, Burke worked his way down a darkened hallway into another office, also unlocked. He saw a photo of Charles Barkley and Kevin Johnson – two Phoenix Suns of yesteryear – posing with a middle-aged man in a dark blue suit. In another photo, the same man was shaking hands with Arizona's legendary U.S. Senator Barry Goldwater. The photo was signed, " To Mark Truman, Best Always, Barry."

Burke surveyed the office. Except for two dirty coffee cups on the desk, this office was as neat and clean as Jansen's. Burke shopped from drawer to drawer, coming up empty. He routinely inspected the trash cans. In one, he saw a business card. "KBLT/Action 4 News," it said. The card belonged to Jack Summerland.

Burke picked up the card and slipped it into his pocket. He rifled through a drawer file in a credenza behind the desk and quickly scanned a file labeled Carl Jansen. There wasn't much helpful information, except for an employee records form. Burke jotted down Jansen's home address and put the folder back in the drawer. He paused a few seconds, then re-opened the drawer and snatched the employment form. He thought it might come in handy later.

Burke quickly left the building, re-setting the security alarm and re-locking the front door on his way out. He smiled, thinking about how easy it was to break into a security company's office complex.

Once settled into his car, Burke lit another cigarette, pulled out of the glove compartment a folded map of Tucson, then drove four miles to Jansen's apartment complex. Getting into Jansen's apartment was easier than breaking into the Desert Security office.

Burke's first stop was the desk in the bedroom. He turned it inside out but found nothing of value. He searched every room in the apartment. Burke walked into the kitchen and opened the refrigerator door, hoping Jansen had left a few beers behind. Then it hit him. The freezer! Many people keep valuable papers in their freezer to avoid having to rent a safety deposit box. The freezer protects the papers in case of fire and it's a great hiding place.

Burke opened the freezer door and there it was under a frozen steak, a manila envelope stuffed with documents and a half-dozen news articles about Johnny Callahan. Burke sat down at the kitchen table and scanned the stories. One of articles, a brief story from *USA Today*, was written while Senator Edelstein was still alive and was headlined, "Moses to the Senate?"

> **Washington** — California Sen. Bernie Edelstein remains in a medically induced coma after suffering a major stroke, doctors at George Washington University Hospital said Tuesday. Doctors said the senator's life expectancy is "hours, rather than days."
>
> If Sen. Edelstein, a Democrat, should die, Republican Governor Colin Frank will name a replacement. Sources indicate that California GOP Assembly Speaker Johnny Callahan, nicknamed Moses during his successful football playing days at the University of Southern California, has emerged as a top candidate to replace Edelstein.

Burke dialed Dreiser's cell phone. He knew he'd get his voicemail at this hour and left a simple message. "It's early Monday morning, Arizona time," he said. "Your information was correct. And the reporter was here, too."

Twenty-Three

Twenty-Three

Jack Summerland clicked his mouse cursor on the Associated Press icon. Up popped the AP's Daybook on his office computer screen, listing the major news events at the Capitol for Monday. Reviewing the calendar, as well as the Capitol Morning Digest, was a daily ritual for every government reporter in Sacramento.

There was nothing earth-shattering on the agenda this day. A victims rights group and its legislative sponsor were holding a news conference to discuss legislation to strengthen reporting requirements for convicted child sex offenders. The California Chamber of Commerce scheduled a briefing for reporters to update them on the business group's legislative agenda. A San Francisco environmental group Jack had never heard of was holding a noon rally outside the Capitol to urge the governor to include more budget funds to fight global warming.

Jack had a tiny office cubicle on the 11th floor of the Boxcar Building across the street from the Capitol. Newspapers and government reports were piled high on the floor against the walls. He shared a larger office with a reporter from the California Newspaper Group. Outside the door, on a small table in the building corridor, were two three-inch-deep baskets that housed the dozens of news releases delivered every day from legislators, government offices and public relations people representing every issue and special interest under the sun.

Jack read every release, even the inane, self-congratulatory releases that provided no news value. Sometimes, he picked up on a story idea by reading them. Usually, though, he simply bemoaned the incredible waste and tossed them into the trash bin. He wondered how many trees were lost in the name of good government.

Jack dialed the office and asked for Clay Bertrand, the assistant news director. Every story he covered had to be cleared by management in advance, usually with an eye on its ratings potential.

"Look, there's nothing big over here today," he said. "The two houses have floor sessions but they look pretty weak. Here's what I'd like to do. Tomorrow, the governor's finance director will announce the May Revise, which analyzes all the tax returns. Rumor has it that the state brought in about $3 billion more in personal and businesses taxes than expected. If that's true, the deficit will mostly be eliminated and the state won't have to go through some of the projected cost-cutting plans that are on the table. I could work on the story today, and scoop everyone before the May Revise is announced."

"For Chrissakes, Jack," Bertrand shot back. "You've seen our surveys. People don't care about budgets; they want exciting news. Last week's Nielsens dropped a little. I don't know about a budget story. What about that bill requiring convicted sex offenders to be tracked by global positioning satellites? That's a winner. And isn't there some bill about regulating tattoo parlors?"

"Come on," Jack said. "Give that to someone else. Why in the hell do you have me covering government if you're not going to let me do important stories that take advantage of my sources?"

Bertrand acquiesced. "Okay, but you know the drill. Make it relevant to the viewer with an eighth-grade intelligence. Will they pay less in taxes? Will they be safer in their homes? Will their kids get a better education? And how can we promote this during the day?"

Jack did, in fact, know the drill. "You mean something like, 'New and exclusive tonight at five – the state has new budget numbers. How will it affect your pocketbook?'"

"Yeah," Bertrand shot back.

"And one other thing," Jack continued. "I've got a new lead on the Callahan story. It's going to take some digging but it has great potential. I'll talk to you about it this afternoon when I'm back from the budget story."

Jack wrapped up the May Revise preview shortly after the lunch hour. The governor's budget director was tight-lipped, but two sources indicated "off the record" the state's tax income was $2.6 billion greater than anticipated. While he worked the phones, he sent Middleton to the Franchise Tax Board to shoot video of its cavernous work area with hundreds of state employees processing tax returns.

Jack's ace-in-the-hole – a source he never betrayed or acknowledged publicly – was a friend who worked in the state printing plant who ripped off a copy of the executive summary, which confirmed that the Department of Finance was printing a comprehensive revised budget document that included the suspected multi-billion dollar windfall.

To keep the station's executives happy, Jack interviewed a handful of ordinary citizens – man-on-the-street interviews – and asked them what they thought the state should do with the money. One said, "Buy out Governor Frank's contract." Jack decided to use it on the air.

Once Jack finished writing his script, Middleton started editing the story. It would take about an hour for the minute-and-a-half story to be completed.

Jack walked into the office of the station's news director, Jimmy Johnson. He sat down in a chair across from Johnson's desk, piled high with resumes from ingénue reporters in small towns who wanted to be in show business. Clay Bertrand joined them. Once again, Jack started selling the Callahan story to management when he was interrupted.

"Hold on, Jack," Johnson said. "Before you start, we need to get Meredith in here."

"Meredith? Who's Meredith?"

"Meredith Layne. She's our new Promotions Manager. Technically, she's supposed to start in June, but she's spending a little time with us to take a look at our product as we move through sweeps. You'll like her. She's real smart."

Jack shot back angrily. "Aren't we a little premature with trying to figure out how to promote this story? We don't even know what the story is yet because you won't give me time to work on it."

"Look, Jack," Johnson said. "Enough of this. I don't like it any more than you do, but New York is bitching about our falling numbers so we've hired someone to, uh, help us make decisions as to what stories we cover. She's originally from the Collins Agency."

Jack was incredulous. "You mean we've sunk so low that we are now making news judgments based on how well they sell instead of their news value? This is ridiculous."

Johnson glanced at Bertrand, then back at Jack. Clearly, the two veteran broadcasters didn't like the new paradigm either. But business was business and Johnson was getting tired of Jack's constant whining. "Nonetheless, it's the way we have to do things around here. Let's all make the best of it. If you don't like it, I can always find someone who will."

Jack knew about the Collins Agency. It was a media consulting firm out of Denver that advises television news departments on their presentation and appearance, as well as news content. It received hefty monthly fees to tell stations how to cover the news in order to maximize ratings. These firms were first in vogue in the early 1970s and transformed television news into "flash and trash." Stories on crime and sex were designed to keep viewers entertained, if not informed. Shortened story length was aimed at viewers with short attention spans. The subliminal message was: "Don't touch that dial – we've got more entertaining and exciting news coming up in just a few seconds."

Jack remembered seeing a memo from the Collins Agency during the Iraq War. It noted that millions of viewers were glued to late-night television news programming for war updates. It suggested that its client stations do stories about how the war coverage was interfering with their sex lives. Jack remembered that KBLT chose not to do the sex story, but he wondered how many other stations succumbed to the ratings ploy. And what would the station do today if it found itself in the same situation?

Johnson invited Meredith Layne into his now-cramped office and introduced her to Jack. She couldn't have been older than 30. She was tall and thin, with long blond hair cascading over her shoulders. She had no journalism experience. Ever since she graduated from the University of Colorado with a degree in communications and a minor in public relations, she had been employed by the Collins Agency. KBLT was one of her major clients, until the corporate suits at KBLT's parent company in New York hired her away, placed her in Sacramento, and tapped her to add some spice to the local newscast.

Jack pitched his story.

"On my own time, I spent the weekend in Tucson following leads on the Callahan story. I talked to a number of sources, a reporter friend of mine, and others, who gave me some good information on that dead former FBI Agent, Jansen. You know, the guy who was killed in Sacramento just before meeting me."

Johnson, somewhat dismissively, picked up the conversation. "Okay, so what do we know?"

"We know he once was a rising star in the Houston office of the FBI until he was fired. And I found a note in his rolodex that further confirms he came to Sacramento to see me. There's something going on here."

"Okay, Jack, you tell me what's going on." Johnson shot back.

Jack took a deep breath, glanced quickly at Bertrand, then created a likely – if unproven – scenario for his news director.

"Here's what I think is going on. This guy Jansen used to be an FBI agent. He once investigated the state legislature in Texas, and I think he investigated Johnny Callahan at some time. In any event, he had something on Callahan and was going to tell me. But before he could, he was killed."

Jack paused and looked directly at Johnson. "Tell me this isn't a great story."

"Maybe," Johnson shot back. "Maybe it's a good story. I'm willing to give you some latitude here, but you'll have to wait until sweeps is over."

Johnson turned to Bertrand. "Have you got the numbers and the last Collins Report?"

Bertrand fished through a pile of papers in a folder on his lap and pulled out the overnight Nielsen ratings and a memo from David Collins. He handed them to Jack.

"Look, Jack," Johnson said. "The numbers are down – not terribly – but they're not what they used to be. Overall viewership is still hemorrhaging, and we're no longer on top with the 25-to-54-year-old demographic."

Jack was keenly aware of recent industry trends that had fractured the audience. In the 1960s, 91 percent of the television audience relied on the three networks – ABC, NBC and CBS – and their affiliated stations. Since then, the growth of independent stations and networks, as well as cable and satellites, eroded viewership of the three major networks to less than 40 percent. And the percentage of overall television news viewing continued to drop as the Internet became a more viable and accessible news source.

"Collins is convinced we've got good sweeps series between now and the end of the month," Johnson said. "He really likes our reporting staff. But he stresses we have to have our top reporters on the air every night. We've got two weeks until the end of sweeps, and I simply cannot afford to have you off the air while you chase this story. After sweeps, I'll give you plenty of time, I promise, to develop this Callahan thing."

Summerland gave it one more shot. "But in a few days, Callahan could be appointed to the U.S. Senate. We can make a difference with this story. Besides, it has intrigue and murder. If I can dig up a little sex, then we'll have all the bases covered with an exclusive that will blow the lid off ratings. Remember, our numbers spiked higher when we were running that *Starlight* crap."

"Sorry, Jack," Johnson said. "All you've got right now is a hunch. Nothing concrete to go on. Two weeks. If timing won't let us nail a *potential* senator, then maybe we can nail a *sitting* senator after he's appointed. That could be an even better story."

There was an awkward silence. Meredith actually agreed with Jack but thought it best to keep her mouth shut. After all, she wasn't even on the payroll yet. Johnson and Bertrand waited for Jack to say something, but he sat silent, simmering. He wanted to say, "This is a bunch of bullshit," but he held back. Why piss off management more than he already had. It was time to fold his hand. His mind wandered to his earlier conversation with Johnny Callahan. Maybe, he thought, forgetting about this story and going into politics wasn't such a bad move after all.

Johnson looked at his watch. "Well, I've really got to go. I'm five minutes late for our west coast news directors conference call."

Jack rose from his chair. His eye caught the image on one of three silent television monitors in Johnson's office. It was a promo, on a rival station, of that night's sweeps series installment. "Where the Sacramento singles go after dark – Tonight at 11," it read. Jack rolled his eyes and left the room.

Twenty-Four

Jack reported his budget story for the five o'clock news and then wrote a second version for the late news. He and Ron Middleton, who usually went their separate ways after work, shared some beers at Garcia's a few blocks south of the Capitol.

"Shit, Ron. I still don't know what to do about this job offer from Callahan. It's really tearing me up inside."

Middleton shot back. "You're kidding. This should be a no-brainer. Think what you'd be missing. More money, more stature, those D.C. parties and think of all the women back there."

"I know," Jack said, "but I'm not sure if my heart is in it. I know I complain about TV news all the time — you must be sick of my whining — but even with the crap I've got to put up with on a daily basis, it's in my blood. And you've got to admit I could do a lot worse than KBLT. More importantly, and I haven't discussed this with you, there appears to be a connection between Callahan and a murdered private investigator. Something tells me I've got to let this story run its course. I've got to figure this out before I make any career move."

Ron reached for the menu and spied the dessert section. "Look, this whole story could turn out to be nothing. If I were you, I'd keep my options open. Don't close any doors, okay? Besides, a senator needs a staff photographer, right?" he said with a broad smile.

At dusk, Jack made the 20-minute drive from the Capitol to his condominium complex east of downtown, several blocks of brown townhouses that all looked the same. He favored quiet, less-congested surface streets to the freeway. After a dinner of minestrone, macaroni and cheese and sourdough bread, he settled into the recliner chair in his den. A baseball game droned on the TV, but Jack wasn't paying attention.

Jack stared at the wall a few seconds. One was covered with photographs of Jack interviewing politicians, even a few presidents. Jack's Northern California Emmy Award, won for a documentary on California's energy crisis, was placed conspicuously in a ceiling-to-floor bookcase. A dozen other journalism award plaques filled another wall, along with two framed *Kansas City Star* front pages featuring Jack's byline on banner headline stories — a multi-part series on widespread corruption in City Hall and an exclusive report on sexual abuse of foster children. He couldn't help but think that he reported and uncovered important stories back then instead of chasing a tabloid report about a politician's phantom sexual tryst.

Jack was nodding off, an empty can of beer in his hand, when he heard a noise at his front door. Startled, he thought someone was breaking into his home. He quickly turned off the lights in the den, squirmed out of his chair and crouched behind his desk, his heart pounding. His eyes darted across the darkened room as he looked for something he could use as a weapon. He didn't own a gun, and his baseball bat was in the garage. Was he about to suffer the same fate as Carl Jansen? He had been threatened a few times during his journalism career, but he never was harmed, or even attacked. True, someone once pumped a half-dozen bullets through the front window of the KBLT studios, but the police traced the shooting to a mentally ill man who thought anchorman Conrad Dalton was sending him messages through his television set.

Without making a sound, Jack gingerly reached for the middle drawer of his desk. He opened it a crack, then an inch, then two inches. He reached inside and quietly fumbled until his fingers found it. A letter opener. It wasn't very sharp, but it'll have to do.

From a room away, Jack heard the front door squeak as it opened, slowly at first. Sweat formed on his forehead. Jack thought he was going to have a heart attack. He tried to remain deathly quiet, but he was starting to hyperventilate. Stop breathing so hard, he commanded himself. He squeezed the letter opener in his right hand and crept to the door separating the den from the apartment's small entryway.

The den door was slightly ajar. Jack peered through the tiny opening but could see nothing in the darkness. Then, a soft voice pierced the air. Jack was startled. It was a woman's voice, a familiar voice.

"Jack, you here? Jack?"

"Jesus, Karen," he said. "You scared the shit out of me."

"Don't tell me you forgot you gave me a key?" Karen replied. "Jack, we've got to talk."

Jack grimaced. "That has an ominous ring to it. Actually, I've got something to tell you, too. You go first."

"Okay," she said. "What the hell is going on with you? Are you investigating my boss?" She paused a second, then pushed the conversation forward. "Johnny is a good man, an ethical man. He has a bright future. You and I can be part of that future, but I know you're up to something."

"How do you know?" Jack replied.

"I saw your notes after you got that phone call in the middle of the night. I know you had a meeting at Christy's. I tried to reach you all day Sunday, but you weren't home. Where were you? Were you working on this story?"

"Look, I'm a journalist and I'm just following the facts," he told her. "I have no idea where it's going to lead – if anywhere – but I've got to pursue it." He paused a few seconds. "I went to Tucson last weekend, and I might go to Houston this weekend, as well. But so far I don't have a story."

Karen pursed her lips and looked at Jack sternly. "Listen, I want you to drop this. Now. It's turning personal. You're jeopardizing my career. Johnny will think I've been feeding you this stuff. I could get fired. And what if your investigation goes nowhere but it comes out in the press? You've always said that perception is reality. How many times have you seen a politician hurt by inaccurate accusations? You could ruin an innocent man's career."

"You don't understand," Jack said. "Ever since I was in college at Missouri, I wanted to be a journalist. I was editor of the school paper, which helped me get a job at the *Star*. To this day, one of the greatest thrills in my life was that first byline. I still remember every detail of that story. I remember waking up at six o'clock in the morning – six in the morning, for Chrissakes – and running to the front door to open the newspaper."

Karen quivered. Jack thought she was going to cry.

"For years you've been griping about how the news business, particularly TV, has changed. You get sick of the superficial stories and lack of investigation. You tell me you're embarrassed at some of stuff you put on the air. You're not going to go back to newspapers. They're shrinking and there's no future in it. Jack, you're not getting any younger. I know Johnny has talked to you about being press secretary. If you turn down this opportunity, you may never have another chance to start a new career."

"You know about the job offer?" he asked.

"I've been told about it. You need to take it."

Jack walked over to the refrigerator and grabbed a beer. He pulled out a half-filled bottle of chardonnay, poured Karen a tall glass and exhaled deeply.

"You're right," he said as he handed her the glass. "I do hate what the TV news business is becoming. We even have a new promotions director who is helping to make judgment calls about what stories we cover. I don't like the idea that I have to research a story over the weekend because I have to grind out a story a day during sweeps month. I don't like the fact that we've turned into a headline service instead of giving the public in-depth, important stories. I don't like the idea that we have thirty-something graduates with degrees in communications running the newsroom even though they've never covered a story in their entire lives. I don't like the goddamn bean counters who rake in millions of dollars in political ads but don't want their news divisions covering political stories.

"You're right. It *is* a pretty screwed up industry right now and I'm not very confident it will get any better. But..." he paused, obviously in conflict. "But every once in awhile we do a damn good job of breaking *real* news that's important to our community. And that makes me feel good." He paused again. "I just don't think I'd be happy as a flack fronting for a senator. In a couple of years, maybe. But not just now."

Karen shot back. "Jack, it's time to settle down. Get a *real* job. Nights, weekends and holidays off. When was the last time you had Thanksgiving or the Fourth of July off? You've had your glory. You've been on TV and have had your bylines. You've won your damn awards and people recognize you on the street. How much longer are you going to put up with other people – so-called 'journalists' – telling you what to do and how to do it? These people may have a college communications degree but they don't have one-tenth your brains or experience. And don't forget. Who has cut your salary while you worked your ass off? I'll be getting retirement benefits. Will you?"

For once, Jack was speechless. He rubbed his forehead as if he had a migraine.

Karen continued. "Johnny is going places. The talk around the office — from Marty, Sam and the others — is that he could be president some day. President, Jack. You'd be press secretary to the president. If that doesn't validate your life, what the hell would?"

"Look," Jack said. "I don't disagree with anything you said, but I can't follow this Callahan story while I'm considering a job offer. I have to see this story through, no matter where it takes me."

"You do that, Jack," she said scornfully. Her emerald green eyes were throwing darts. "Go ahead and do that and you'll be burning a bridge forever. Even if you turn up nothing, as you will, don't expect Johnny to say, 'Let's let bygones be bygones. We'll hire you anyway.' Forget it. That'll never happen."

Jack walked towards Karen and tried to put his arms around her. She recoiled, tears streaming down her face, smearing her mascara. She turned toward the door and gently dropped his house key on the kitchen counter.

"This is goodbye, Jack," she said as she walked out the door.

Twenty-Five

Twenty-Five

Johnny Callahan, with Marty Frank and Billy Galster in tow, gingerly stepped off the curb outside the Hyatt Regency, let the traffic pass and walked across L Street to the edge of the Capitol grounds. They were working their way back to the Capitol after a breakfast meeting at the Hyatt Regency with well-heeled business leaders.

"I thought that went very well," Galster said to no one in particular.

The Assembly speaker had discussed the prospects of his tax cut proposal before a few dozen of California's most influential captains of industry, an audience hand-picked by the influential California Chamber of Commerce. It was common knowledge at the Capitol that business and conservative groups booked the Hyatt, which was nonunion. Teachers, nurses and other labor groups booked the Sheraton. There hadn't been pickets outside the Hyatt for several years, but some Democrats still refused to set foot in it.

As they crossed L Street, Galster motioned over his shoulder to the Senator Hotel. "I'll bet you don't know the history of this place."

He didn't wait for a response. "It was built in 1924 and once was home to some of the mightiest and most corrupt lobbyists in history."

With its terrazzo marble floors and pillared foyer, the Senator Hotel was a Sacramento landmark, modeled after the Farnese Palace in Italy. Since the 1980s, the hotel had become an office complex.

"And you know, we're following in President Ford's footsteps."

Callahan wasn't paying attention. Frank had a quizzical look on his face.

"Don't you know your history? This is where President Ford barely escaped assassination back in 1975. He was walking from the Senator, across L Street, about a half-block through the edge of Capitol Park and up the east steps of the Capitol to deliver a speech to a joint session of the Legislature.

"On the walk through Capitol Park, Lynette Fromme, a disciple of Charles Manson, pointed a loaded gun at the President and pulled the trigger. As it turned out, she had loaded the gun improperly. There was no bullet in the firing chamber."

"So here is where that happened," Frank said. "I remember seeing film of the incident, but I didn't know it was here."

"I covered it for the *Times.* I'll never forget the stunned look on Ford's face as Secret Service agents grabbed him and literally pushed him up the steps and into the Capitol."

Callahan and Galster worked their way to the Capitol's east entrance; Frank peeled off to go to his office. They skirted a small knot of protesters. A woman with a bullhorn yelled, "What do we want?" The small crowd replied, "Freedom." "When do we want it?" "Now." Callahan had no idea what they were protesting for – or against. He smiled and nodded at one of the participants then walked on to the Capitol entrance.

"It's not like the old days," Galster said. "During the Vietnam War, they'd have rallies that routinely attracted 10,000 people."

To be sure, rallies – usually very mild – still occurred almost daily at the Capitol and captured more television coverage than they deserved. Capitol security required rally permits and kept a watchful eye in case of problems. But over the decades, the Capitol had gradually become a fortress as law enforcement steadily reacted to threats and actual terror incidents by gradually tightening public access to the building.

On May 2, 1967, 26 Black Panthers, wearing distinctive black berets and black leather jackets, and toting rifles and shotguns, marched up the Capitol steps and straight onto the Assembly floor to protest a bill being debated on gun control.

The bill, later approved by the Legislature and signed by Governor Ronald Reagan, rescinded the law that allowed citizens to carry weapons in public as long as the weapons were clearly visible and not hidden. The Black Panthers accused the "racist" Legislature of trying to keep black people unarmed and powerless.

State police couldn't arrest the Panthers on weapons charges, because their loaded weapons were not concealed. Six Panthers, however, were arrested for creating a hazard to public safety. In response, electronic door locks, peep holes and bullet-proof windows were installed in the governor's office, while state police officers were armed with rifles, shotguns and chemical gas.

Decades later, the Capitol underwent another significant security upgrade. On January 16, 2001, a 37-year-old parolee from Sacramento, apparently with a grudge against Governor Gray Davis, crashed a truck loaded with evaporated milk into the south portico of the Capitol building just as the Assembly adjourned an evening session devoted to the state's energy crisis.

Witnesses said the truck had circled the Capitol, its horn blaring, before plowing up the marble steps and smashing into the granite pillars just below the Senate chambers.

On impact, the truck's fuel tank ruptured and the south side of the Capitol was engulfed in flames. The driver was trapped inside the truck and died instantly. The fiery crash prompted new security measures at the Capitol, including denial of public access to the basement through two driveways – one on the north side of the building, the other on the south.

Before the crash, wooden security gates had guarded the two driveways leading to the Capitol basement. They were placed strategically at the beginning of the long, 50-yard driveways – one entering the Capitol from the north off L Street, and the other entering the Capitol from the south, off N Street. After the crash, state officials installed thick metal hydraulic barriers in each driveway behind the gates. Instantly, upon a security breach, they could rise from the ground and block even the heaviest truck from reaching the basement where legislators parked their state-leased cars.

Once safely inside the Capitol elevator reserved for legislators, Galster returned to the subject of business political support. "When you get to the Senate, those folks are going to be real good friends," he told Callahan.

"I particularly loved it when the head of that theater chain asked you about the presidency. I tell you, there's a buzz out there. It's great. And it certainly can't hurt us."

"Yeah, I suppose," Callahan said. He seemed to have his mind on something else.

The duo whisked through the front door of the speaker's office like a gust of wind. Once through the door, each went in separate directions.

The speaker walked into his lavish office, sat at his desk and started to scan the daily newspaper clip file. Every day, the speaker's staff downloaded public policy and political articles from the major California newspapers. Callahan started reading a *Riverside Press-Enterprise* article about a local assemblywoman who opposed the speaker's tax plan. Then he noticed a small "While You Were Out" memo. "Please call Mr. Dreiser," his secretary had written in the space for comments.

Callahan closed the door to his office and dialed the Hollywood producer.

"Gladstone, my friend, how are you?"

"A little worried, Johnny. I hope your Senate nomination isn't unraveling."

Callahan seemed incredulous. "What are you talking about? Everything is going great." He glanced at his watch. "I have a meeting with the governor in ten minutes. Marty tells me the governor wants to finalize details for the announcement. I'm pretty sure…"

Dreiser interrupted. "Don't get ahead of yourself. This reporter is stirring up shit about you."

"What reporter?" Callahan asked.

"That TV reporter, Jack Summerland."

Callahan leaned back in his chair and took a deep breath. "What about him? I've offered him a job to be my press secretary when the Senate appointment comes through. He's thinking it over. He's actually a good guy. He made a stupid mistake by jumping on the *Starlight* story without verifying it, but he apologized. That's more than most reporters would do."

"Then I hope you're sitting down for this one," Dreiser said. "Your boy is investigating you. He was in Tucson last weekend and it has something to do with you. My investigator found a document hidden in some guy's freezer that could ruin your life if it ever becomes public."

Again, Callahan seemed incredulous. "What the hell are you talking about, Gladstone? I'm squeaky clean. Nobody could possibly have anything on me."

Dreiser decided not to push the conversation any further. "Okay, maybe it's another phony story. But I'm telling you, this reporter could burn you and your political future could be in jeopardy. If that happens, you won't be the only loser. My friends and I won't be very happy about it, either."

Callahan hung up the phone, then dialed Marty.

"You've got to get over here now," he barked. Marty's consulting office was across the street from the Capitol. He could be in Callahan's office in five minutes.

Enjoying "most favored" status had its perks. In a blur, Marty slipped past Callahan's receptionist with not so much as a nod. Without knocking, he walked into the speaker's private office.

"Marty, I just had a conversation with Gladstone Dreiser, and he says Summerland spent last weekend snooping around Tucson. He says Summerland is trying to come up with another story about me."

Anger showed on his face. "What the hell is going on here?"

"Look," Marty responded. "I didn't want to bother you with this, because I can handle it. But Summerland has been digging around. Karen told me he's not going to take the job. He thought he had a source that would take you down, but that source is no longer a threat."

"Take me down? What are you talking about?"

Marty continued. "It appears that an ex-FBI agent tried to plant that story about you in the *Starlight*. When that backfired, he tried to trap you into accepting a bribe. That also failed. He then sent me an e-mail demanding $200,000 to keep his mouth shut."

Callahan was stunned, in disbelief. "Keep his mouth shut about what? What did I ever do to this guy?" Callahan paused a few seconds. Marty remained silent. Suddenly remembering something that had happened long ago, Callahan broke the awkward silence. "Ohmigod, ohmigod." He covered his mouth with his right hand. "It can't be."

Marty tried to reassure his friend and benefactor.

"Don't worry. I have it handled. This guy won't be bothering us anymore."

Callahan put on his suit jacket and headed for the door.

"Marty, I hope you're right," he said in a hushed voice. "I'm going downstairs to see your father. I want to get this thing over with."

As soon as Callahan cleared the front door, Marty sidled over to Karen's desk. "Come here," he said, as he motioned to an empty conference room. Closing the door behind him, he asked her point-blank, "Thanks for all your help. Do you know what Summerland knows?"

"I don't think he knows anything. At least, that's what he told me. Is there something going on?"

Marty started to lecture. "Nothing is going on. It's all bullshit. But you do know what's at stake here, don't you," he said. "Stay on him and find out if he knows anything."

"That's going to be a problem," Karen responded. "We broke up last night. I think it's over."

Marty was angry now. Karen could see the veins on his neck. "Dammit, that's not good enough. Johnny Callahan could be president one day, but if your boyfriend snoops around too much, it'll be a pipe dream – or worse."

Karen was stunned. "What are you talking about, Marty?"

Marty realized he had been too forceful. He relaxed and exhaled. "I'm sorry if I made this sound like a mystery novel with conspiracies everywhere. I've known Johnny for most of our lives. There's nothing in his past to find, but you know how bad publicity can screw everything up. One more phony story could ruin his career – our careers."

He started for the door. "Now forget we had this conversation, but try to stay close to Summerland and tell me if he finds anything on Johnny. Okay?"

Karen nodded and walked out of the conference room, still confused and more than a little curious.

Twenty-Six

One floor below the speaker's office, in the governor's private sanctum, a secretary knocked weakly on the door, then brought in two cups of coffee. The governor took both cups, then handed one to the Assembly speaker. The secretary closed the door on her way out the office.

Speaker Callahan sat in a plush chair directly across the governor's desk. There was an awkward silence for a couple of seconds, then Governor Frank smiled, as if he knew a secret.

In fact, Frank did know a secret. And it was a beauty.

He smiled broadly. "Johnny, what would you say if I told you that Harold Barnes, that sanctimonious hero of conservatives and would-be United States Senator, was once a member of the Taney Society?"

Callahan was dumbfounded. He had a quizzical look on his face and at first didn't say a word. The defunct Taney Society was a thoroughly discredited white supremacist group that advocated the merging of Idaho and Montana into a whites-only enclave. It was named for U.S. Supreme Court Chief Justice Roger B. Taney, who authored the Court's majority opinion in the infamous 1857 Dred Scott case. The Taney Court ruled that the U.S. Constitution did not recognize the citizenship of an African American who had been born a slave. The decision was a flashpoint as the nation headed toward Civil War.

Ironically, three decades earlier as a lawyer Taney had declared, "Slavery is a blot on our national character."

In the 1960s, as the nation's civil rights movement was at its peak, a small group of white supremacists started the Taney Society at a southern university. By 1971, 28 college chapters had been formed, including one at Sacramento State. Most students didn't even know it existed, and those who did, didn't take it seriously.

"What are you talking about, Colin?" Callahan finally said.

"I'm talking about Harold Barnes advocating white supremacy when he was in college at Sacramento State. There was a small chapter of the Taney Society on campus. It didn't do much, except for handing out leaflets on campus on occasion. But Barnes was right in the middle of it."

"Jesus," Callahan said. "I know he's pretty conservative, but this?"

Callahan knew this revelation killed any long-shot hopes Barnes might have of being appointed to the U.S. Senate. "How do you know all this?" he asked.

"I know this from the best independent source available, the *L.A. Times.* Kellen Foster is going to run a story in tomorrow morning's paper spelling it all out."

The governor smiled broadly, like the cat that swallowed the canary. "Apparently, someone leaked this information to the *Times.* I have no idea where it came from," he lied. "Foster has references in the school paper and interviews with fellow Society members. He called me for a comment, and he'll probably call you, too."

"I'm shocked," Callahan said. "Why has this never come out before? What did you tell him?"

"Nothing, except to say that I'll reserve judgment until I hear all the facts. I did, however, tell him that I thought the Taney Society, while ineffective, was an organization whose ideas I abhor. You know what this means," he continued.

"What?" Callahan responded.

"This means that I can now go ahead and make your appointment. But I've got to tell you that I did my own opposition research on you, too. It was a precaution. I had to protect myself."

Callahan appeared startled. "Will all due respect, Colin, we've had these discussions. What kind of research did you do?"

"Out of campaign funds, I hired an op-research firm to check your past. You know, stuff like marijuana in college, or knocking up a cheerleader. But don't worry. Except for a couple of parking tickets and that disturbance at your fraternity house, you're a Boy Scout."

"I told you I'm clean."

The governor rifled through a pile of papers on his desk and pulled out a letter from New Mexico Senator Hernando Gomez. "Look at this," he said, smiling broadly. "The esteemed Senator Gomez tells me that since Senator Edelstein was a Democrat, it is my duty to appoint a Democrat to occupy his seat." The two shared a laugh.

The governor tossed the letter back onto his desk. "Your competition is out of the way now. Let's set the announcement for next week. Let's see what the good Senator Gomez thinks about that. Clear your calendar for Tuesday morning. I'm sure I'll get tons of questions once the Barnes story breaks, but I'll keep a lid on the announcement until then."

Callahan took a deep breath. "I'm grateful for the confidence you have in me, Colin. Needless to say, I'll make you proud."

"Just do a great job in D.C., Johnny. You deserve it and the party deserves to be in charge. But there is one thing you can do for me."

"What's that, Colin?"

"Tell Dreiser to stop running those ads," the governor said with a half-smile "We're getting swamped with e-mails and letters. Enough already."

Johnny laughed. "I'll make sure he gets the message."

Johnny smiled at the secretary as he left the governor's private office, then walked through a long L-shaped hallway to the outer office leading to the main hallway on the Capitol's ground floor. As he opened the door to the large reception area, the lights of three television cameras blinded him. It was a media ambush. How in the world did all these reporters know he was inside the governor's office? All of a sudden, questions were being thrown at him.

"Mr. Speaker," one reporter shouted as he thrust a microphone three inches from Johnny's bright, white teeth. "Senator Harold Barnes has called an urgent news conference that is supposed to start in ten minutes. We suspect it's about the Senate appointment. Do you know what that's all about?"

"No, I don't. Sorry."

"Mr. Speaker, were you talking to the governor about the Senate appointment?"

Johnny thought for a second, then decided it would be best to obfuscate. "The governor and I talk at least once a day on critical matters affecting California, not the least of which is the state budget. As you know, our tax receipts are nearly $3 billion higher than anticipated, which is great news for the upcoming budget. I now expect pretty smooth sailing in the Assembly for the governor's spending plan. Now, if you'll excuse me, I've got to get going."

Callahan pushed his way through the heavy double doors into the first-floor hallway that was crowded with a curious mixture of fourth-grade students on a field trip and grown men and women of the press corps filing into the news conference room across the hall.

Callahan scurried to an elevator and the safety of his office. He had trouble processing what had just occurred the past half-hour. Events happened so quickly.

He smiled ever-so-slightly and thought of Daniel Webster, John C. Calhoun and Henry Clay. The reality was sinking in that he was on the brink of becoming one of only a handful of Americans who ever has the chance of sitting in the United States Senate.

Then, as if suddenly awakening from a dream that hadn't reached its logical conclusion, his mind raced back to his conversation with Marty. Summerland? Blackmail? That secret from so long ago?

He exhaled deeply. After all, Marty said he has it handled.

Twenty-Seven

Twenty-Seven

News reporters, like a herd of cattle, many carrying heavy tripods and bags of television equipment, filed into Room 1190, the Capitol's news conference room.

News conferences were a dime a dozen during a typical day at the Capitol. Sometimes only one or two reporters would show up, although journalists could monitor events via closed circuit audio feeds.

The Barnes news conference was one of those stories that spread like wildfire through the press corps. Most reporters received cryptic phone calls from Barnes staffers. "The senator is having a news conference in 30 minutes in Room 1190," the caller said. "I can't tell you what it's about, but you'll want to be there." The definition of a hastily called news conference.

One reporter, sitting in the third row, looked over his shoulder and surveyed the larger-than-normal attendance of reporters.

"It must be a slow news day," he said to no one in particular.

No one professed to know why Barnes had called the news conference, but Kellen Foster, sifting through notes at his desk in the first row of the news conference room, had a pretty good idea.

Barnes had been tipped off to the *Times* story an hour earlier as he ate a bagel at his desk shortly after arriving at the Capitol. The Senate Democratic floor leader had been called for comment by Foster and, as a courtesy, told Barnes about the phone call. The two had gone to college together and remained friends despite their political disagreements.

Barnes, himself, hadn't been called to comment on the story, but he figured that call would come late in the afternoon after most of the story had been written. That's how the media work, Barnes knew. They write the story, and save a paragraph or two for response.

Barnes and his two advisers, Roger Nicholson and Jim Postelwhite, had debated how to handle the budding scandal. They could wait until the article appears and is repeated on websites and television. Or, they could try to seize the agenda and scoop the *Times* by admitting Barnes had a youthful college dalliance with the Taney Society, which he later repudiated.

"But what if the story never runs?" Nicholson asked. "You'd be committing suicide if you admitted something that no one was going to find out in the first place."

"That's a calculated risk," Postelwhite interjected. "I think we need to assume the story will be written and we should be the ones to release our own bad news. It'll take some of the sting out of the story."

Barnes remembered the advice of a former White House speechwriter, "A mistake stays a scandal until it is explained."

The Barnes brain trust decided to call a news conference to spin the story their way before the *Times* story even made it into print. They hoped this would make it a one-day story that would be over as quickly as it appeared. It was risky, but they felt they had no choice.

Barnes, flanked by his two advisers, hurriedly walked into the news conference room. Barnes seemed to exude confidence and, with pursed lips, there was a trace of defiance in his face as he walked to the podium.

A hush fell over the room. Then came the cacophony of still cameras clicking and whirring as Barnes approached the podium. About 15 reporters, sitting in several rows of desks, grabbed their pens. On a riser behind the print reporters, television reporters made gestures to their photographers telling them to start rolling their cameras.

Barnes waited for the commotion to settle down. "Ladies and gentlemen," he began. "I have received information that the *Los Angeles Times* is working on a story involving my one-time membership in a campus group that has come to symbolize intolerance." Barnes could hear mumbling from the assembled reporters. He paused a few seconds and waited for quiet.

"It is true that for one year as an undergraduate more than three decades ago I belonged to what was called the Taney Society, which advocated for separate but equal rights for everyone."

While most of the reporters had heard of Roger B. Taney and his controversial court decision, few knew anything about the Taney Society.

Barnes continued.

"I was young – a sophomore – and misguided. Perhaps my ideas were clouded by the fact that I had been raised, until the age of 14, in Mississippi. Whatever the reason, I clearly made a mistake and I take full responsibility for it. The extent of my participation was speaking at one informal rally on campus. The following year, I dropped out of the group.

"I strongly disavow the tenets of the Taney Society, and I ask the public to judge me by my actions and public record over the years, both as a private citizen and as a state legislator. I believe my record for integrity and fairness is unimpeachable.

"This is a very difficult news conference for me. I realize it will forever be a blemish on my career. But I was afraid that the *Times* article might not let me explain the whole truth." Then, staring directly at Kellen Foster, he said, "That's why I'm here today. It is very important to me that I clear the air on this sad chapter in my life, so I will stay here until all your questions have been answered."

Foster fumed. Barnes had scooped him. Now, every television station will have the story before the *Times* goes to print, even before it gets the story on its website. Every newspaper in the state will lead with the Barnes rebuttal instead of the *Times* allegations.

Almost in unison, five reporters shouted questions at Barnes.

"Tell us more about this Taney Society," one radio reporter asked.

"Why do you think this came out now?" asked a reporter from the *San Jose Mercury News.*

Two other questions were unintelligible in the din.

With a voice rising above all others, the unmistakable voice of Jim Raymond of KSFT television in San Francisco could be heard.

"Senator," he shouted. "Senator, given the timing of this article, do you think someone is out to scuttle your chances at being appointed U.S. Senator?"

Barnes again looked at Foster, then addressed the reporter in the back of the news conference room.

"I will tell you this: the timing is suspicious. I have tremendous support up and down the state from some of the Republican Party's brightest stars. There is no doubt in my mind that the news coverage of this story is intended to hurt my chances."

"Who do you think is behind this?" another reporter followed.

"I can't tell you, because I don't know. But it is this type of dirty politics that has soured the electorate on the valued profession of public service."

As Jack pulled a cell phone out of his pocket, he whispered to Middleton, "Keep rolling. I'm calling the office to get a live truck over here."

Jack called Janine Robards on the assignment desk. He whispered so as not to disrupt the news conference. "A big scandal involving Senator Barnes has just broken here at the Capitol. Get the live truck over here for the noon show."

The Barnes story would be big for two reasons. The most obvious was that it seemed to kill his chances to become a U.S. Senator. The second reason was that it involved a home-grown legislator who had been a local fixture since his college days. Former U.S. House Speaker Tip O'Neill once coined the phrase, "All politics is local." In the broadcasting business, it seemed, "All news is local."

The Barnes news conference took 42 minutes – long by normal standards. Afterwards, a knot of reporters surrounded Kellen Foster and peppered him with questions about the Barnes story. Foster gave away nothing. "I'm sorry," he said. "You'll have to read my story. It'll be on our website shortly."

Jack looked at his watch. Only about an hour until he'd undoubtedly be the lead story on the noon news. "Quick, let's go," he said to Middleton, who grabbed the camera and folded the tripod. They sprinted out the back door of the news conference room, walked hurriedly down the main Capitol hallway, then rushed through a door leading to the stairs. On the second floor, they whooshed through a door under a blue and gold sign that read "Assembly Speaker." Once inside the speaker's waiting room, they saw two print reporters and a political blogger waiting for Johnny Callahan.

Another television crew, a radio reporter and two other print reporters joined the crowd in the waiting room. Billy Galster, who had watched the news conference with Johnny Callahan on the Capitol's internal video circuit, walked out and handed the reporters a single piece of paper on the speaker's letterhead. "The speaker has a brief written statement. That will be the extent of his comment on the events surrounding Senator Barnes," Galster told the reporters.

"Harold Barnes has served California with distinction in the Assembly and Senate," the statement read. "The public should be cautioned not to jump to conclusions about a singular event, since renounced, that occurred nearly four decades ago."

"That's it?" one of the reporters asked Galster. "Isn't the speaker going to comment about how this affects the U.S. Senate sweepstakes?"

Galster started to turn, to retreat into his office. "That's all the speaker has to say about this. Period."

The governor's office had no comment on the Barnes announcement.

Running out of time as his deadline approached, Jack corralled a half-dozen tourists outside the Capitol to comment on the Barnes developments, then sat with Middleton as they edited the story in the video truck. He didn't have time to record a narration track; he'd have to deliver the story live, as he had done hundreds of times before.

Standing just off the sidewalk along Tenth Street – the Capitol's west side – Jack rehearsed his script only seconds before airtime when some joker on a bicycle wheeled into view and yelled, "Hey, Summerland. Bite me." The live truck engineer ran the intruder off the make-shift set, and Jack smiled as he thought how people would do anything, no matter how idiotic, to get their five seconds of fame on television.

"Topping the news at noon," intoned anchor Vern Carson, "a bombshell at the State Capitol."

"That's right, Vern," responded co-anchor Carly Benjamin. "Action 4 has uncovered a secret in the past of Senator Harold Barnes."

Jack winced. Action 4 hadn't uncovered anything, and that was not the lead-in he had dictated to the news producer. Jack knew he had to be very careful about what he reported. Naturally, he wanted to scoop the competition, but he had been given inside information from Johnny Callahan about his upcoming Senate appointment. He didn't dare reveal it. He could use information only obtained from other sources.

Carson picked up the introduction. "Our political reporter Jack Summerland is live at the Capitol with the story. Jack?"

Summerland on camera

Vern, long-time State Senator Harold Barnes of Sacramento County acknowledged today that he joined the white supremacist Taney Society while a student at Sacramento State University.

Barnes made the stunning announcement in anticipation of a critical article in the *Los Angeles Times* outlining the senator's youthful dalliance with the now-defunct organization.

Video – news conference

At a news conference that concluded about an hour ago, Barnes said he joined the group as a sophomore, but resigned a year later and conceded he made a mistake.

Audio/Video – Barnes

"I was young – a sophomore – and misguided. Perhaps my ideas were clouded by the fact that I had been raised, until the age of 14, in Mississippi. Whatever the reason, I clearly made a mistake and I take full responsibility for it. The extent of my participation was speaking at one informal rally on campus. The following year, I dropped out of the group.

"I strongly disavow the tenets of the Taney Society, and I ask the public to judge me by my actions and public record over the years, both as a private citizen and as a state legislator. I believe my record for integrity and fairness is unimpeachable."

Video – Barnes campaigning

Barnes has never faced a serious political challenge during his lengthy tenure in the Legislature. He acknowledged, however, that his record could be blemished forever.

Video – Bernie Edelstein

Barnes has been considered one of two front-runners – along with Assembly Speaker Johnny Callahan – to be appointed to the U.S. Senate to fill the vacant seat of Bernie Edelstein who died recently.

Video – Callahan statement

Callahan released a brief statement noting that Barnes joined the Taney Society nearly four decades ago and that Barnes has served in the Legislature with distinction.

Summerland on camera

Today's announcement would seem to be the last potential obstacle preventing Speaker Callahan from being appointed to the Senate. Vern and Carly back to you.

Carly Benjamin on camera

Jack, any idea when Governor Frank is expected to make his announcement?

Summerland on camera

Sources in the governor's office have told me an announcement is imminent.

Twenty-Eight

Once back at his cubicle in the newsroom, Jack tried calling Karen at the office to apologize for their fight the night before. She was out to lunch. Jack knew Callahan's appointment would be announced in a matter of days. If there was anything in the speaker's past that needed to be revealed, time was running out. He thought about giving it one more try, a whirlwind weekend trip to Houston to touch bases with some of Jansen's old FBI mates.

Originally, a part of Jack wanted to come up empty-handed. Then, he could have taken Callahan's job in good conscience and begun a new career working for a U.S. Senator. He'd be set for life.

But his mind always returned to Jansen. There was a reason Jansen called him and tried to set up a meeting. There was a reason he ended up dead in the Sacramento River. And there was a reason that a decades-old secret by Callahan rival Harold Barnes all of a sudden was leaked to the *Los Angeles Times.*

Jack accessed the Internet on his computer and checked flights to Houston. He suddenly stopped typing and shook his head. Christ, he thought, I'm not even sure what I'm looking for. And a round trip fare of more than $750. Jack thought a trip to Houston could be a colossal waste of time and money – or his last chance to break the story of his career.

Just then, Jimmy Johnson stepped out of his office. "Jack," he yelled across the newsroom. "Come here for a second."

Wary, Jack sat across Johnson's desk and waited for the next shoe to drop. What if he wants me to cover that bill regulating tattoo parlors?

"Jack, do you agree that it seems like this Callahan episode is coming to a close?"

Jack fidgeted in his chair, then responded. "I do agree that Frank is probably only days away from naming a replacement for Edelstein. But you know I think there is more going on here. I have no clue what, but I'm convinced there is something in Callahan's past that needs to be investigated."

"Okay," Johnson said. "I know where you're coming from. And we've discussed this before. What I want you to do is work your regular beat unless something breaks on the Callahan story. Spend your spare time digging some more. I want you to do a brief live update piece for Saturday and put together a big "thumbsucker" for Sunday."

"Thumbsucker" is journalism lingo for a large wrap-up piece, sometimes advancing the story but often merely giving the story what reporters called "legs."

"Weekend?" Jack shot back. "I, uh, I'm planning to be out of town on this weekend."

Johnson continued. "Look, there's a flu bug going around and we're short-staffed this weekend, so we could use the product on both the Saturday and Sunday shows. Do them both live. I'll give you two days comp time and I'll make sure you get extra time on Sunday so you can talk about Edelstein, the governor's dilemma, the *Starlight* – all that stuff. One other thing, the *Today Show* is interested in a shortened version for Monday. I told them you'd feed the story late Sunday afternoon."

Jack returned to his desk, thoroughly confused. On the one hand, station leadership seemed to recognize the importance of the senate story. And his sister in St. Louis would be able to see him on network television. But he'd be stuck to his desk for the next several days, likely unable to break new ground on Callahan.

To Jack's knowledge, no other reporter had a clue about the Callahan-Jansen connection. In the meantime, Callahan's appointment to the U.S. Senate seemed imminent, perhaps only days away. It had the makings of a blockbuster exclusive that would cover KBLT in glory. And what was the response of the news leadership at KBLT, Sacramento's leading television news source? "We'll get to that story later."

Jack put the finishing touches on the Barnes story for the early evening newscast, reviewing the final version in an edit booth. As he walked back to his cubicle, he noticed that the big clock on the wall next to the bank of four video monitors said 4:32. There still was plenty of time. Jack had gone through this drill hundreds of time. It took him about six minutes to drive from the KBLT parking lot to the west side of the Capitol. Jack's story would air in the lead news section, about 5:03.

Jack decided to check the Associated Press wire to see how it treated the Barnes story. Just then, his private line rang.

"Jack, Karen. Are you on deadline?"

Jack looked at the clock for the second time in 30 seconds. "I'm okay for few minutes, Karen."

"I got your message and I want to apologize, too. I…we… both of us have been under a lot of stress lately."

Why the sudden change of heart? Jack wondered. "I know," Jack said.

Karen continued. "I realize that I don't have the right to interfere in your work, even though I think you're chasing a story that doesn't exist. I just wanted you to know that."

"Thanks, Karen." Jack wasn't quite sure how much he could trust Karen, despite their fondness for each other. It's true they were lovers and in the back of his mind he always thought he might make Karen wife number three. But she did work for the man he was investigating and the doubt lingered in Jack's mind.

"I'm still working on the story, but the station is in no hurry. I'm not sure when I'll be able to get back to it."

"Jack, I know you've got a show starting in a few minutes and I have to get back to work. I'm glad we were able to clear the air on this. Can we get together tonight?"

"Sure," Jack responded. "Come on over."

Jack hung up the phone, glanced at the clock again, then grabbed his coat and headed for the Capitol.

Inside the speaker's office, Karen gently lowered the telephone receiver. She stared at the phone for a few seconds, took a deep breath and dialed.

The voice on the other end responded.

"This is Marty Frank."

"Marty, this is Karen. I've got an update for you."

Twenty-Nine

Twenty-Nine

Marty Frank hung up the phone and leaned back in his chair. Finally, he thought, things were going pretty good.

Karen, the loyal soldier who recognized the need to protect the speaker, had just relayed Jack Summerland's frustration with his news bosses over pursuing the Callahan story. Callahan's main competition for the U.S. Senate post, Harold Barnes, was out of the way, a victim of his own stupidity decades earlier. And, most importantly, a blackmailing ex-FBI agent who had threatened to derail Johnny Callahan's career was killed before he could reveal his story. The news reports said the police had no suspects or clues.

Once again, Marty was leading a charmed life and succeeding without putting much effort into it. He had skated through college without breaking much of a sweat and was one of the stars on the school's perennially successful football team. His best friend, Johnny Callahan, made sure Marty wouldn't have to worry about making a good living. He even had the foresight of being born into what turned out to be one of California's most prominent political families. Looking ahead, Marty planned to open a small political consulting firm in Washington, D.C., and charge clients fabulous sums in return for access to one of the country's most influential senators.

Marty heard that familiar ringing sound on his computer, which told him he had received a fresh e-mail.

His heart started pounding as he read the return e-mail address: 657xyq.

"What?" Marty said, loud enough for Jennifer to hear in the adjacent office.

"Everything okay, Marty?" she asked.

"Uh, yeah," he said.

But everything wasn't okay. With trepidation, Marty clicked his mouse on the e-mail entry.

"My offer still stands," it read. "Send me $200,000, and I'll forget what I know. If I don't hear back from you by 10 p.m. tonight I will go public. You and Johnny Callahan will be spending the rest of your lives in prison. What an awful way to ruin two promising careers."

Marty couldn't comprehend what he was reading. Wasn't this guy found floating in the Sacramento River? If Carl Jansen is dead, then who else is sending me e-mails?

Marty got up from his chair and gently closed the office door. He returned to his desk, picked up the phone and punched in ten numbers.

"Gladstone, we've still got a problem."

Thirty

The first thing Jack noticed were a dozen well-scrubbed six-year olds in a greeting line. A few fidgeted as their teacher warned, "All right children. Big smiles." California's ambitious lieutenant governor, Gardner Tyson, invited reporters to join him on a tour of a successful suburban Sacramento charter school.

Jack had no illusions about the story. He was being used and he knew it. It was part of the symbiotic relationship between elected officials and the media. Each needed one another.

Tyson wanted to succeed Governor Frank, but as lieutenant governor he was a low-profile political figure with few official duties and was forced to create news in order to get on television. Every lieutenant governor before him had tried to force-feed manufactured news to the public. It rarely worked. Only a handful had ever climbed the mountain to the governorship.

Jack dutifully covered the photo-op. Actually, he had no choice because this type of story was a no-brainer at KBLT, even if it did involve a politician.

It was no secret that 25-to-54-year-old females were the station's primary audience target. They dictate the family viewing habits during the critical 5 p.m. – 7:00 p.m. news hours. Most important, this particular audience demographic spent money. They are the golden icons of advertisers.

Over the years, KBLT spent hundreds of thousands of dollars on research trying to pinpoint exactly what their target women want from news programs. Number one, the research showed, they want to know if their family is safe. Ironically, since the early 1970s, local television had given viewers a steady diet of crime news – shootings, stabbings and rapes – even as crime statistics indicated the rate of violent crimes had dropped significantly.

Number two, women want to know how they can improve their lives and the lives of their children – one news executive derisively calling this the "Botox and baby food" factor. Number three, they want stories on education. What's happening in the schools? Are they safe for my children? What new advances are available to help my child learn?

Jack turned the Tyson story into a more comprehensive report on public charter schools in California, a relatively new phenomenon, and questioned Tyson about academic achievement and reported fraud and abuse at some of the schools.

For this story, Jack was guaranteed good placement on both the early evening newscasts – a rarity, since the station tried not to rerun the same stories only an hour apart. But the powers that be had decided that charter schools might make a good "Question of the Day," a segment designed to entice viewers by inviting them to comment on news stories via e-mail and, perhaps, to have their votes recorded on the station's website and comments read on the air.

Every question, usually crafted by a twenty-something producer, was supposed to be provocative. Do state legislators deserve a pay raise? Should convicted sex offenders be allowed to get Viagra? Usually, the results were a foregone conclusion. But that wasn't the point. The station wanted people talking about and responding to the newscast. It was a marketing ploy, pure and simple.

Of course, it almost turned into a public relations disaster. During one "Question of the Day" segment dealing with the state budget, the station had received no comments at all. Stunned, a young producer fabricated a response and had the anchors read it on the air. Keeping a secret at a television station is like trying to prevent leaks in Congress. The producer was reprimanded but the ethical lapse never made it to the public.

Jack remained at the station through the six o'clock news to check the comments on charter schools. Two of them, carefully selected to represent both sides of the issue, were read on the air.

Later that evening, long after putting his evening story to bed, Jack sat at his desk at home and wrote an e-mail to Ed Stewart, his Berkeley friend.

"Ed: It looks like I'm going to have to take you up on your offer. There is no way I can pursue the Callahan story and work my day job at the same time. If you're still okay with it, I suggest we begin immediately. The Callahan announcement is imminent. Only you can help me forestall it. Call or e-mail me back. Jack."

Thirty-One

Jack Summerland listened to the morning commute traffic report on an all-news radio station as he exited Highway 24 at Fish Ranch Road. At seven-thirty, every freeway in the San Francisco Bay Area was as clogged as a beef fanatic's arteries. Jack had calculated the crawl and took the road less traveled, a back door route to Berkeley that avoided the usual back-ups. It was a semi-secret approach he often used when attending Cal football games.

Jack had left an early message with the station's assignment editor, saying he had a doctor's appointment that could not be changed. It was a lie, of course, but he didn't feel in the least bit guilty. He told the station he'd be at his Capitol office by eleven o'clock.

Ed Stewart's graduate seminar in investigative reporting met for two hours, beginning at eight o'clock. Jack would brief the class on their assignment, then return quickly to Sacramento and hope the students would find some results.

Jack turned off Fish Ranch Road onto Grizzly Peak, a winding tree-lined two-lane road that rims the East Bay and offers spectacular panoramic views of Oakland, Berkeley and San Francisco. He pulled off the road at an overlook and marveled at the picture-perfect sight – San Francisco's gorgeous skyline, the morning sun glistening off high-rise windows as the sun rose in the east. Jack had a view of both the Bay Bridge and the Golden Gate Bridge and could still see evidence of the devastating 1991 fire that destroyed thousands of homes in the Oakland hills and, for a while, threatened the university campus.

Much of the landscape had repaired itself in the years since the fire, and many burned out residents re-built bigger and more expensive homes on the hillside – often with considerably better views of the bay than they had originally.

Jack remembered watching live reports of the fire during a telecast of a San Francisco 49ers game. Throughout the game, cameras showed the progress of the fire, propelled inexorably down the hills by torched eucalyptus trees that literally exploded when hit by flames.

In the foreground, Jack saw his destination – the University of California. Many of the buildings on campus, particularly those built near the dawn of the twentieth century, had distinctive red tile roofs. The majestic Sather Tower, a replica of Venice's campanile, dominated the landscape as it had since 1913.

Jack got back in his car and continued north along Grizzly Peak, taking the hairpin curves at no more than 20 miles an hour. Suddenly, his steering wheel yanked to the right on the narrow two-lane road. He had little time to react and careened into the side of the hill, coming to rest only a foot from a giant eucalyptus.

As his car came to an abrupt halt, Jack's face slammed into the steering wheel, opening a small cut on his forehead. The back half of his car was jutting into the road and he feared a following car might plow into him. He sat in the car a few minutes and re-lived the entire episode.

Stunned and shaking, Jack opened the driver's door and gingerly stepped out of the car. For a few seconds, he thought of Carl Jansen and wondered if Jansen's killer had now targeted him. Was there a gunshot? Jack was relieved to see he only had a shredded right front tire. Except for some body damage on the bumper, the car seemed to have come through the ordeal in fairly good shape.

Jack could feel his heart beating wildly. His hands shook. A few drops of blood meandered down his forehead. Maybe I'm seeing conspiracies everywhere, Jack thought.

Twenty minutes later, after replacing the tire with a well-used spare, Jack was on the road again, slowing making his way east toward the hills above the campus.

Jack worked his way down the hill along a narrow 1.7 mile road leading to the university's east entrance. He passed the Lawrence Hall of Science, named for Berkeley's Ernest O. Lawrence, the winner of the first Nobel Prize ever awarded a faculty member of an American public university.

Still in the hills, Jack saw the huge botanical gardens, the Berkeley lab, the rugby field, another research lab, then the huge, venerable football stadium. Memorial Stadium, built in 1923 for the then-whopping sum of $1.3 million, had been the scene of some of the greatest games in college football history – not the least of which was that Cal victory in 1982 involving five laterals and the Stanford band as time expired.

Jack made his way to the north side of campus. It wasn't even eight o'clock and the campus was teeming. Jack cruised Hearst Avenue, adjacent to the university, looking for a place to park. Failing that, he circled several other blocks until he finally found a space on Virginia Avenue, a tidy half-mile walk to Stewart's class.

Jack arrived at Northgate Hall ten minutes late. He walked into the seminar room and saw Professor Ed Stewart talking to the class.

"Class, take five, okay?"

"Ed, great to see you. Sorry I'm late. There's absolutely no place to park around here."

Stewart laughed. "Parking is always a problem. It's a running joke. After Professor George Smoot was awarded the Nobel Prize for Physics in 2006, the chancellor introduced Smoot at an alumni dinner. He briefly recalled the professor's work on the origins of the universe, then congratulated him for winning the big prize — a guaranteed parking place on campus that is awarded to any faculty member who becomes a Nobel laureate. I remember former university president Clark Kerr once saying, 'Students want sex, alumni want a winning football team and faculty want a campus parking place.'"

Jack smiled. "This place is amazing. I can't thank you enough for helping me out."

"The class is really pumped about doing this," Stewart said. He noticed that Summerland has smudge marks on his shirt, his hands looked filthy and he had a small cut on his forehead.

"You need to wash up?" he asked.

"Yeah. On my way here I got a flat tire and sort of crashed into a tree on Grizzly Peak."

"You okay? Are you hurt?"

"I'm fine. Just a little cut."

A few minutes later, Stewart opened class and introduced Jack to eight graduate students who wanted to be investigative reporters. One by one the students briefly talked about themselves. Only one of them expressed any desire to have anything to do with television; they considered TV to be entertainment, not real news.

Robert Michaels, who had interned at the Capitol bureau of the *Sacramento Bee* while an undergrad at Berkeley, said he had seen Jack in action on many occasions and praised his work. Another student, Kaitlin Brown, said she watched Jack while growing up in

Stockton.

Professor Stewart asked Jack to outline the situation.

"I'll be brief. You're probably aware of most of what I'm going to tell you, because it's been in the papers for several weeks. As you know, U.S. Senator Bernie Edelstein, a Democrat, died recently. It is now up to Governor Frank, a Republican, to appoint his successor. With Edelstein's death, the Democrats narrowly control the Senate with a 50-49 advantage. If Frank appoints a Republican, which is all but certain, we'll have a 50-50 split in the Senate. That means, of course, that any tie votes will be broken by Vice President Hollings, a Republican. You can see there's a lot at stake with the governor's appointment."

Jack was careful not to divulge privileged, off-the-record information.

"A couple of prominent Republicans have been mentioned as likely successors to Edelstein. The most prominent is Johnny Callahan, the Republican state Assembly speaker in Sacramento. Callahan is young – not even in his 50s." Jack could hear a few snickers among the students, who probably considered 50-years-old to be ancient.

"Okay," Jack said with a smile. "Just wait. Take it from me, one day you'll look back on your 40s and think those were the golden days. Anyway, Callahan is the front-runner. His right-hand man and best friend is Marty Frank, who just happens to be the governor's son. They played football together at USC."

One of the students booed. A couple of the others laughed.

"Just a couple of days ago, Callahan's major competition, a state senator from the Sacramento area, was discredited in an investigation by the *L.A. Times.* He's out of the running now, so the coast is clear for Callahan."

A student in the front row interrupted. "Isn't Callahan considered future presidential material? I've read about his high-profile tax cut proposal. He's really accomplished quite a lot so far in his career."

Jack replied, "You're absolutely right. I can see a scenario in which Callahan is appointed a senator, wins election outright next year, then re-election to a six-year term. He'd be in his early- to mid-50s with eight years in the U.S. Senate under his belt."

Jack, of course, knew much more than he offered the students. After his conversation with Callahan and the job offer, he knew for certain that the Assembly speaker had his sights on the White House.

"He's conservative, but not a right-wing crazy, so he'd appeal to a broad cross-section of voters. Plus, he's a former football hero who is smart and articulate and looks good on television."

A few students groaned at that last remark. Kaitlin, who had earned her undergraduate degree in political science at Princeton, raised her hand and started talking without waiting to be acknowledged.

"This is a bit off track, but the Senate really isn't a good stepping stone to the presidency, is it? There have only been three presidents who have jumped directly to the presidency from the Senate."

Stewart interrupted. "Kaitlin, I think you're right but a little off subject right now."

"Sorry," she said sheepishly.

"So, we have Speaker Callahan as the likely appointee," Jack continued. "Now, here is where it gets interesting. And this is all confidential, between us.

"One night at home, I got a phone call from some guy who didn't identify himself. I later learned his name was Carl Jansen – that's Carl with a C… J-A-N-S-E-N. I know this much about him: he was an FBI agent in Houston before he lost his job after a botched sting operation involving Texas legislators. He moved to Tucson and worked with a security firm. I've got a few news clippings that I'll give to you. He told me he knew something about Callahan and he wanted to meet me in Sacramento.

"We set up a meeting but it never took place. Right before we were supposed to talk, he was killed – murdered and dumped into the Sacramento River. As he prepared for our rendezvous, he sent me another voice message."

Jack hit the play button on his micro recorder. "Jack Summerland… arrived…Tucson…to Christy's…information about… Cal…minutes…"

"The recording breaks up, but it's pretty easy to piece together the message. He had just arrived at the airport and was on his way to Christy's – that's a bar in Sacramento where we had scheduled the meeting – to give me information about Callahan. I have no idea what he was talking about and I've been unable to dig up anything that's useful. Whatever information Jansen had, it must have been important for him to be killed over it.

"That basically brings you up to date. I wouldn't involve you if I wasn't getting some static at work. It's not political, I'm sure. It's just that we're in the May sweeps and the station won't let me take a few days off the air to investigate. I need help if I'm going to get to the bottom of this story before Frank appoints Callahan, which could be any day. We have very little time to figure this out."

"Who knew that this Jansen guy was meeting you that night?" one student asked.

Jack paused a few seconds. "I've thought about this a lot. My girlfriend knew about it, but there's no way she'd be involved. I mentioned to a few people at work that I had this meeting, but I was pretty vague about it."

Stewart stepped to the front of the class. "Thanks, Jack. So this Jansen fellow possibly knew something incriminating on Callahan. As I told you before, your class projects are done, and there is no final, so I thought you might want to help Jack with his research on a real-life project.

"Jack and I talked it over. If you are interested – and this is purely voluntary – you do the research, pass it on to me and I'll then pass it on to Jack. I won't make you do this exercise as an official part of the class, and anyone who wants to say 'no' can do so. No one's grade will be affected. But I will say this could be a great opportunity to give you some real experience about investigative reporting."

A student in back, dressed in shorts, sandals and a Cal T-shirt spoke first. "Let's do it."

Other students chimed in their assent. They relished the intrigue.

"Last chance," Stewart said. "Is there anyone here who does not want to undertake this project? It would be quite understandable."

No one responded.

After a brief pause, Stewart broke the silence. "Okay, then, let's get to work."

Thirty-Two

Professor Ed Stewart divided his Journalism 250 class in half. He liked the idea of two teams, four students to a team, collaborating on an investigative project. Each team would work independently of the other, then the two would compare notes and conduct further research together.

Group One, dubbed the Blue Team, concentrated on Johnny Callahan and his personal and professional history; Group Two, the Gold Team, focused on Carl Jansen.

The Blue Team decided to start with basic Internet research on Callahan and Marty Frank. Eventually, they expected, their research would take them to Berkeley's renowned library system and archives of California newspapers.

In class, each desk was equipped with desktop personal computers.

"I've got Callahan on Google," said Chris Northcutt, a Berkeley graduate who had worked for three years as a general assignment reporter with the *San Francisco Chronicle* but decided a post-graduate degree in journalism would help his career.

"Jesus, there are a million entries. I don't know where to start."

"Look at them all," said Kaitlin. "We don't know what we're looking for but something might hit us."

Andrew Callaway, a 23-year-old graduate of Michigan, pulled out a pad of paper and suggested the team make a timeline of events in Callahan's life, going back to his teen years in Los Angeles. "Let's list everything we can find and maybe Carl Jansen will intersect."

"Maybe it's right in front of our eyes," someone interjected. "Perhaps Jansen was investigating Callahan for the FBI."

"Right now we don't know anything," Callaway said. "Look, it's a long shot, but does anyone have a better idea?" No one answered.

Andrew walked to the other side of the classroom, where the Gold Team was doing its initial research on Carl Jansen. He suggested they make a similar timeline.

The Blue Team read biographical articles from the *Los Angeles Times, Orange County Register, Orange Coast Daily Pilot,* and even a feature story in the *New York Times* touting Callahan as an up and coming political star.

Slowly, methodically, they assembled fragments of Johnny Callahan's life – high school in Orange County's affluent Mission Viejo, where he was a star quarterback, all-conference basketball player and senior class president; football scholarship to USC where he enjoyed all-star status; USC law school; marriage to high school sweetheart Colleen Vernalis; assistant district attorney in Orange County; attorney in the prestigious Los Angeles firm of Kerr, Brownlee & Jackson; cancer death of Colleen before the couple could have children; election to the Newport Beach City Council; election to the Orange County Board of Supervisors;

election to the California State Assembly and ascendancy to the speakership.

Marty Frank's resume was considerably shorter. He was raised in Pasadena, the son of Colin Frank, who rose through the Republican ranks to become attorney general, then governor. Marty's high school career was undistinguished academically, where his grades were mediocre, at best. But he was nicknamed "Mr. Stickum" in high school because it seemed he never dropped a ball as a wide receiver on the football team. Overlooking Marty's lack of academic achievement, USC offered him an early football scholarship. The athletic department thought the Callahan to Frank tandem would light up the Pacific Ten conference. It didn't hurt that his father, also a USC alumnus, was starting to make his name in politics.

After a solid, all-conference football career at USC and brief tenure in the National Football League, Marty Frank concentrated on surfing, drinking and girls. Once Johnny Callahan became a city councilman, he hired Marty out of the blue to be an aide, and Marty had been by Callahan's side ever since, currently serving as a connected political adviser.

The students found the Callahan-Frank connection strange. Callahan was a solid citizen who seemed poised for stardom. Frank, on the other hand, was a classic underachiever. The pair had become long-time friends since playing football together in college. It seemed that Frank rode Callahan's coattails – from city government all the way to the highest reaches of state government.

Two of the Blue Team members volunteered to trek to Doe Library on campus to do more research on this inseparable pair.

Meanwhile, the Gold Team concentrated on Carl Jansen and the FBI, convinced their research would reveal the secret they were looking for.

If the secret was there, they couldn't find it. Jansen went to college at Texas Tech then he spent four years in the Marines.

After Jansen's military service, an FBI recruiter hired him, by then married, because he thought Jansen had the combination of intellect and brawn that the FBI wanted. Stories in the *Houston Chronicle* and *Dallas Morning News* detailed Jansen's role in nabbing an abortion clinic bomber in Houston.

"Hey, look at this," one student shouted as he pored over his computer screen. "According to some magazine, this guy was here at Berkeley for awhile, in 1985, doing some sort of research and teaching a class in criminology."

"That's a big help," another student said derisively. "What good does it do us?"

"How the hell should I know," the first student responded. "Let's put it on the timeline and see what happens."

The Gold Team found another *Houston Chronicle* article detailing the bungled sting at the Texas Legislature.

The final entry, a brief introductive biography retrieved off the Internet was included in a newsletter for a Tucson civic group that had reviewed a speech by Jansen, then an executive with a local security firm.

Every tidbit of information on Callahan, Frank and Jansen was noted on the timelines. As the two-hour class ended, the students didn't want to quit working. Their interest had been piqued. Several of the students headed for the library. Others stayed after class and reviewed their notes with Professor Stewart, agreeing to press on.

They hadn't found out anything yet, but they felt they were in the thick of a mystery, and it was exciting.

Thirty-Three

Thirty-Three

Jack Summerland and his newly dented Camry gingerly merged onto eastbound Interstate 80 from University Avenue in Berkeley. Without heavy traffic, he figured, he could be back at his downtown office in 75 minutes. He quickly calculated the mileage and glanced at the clock on the dashboard. He grabbed his cell phone and called the newsroom.

"Hey, Janine, this is Jack. Give me Ron, would you?"

There was a brief pause, and he could hear Janine yelling across the newsroom. "Ron, it's Jack."

"Ron, I'm on my way back to town. I should be back around 10:45 or so. Anything going on?"

The photographer was now sitting at Jack's desk. "Not much. The bill expanding penalties for hate crimes is on the Assembly floor, but Dawson is covering that. The teachers union has a news conference about the budget at eleven and a big anti-tax guru, some guy named Crickfield, is meeting with the Chamber of Commerce at noon. We could do a budget wrap if you want."

"Sounds good," said Jack. "Thanks for backstopping me. Look," he said, then paused. "Look, I didn't really have a doctor's appointment this morning. I'm still working on the Callahan story. Don't tell anyone, okay?"

"Don't worry. You're secret is safe with me. Any way I can help?"

"Not really," Jack said, "but I'm sure the time will come."

"Where are you?" Middleton asked.

"I'm coming back from Berkeley where I met an old friend of mine, a journalism professor. His students are doing some of the basic research that I simply don't have time to do. They may get nowhere, but I've got to try. It's already been a little exciting. I got a flat in the Berkeley hills and rammed my car into a tree."

"Christ, Jack. You okay?"

"Yeah, I'm fine, but my car is a little banged up. No big deal."

Middleton probed, "Jack, how can you do this and still think about Callahan's job offer?"

"I'm not going to take it." Jack abruptly ended the conversation. "Look, let's talk about this later; I'm at the Carquinez Bridge."

Jack reached into his pocket for the bridge toll. Every time he drove in the Bay Area it irked him that he had to pay a four-dollar toll to cross the Bay, Golden Gate and Carquinez bridges.

Jack pulled a wad of ones out of his pocket. Tangled with the money was a business card. He handed the toll taker four crumpled dollar bills, then looked at the card as he accelerated on the freeway.

"Cameron Towne, Esq.," it read. "Houston, Texas."

"What a dumbass," Jack said out loud to himself. "I should have called this guy." Jack entered the phone number on his cell phone and, noting the time difference, hoped Towne hadn't left the office for an early lunch.

"Good morning," Jack said to the receptionist. He decided to fib a little in order to talk to Towne. "My name is Jack Summerland and I was working with Carl Jansen on a project. Mr. Jansen suggested I give Mr. Towne a call if anything should happen to him."

Jack was put on hold for several minutes. Finally, as he passed Vallejo and headed for Fairfield, a deep voice with a thick Texas accent asked, "Mr. Summerland, this is Cameron Towne. How can I help you?"

Now that Jack had Towne on the line, he decided to be direct. "Mr. Towne, I'm a reporter for KBLT, the NBC affiliate in Sacramento, California."

"How did you get my number?" Towne asked.

Jack decided it best not to reveal that he had lifted his business card from Carl Jansen's rolodex.

"Your client, Carl Jansen, had corresponded with me about information he had concerning our Assembly speaker here in California, Johnny Callahan. He was about to meet me and tell me everything he knew when he was murdered here in Sacramento. I got your name from him."

There was a five-second pause. Towne then responded curtly. "And?"

"And, I want to know if Carl gave you anything or told you anything that might help me. He wanted me to have this information."

Towne seemed suspicious. "And who are you again?"

"I'm a political reporter in Sacramento and I've been investigating Johnny Callahan. I'm getting nowhere. Only Carl – even in death – can unravel this."

There was a long pause on the phone.

"Mr. Towne, you still there?"

Another pause, then, "I'm here. I'm not sure if I should reveal client communications."

"But he's dead."

"I'll tell you what, Mr. Summerland. I'll think it over."

Thirty-Four

Thirty-Four

Gladstone Dreiser worked two phones at once as he sat in the backyard of his Pacific Palisades mansion. It was unseasonably warm in Southern California, even along the usually foggy Pacific Coast.

"Dammit," he yelled into one phone. "You tell Lucerne to have that contract to me by the end of the day tomorrow. Got it?" He hung up.

He glanced up at his housekeeper as she re-arranged a couple of lawn chairs. He watched her re-enter the house, then spoke into the second phone.

"Burke, you still there?"

Terrence Burke, sitting on the bed in his hotel room, took one last puff on his cigarette and crushed the butt in a crowded ash-tray. "I'm here – in my hotel room in Sacramento."

"I've got a couple of things to talk to you about, but tell me first about what's going on with the reporter."

"I'm gonna watch the guy for awhile. I want to see where he goes and who he goes with."

"Make sure he doesn't wise up," Dreiser lectured.

"Don't worry, he'll have no clue," Burke responded.

Dreiser wasn't satisfied. "Look, Burke, there's a lot riding on this and Lord knows you're getting paid a shit-load of money. How sure are you that Summerland won't bother us anymore?"

"I figure that in a few hours I'll know everything he knows. He's going to be attacked by a Trojan horse."

"A what?" said Dreiser.

"A Trojan horse," Burke said. "It's a computer trick I learned from a hacker friend. You know the Greek story of the Trojan War?"

"Yeah, sure," Dreiser said. "I was a history professor, remember?"

Burke continued anyway. "Well, the Greeks were fighting Troy. When they gave the people of Troy this giant wooden horse, the Trojans thought it was a peace offering and they dragged the horse inside their city walls. Hidden inside the horse were Greek soldiers. Once inside the city they popped out of the horse and opened the city gates to fellow Greek soldiers who stormed the city and captured Troy."

"I know all about the Trojans and the Greeks. What's your point?" an annoyed Dreiser asked.

"A Trojan horse is a computer program. Of course, you won't find it at your neighborhood computer store. I'm going to send it to Summerland as an e-mail attachment and once he opens it on his computer, I'll have remote access to all his files and e-mails. I'll know what information he has and what he's up to."

"That's amazing," Dreiser said. "So you're going to give his computer a virus?"

"In a way," Burke continued. "Technically, it's not a virus, which spreads from computer to computer. A Trojan horse creates what's called a backdoor, or trapdoor, that will let me into his computer without him suspecting a thing. There are all sorts of Trojan horses. Some erase data on a computer, others corrupt files. Still others spread viruses or seek bank accounts. A few years back, subscribers to America Online's Internet service were victimized by a program that tried to steal members' names and passwords. All I'm going to do is send him a text file. Once he double-clicks on the attachment, I'm in."

Dreiser was fascinated. "What if he doesn't open the attachment?"

"He'll have to open it for it to work," Burke said. "All I have to do is make sure I send him an e-mail that piques his interest."

"It seems like you have a handle on this Summerland fellow, but this whole thing is getting much more complicated," Dreiser said. "There's something else going on here that we're going to need you for. Marty Frank will be contacting you. And, remember, if Johnny goes down, our grand plan goes out the window."

"Yes sir," Burke responded curtly.

Dreiser's second phone rang. "Gotta go. I have another call. Keep me informed."

Burke hung up and got to work. He turned on his laptop and accessed yahoo.com. Three clicks later and he was ready to create a new e-mail account. Because he needed Jack Summerland to read his e-mail and open the infected attachment, Burke knew he'd have to select a user name that would not arouse any suspicion, a name that Summerland couldn't ignore. He entered his new user name on the Yahoo page: "Mark Truman," the Desert Security owner in Tucson who had hired Carl Jansen. Burke found Summerland's business card in the trash can of Truman's office; he knew Summerland would open this e-mail. With his new e-mail account – marktruman-dsi@yahoo.com – Terrence Burke started to set his trap.

He opened his briefcase and thumbed through some papers, pulling out Carl Jansen's employee record he had stolen from Truman's office. Using a portable scanner, he transferred the document to a CD, then uploaded the Trojan horse he stored on his computer. Then, he baited the trap.

He eyed Summerland's business card. Penciled in on the bottom was Summerland's home e-mail address. Burke decided to send the poisonous e-mail to both Summerland's office and his home computer.

Burke started composing a message.

> To: Jack Summerland
>
> Fm: Mark Truman
>
> Re: Carl Jansen
>
> Mr. Summerland: I don't know if this information is helpful to you, but I found it in my files and thought I should pass it on to you. Good luck in your investigation. Mark Truman.

Burke attached the infected file, a copy of a two-page personnel document.

Burke figured the only way this plan would fail was if Summerland figured out that marktruman-dsi@yahoo.com was a phony e-mail address. He hit the send button and waited for the mouse to take the bait.

Thirty-Five

The eight students in Ed Stewart's graduate seminar in investigative reporting were hitting a brick wall. In between their other late-semester studies, they had spent hours in class, at the library and at a campus computer lab scouring the Internet trying to find something that Assembly Speaker Johnny Callahan and former FBI agent Carl Jansen had in common. Nothing.

As the students gathered at Stewart's house in the Berkeley foothills, a woodsy 2,500 square-foot retreat with a gorgeous view of San Francisco and the Bay, the smell of brewed coffee wafted through a living room crammed with books and wall-to-wall framed historical newspaper headlines.

Professor Stewart's neophyte news reporters tried to make sense of where their research had taken them.

From Jack Summerland, they believed that Jansen apparently

had some incriminating evidence on Callahan and was murdered only moments before he was to reveal it to the Capitol reporter. But what?

"These guys never crossed paths, as far as I can figure," Robert Michaels said to no one in particular. "We're obviously missing something. Let's run through the timelines again."

Another student interrupted, "Why bother, it's not getting us anywhere."

"Let's do it," Chris Northcutt said. "There's got to be something."

Kaitlin Brown read the vital statistics of Johnny Callahan's life to the class. Football star at USC, law school, deputy district attorney, prominent attorney, Newport Beach City Council, Orange County Board of Supervisors, California State Assembly. Jeff Farnsworth, a Stanford graduate and the son of an airline executive, read the bits and pieces of Carl Jansen's life. College in Texas, military service, FBI in Houston, private security in Tucson.

"Wait a minute," Kaitlin said. "You've left out his year in Berkeley as a visiting professor."

Northcutt rolled his eyes. "Big deal," he said. "It doesn't advance our story, does it?"

"Maybe it does," Michaels replied. "When was Jansen in Berkeley?"

"I think it was 1984 – no, 1985," Gold team member Ramona Garcia said.

"Nineteen-eighty-five," Michaels said excitedly "That's an odd-numbered year. You know, USC plays Cal in football every year and in the odd years the game is played in Berkeley. That means both Callahan and Jansen were in Berkeley at the same time during one weekend in 1985."

All of a sudden, Kaitlin blurted out, "Wait a minute. Wait a minute." She was so excited, she looked like she had just discovered the Loch Ness Monster. "Remember the message that

Jansen left Mr. Summerland just before he was killed?" She flipped pages in her notebook, searching for an entry. "Here it is: 'Jack Summerland…arrived…Tucson…to Christy's…information about…Cal…minutes…'"

Kaitlin, energized and animated, continued. "We've all assumed that the reference to Cal meant Callahan. Maybe it does. But maybe not. What if he really *does* mean Cal? What if Jansen is saying he has 'information about Johnny Callahan when he visited Cal in 1985?' What if something happened the weekend Callahan was in Berkeley for the football game? And what if Jansen saw it? Or heard about it? Or uncovered some evidence about it?"

Professor Stewart took a large gulp of coffee. "You might be onto to something. How would you go about finding out more about this possible nexus?"

"Simple," Northcutt said. "Let's comb the library and other newspaper sources to see if anything shows up those days both were in Berkeley."

Andrew Callaway jumped in. "What do you think we're looking for?"

"I have no idea," Northcutt said. "But we'll know it when we see it. Callahan would have arrived with the team on Friday, and they would have left after the game Saturday evening. Search the papers for anything unusual, suspicious or interesting, no matter how remote, between Friday and let's say Sunday of the Cal-USC football game that year."

The class decided to split up and meet again later that day on campus. Several students volunteered to continue their computer research. Two others went back to the University's huge Doe Library to scan microfilm of back issues of the *Oakland Tribune, Contra Costa Times, Alameda Times Star, Hayward Daily Review* and *Daily Californian*, Cal's independent student-run newspaper.

The students bemoaned the fact that two East Bay newspapers that likely would have covered events in Berkeley – the *Berkeley Gazette* and *the Albany Times Journal* – folded within two months of each other in 1984, the year before both Johnny Callahan and Carl Jansen spent at least one weekend in Berkeley at the same time.

In 1985, the Cal-USC football game was played on the afternoon of November 9. Painstakingly, the students read every article in each of their targeted newspapers between Friday, November 8, and Sunday, November 10. There was not a single mention of Carl Jansen or the FBI. Johnny Callahan, however, was splashed all over the sports pages.

The banner headline in the *Oakland Tribune* read, "Bears Shock Trojans with 14-6 Victory." The article pinned USC's defeat squarely on the shoulders of its All-American quarterback, Johnny Callahan, and his top receiving target, Marty Frank.

> **Berkeley** – Southern California All-American quarterback Johnny Callahan suffered through the worst day of his career Saturday, as the California Golden Bears stunned the powerful USC Trojans 14-6 before more than 70,000 fans at Memorial Stadium.
>
> Callahan, touted as a leading Heisman Trophy candidate, completed only five passes in 27 attempts, with four interceptions. His primary wide receiver, Marty Frank, also had a day to forget as he dropped several passes and missed key blocks.
>
> "I can't explain it," Callahan told reporters after the game. "I just wasn't myself today."
>
> The Bears, enduring yet another losing season, capitalized on Callahan's mistakes to score two second-half touchdowns behind the power running of tailback Phil Delray.
>
> Delray totaled 78 yards on 23 carries and scored on runs of three and seven yards after a pair of Trojan turnovers. The Cal defense held USC's offense to a season-low 238 yards.
>
> In subdued responses to reporters' questions, Callahan said he was not mentally prepared to play. "I'm embarrassed for myself and the university," he said, "but the fact is I had a lot on my mind besides football and it showed." When asked to

> elaborate, Callahan declined to offer much detail, except to say he was stressed about his class load.
>
> Frank also blamed a lack of concentration for his dismal performance. He refused to discuss specifics with reporters. "I don't blame Johnny for this defeat. He threw some passes my way that I flat-out dropped. I missed blocks, I missed assignments, my head was in the (expletive) clouds."

Professor Stewart met his Journalism 250 class at the FSM Café near the library complex to compare notes. They secured two empty tables in one corner. The café was dedicated to the landmark Free Speech Movement on campus in 1964, which ushered in a generation of student protest throughout the nation.

Every newspaper the students checked had similar accounts about the football game. But what did that prove? There was no mention of Carl Jansen. There were no stories of anything out of the ordinary. No hint of scandal involving Johnny Callahan, unless you considered a bad football game a scandal.

Chris Northcutt joked that a bad game was, in fact, a scandal at USC. Everybody laughed.

"Maybe he and Frank fixed the game," another student offered. "Maybe they took a dive."

There was silence for a second. Then, Michaels responded. "You know, that makes sense. These guys always beat us. They've always been a football factory. It could have been fixed. How else do you explain Cal's win."

"Yeah, right," chimed in one student as he ordered a second cup of coffee.

Jenny Goldwhite, who was a sports reporter while an undergraduate at Penn, cooled the game-fixing excitement. "Wait a minute. Even if they did rig the game, we'd never have any proof, would we? How could we go back decades and trace a money trail?"

Michaels gave it a try. "What if the FBI was investigating the game and they told Jansen, who was on campus at the time, to check it out? What if they had bank records or some other evidence?"

"But we're talking decades after the fact," she said. "If they had something on Callahan back in 1985, why didn't they use it then. Why would that become an issue now?"

"Maybe they dropped the case and it's an issue now because he's about to become a U.S. Senator," Northcutt said.

"It still doesn't make sense to me," Kaitlin offered. "But I agree it's the only possibility on the table right now. I still think there's got to be another link between Callahan and Jansen. Let's go back to the newspaper archives and see if we can find anything else that might turn up."

The students split up again. They pored over more newspaper archives, this time concentrating on news items outside the sports pages. They agreed to meet once again at the professor's house.

For hours they scanned page after page for hints – any hints – of a possible scandal that might link a college football hero to a visiting FBI agent. They came across a number of tidbits, but nothing that stood out as obvious.

The Sunday *Oakland Tribune* ran a story about an alleged rape during a Friday night party at a south campus fraternity house. The newspaper, following traditional journalism practices, did not identify the victim. Coincidentally, the alleged attack occurred at the same fraternity that both Callahan and Frank had joined at USC. The story suggested that three men had slipped a drug to a 20-year-old student late Friday night. She awoke the next morning groggy and convinced she had been sexually assaulted.

With the class gathered for its update session, Professor Stewart called Robert Larson, a long-time friend and a 28-year veteran on the campus police department, who told him no charges had ever been filed because no witnesses came forward and the young woman's story could not be verified.

Most in the Journalism 250 class immediately dismissed the possibility that Callahan, Frank or anyone else on the USC football team could have been involved. After all, teams on the road stick together and have tight curfews the night before games.

Cassie Rumsford, a Stanford graduate, wasn't convinced. She thought there was too much of a coincidence to ignore. She called back Detective Larson, seeking more information.

"As I told your professor," Larson said, "we couldn't find any witnesses. We assume the woman was attacked, and we believe someone may have slipped her some sort of date rape drug, even though such drugs as Rohypnol weren't popular in the U.S. until the mid-1990s. We had seen them in Europe in the '70s and '80s, and then all of sudden they were showing up on college campuses where studies show that as many as 20 percent of women may experience some form of sexual coercion. And even now, only a fraction of such assaults – perhaps about one in ten – are reported to police, and an even smaller fraction, of course, make it to court. You have to remember that there wasn't much public awareness about this sort of crime back then. It wasn't until 1996 that the federal government responded to allegations of a drug-date rape connection by making the use of any drug in a rape a federal crime."

The detective continued. "We interviewed about a dozen fraternity members, as I recall, and no one talked. The woman even went public, identifying herself and pleading for witnesses to come forward. But no one did."

"She identified herself?" Cassie responded.

"Yes," the detective said. "I even remember her name because I led the task force that spent an inordinate amount of time trying to come up with some clues. Judith Camarena was her name. She's Judith Sheldon now."

"How do you know that?" Cassie asked.

"She used to call every once in a while to check on our progress. Last I heard, she lives in Fresno."

Detective Larson gave Cassie the woman's last-known phone number.

"I may be on to something," Cassie told the class. "I've got another call to make." She dialed the Fresno phone number given her by Detective Larson.

"Mrs. Sheldon," Cassie said. "My name is Cassie Rumsford. I'm a graduate student in journalism at the University of California, and I'm involved in a class project that is trying to solve old crimes. Can I ask you a few questions about the attack at the fraternity party back in 1985?"

"I wish you wouldn't," the woman said. "Is this for some sort of publication?"

"No, ma'am," Cassie said, "unless, of course, we find your attackers. Is there anything you can tell me that you didn't tell the police about that night?"

Judith paused a few seconds. Cassie could hear her exhale into the phone. "Okay, I'll talk to you, but there's not much to tell. As I told the police, I attended a party at the Chi house. We were drinking beers with some boys – typical frat party stuff. The next thing I remember is waking up in the basement and my clothes were a mess. I felt groggy and disoriented and my mind was a blank. I felt ashamed and embarrassed."

Cassie pushed. "I know this brings back terrible memories, but is there anything you can remember about your attackers? Anything at all?"

"No. And that's the problem. I couldn't identify anyone. Hell, I couldn't even remember who I was talking to before I blacked out."

Again, Cassie pushed. "Do you have any sense that you might have been talking to some big men – football players – before you blacked out?"

"Again, I have no recollection of most of that evening," she said.

"Do you remember ever meeting or knowing someone named Carl Jansen while you were at Berkeley?"

"Carl Jansen? No, the name means nothing to me."

Cassie thanked the woman and hung up the phone. "Another dead end," she told the group.

Another student found a game preview story in the small Alameda newspaper the Friday before the football game. It featured Callahan talking about how he had frequently visited his older sister, who lived in Berkeley and was an instructor at Diablo Valley College in nearby Walnut Creek.

> Callahan said he loved to travel with his family to Northern California, often borrowing his sister's car for joyriding excursions throughout the East Bay. "There is nothing like taking those turns on Grizzly Peak in a fast convertible on a warm summer's day," he said. "I had so much fun I almost decided to play football at Cal."
>
> These days, however, Callahan confines his joyriding to the football field and is on the verge of winning the Heisman Trophy.

Jeff Farnsworth reported to the class he found a brief article in the Sunday *Oakland Tribune* about a robbery at an Indian restaurant on University Avenue Friday night and a brief story about a hit and run accident late Friday night or early Saturday.

Kaitlin found a similar article on the hit and run accident in the Monday edition of the *Daily Cal.* Ever since the *Berkeley Gazette* ceased publication, the *Daily Cal* had increased its coverage of non-university news in and around the city of Berkeley. It regularly covered the Berkeley City Council and its often-bizarre left-leaning antics. Many critics continued to refer to the city as "The People's Republic of Berkeley," or "Berzerkeley."

> Two hikers in the Berkeley hills found the body of an unidentified woman Saturday afternoon, partially buried under dead eucalyptus leaves near Tilden Park.
>
> Berkeley police said the woman had severe bruises on the left side of her torso. An autopsy is pending.
>
> Police said the woman, likely in her early 20s and wearing

> blue sweat pants, a green T-shirt and blue jacket, had no identification. The coroner indicated she was killed late Friday or early Saturday morning.
>
> "We're looking for any witnesses who may help us solve this case," Sergeant Lionel Rostin told the *Daily Cal.*

Kaitlin flipped through the phone book and dialed the Berkeley Police Department. On a hunch, she asked for Lionel Rostin. A few seconds later, a gruff voice with a hint of Boston accent, said, "This is Rostin. What can I do for you?"

"Sergeant, this is…" She was interrupted. "Chief. This is Chief Rostin."

"Oh, sorry," she said. "I got your name out of an old article in the *Daily Cal* when you were a sergeant. Sorry. My name is Kaitlin Brown. I'm a graduate student at Cal and as part of a class assignment we're looking into old, unsolved crimes. I read that back in 1985 there was a hit and run in the Berkeley hills. Do you remember that?"

"Yeah I do," Rostin said. "Such a shame. A young woman was hit by a car and strangled to death."

Kaitlin had a quizzical look on her face. "Strangled to death? No, I'm referring to another case, a woman who had severe bruises on the left side of her body and was found buried under some tree leaves. It was November 9, the day of the Cal-USC football game."

"We're talking about the same case."

"You mean she wasn't killed in the car accident?"

"No," the captain responded. "As I recall, the autopsy showed that she survived the crash. She died of manual strangulation that restricted blood flow in her neck. She also had fractured bones in her neck."

Kaitlin continued. "The first reports didn't identify the woman, and we're still wading through follow-up articles. Do you remember the woman's name? Was anyone ever arrested?"

"No one was arrested, I can tell you that," Rostin said. "It was one of our longest running unsolved crimes. As for her name, I'm sure I can find it in my files. Hold on."

Kaitlin waited for what seemed like three minutes. "Here's the file," Chief Rostin said. "The woman had no ID on her, but forensics later identified her as Elizabeth A. Cohen, a Cal student from Chicago. As I said, it was pretty apparent she was run over by a car, but the cause of death was asphyxiation. It was several days before her body was claimed — by her parents, as I recall."

"Did you interview any witnesses?" Kaitlin asked.

Rostin paused a second. "We tried. We canvassed the neighborhood in the hills near Tilden Park. Our detectives walked door to door but found nothing but dead ends."

"And what time was she killed?" Kaitlin continued.

"The medical examiner figured she died around 11 p.m. on, let's see…on Friday night, November 8."

"Anything else you can tell me?"

"Not really. Sorry."

Kaitlin Brown had the makings of a top-flight reporter one day. She was smart, inquisitive and tenacious. But she was a neophyte and didn't know all the right questions to ask.

Kaitlin hung up the phone and turned to her colleagues. "Struck out again. There's no way a football player on the road with his team is going to be allowed to drive around town the night before a game."

The students found a few other stories of interest, including a *Tribune* article on an Oakland police officer who shot and wounded a fleeing stolen car suspect on Saturday afternoon. "Maybe this Callahan guy is Superman who can be in two places at once," Callaway muttered. "You can't be stealing a car and throwing interceptions at the same time."

Not a single article mentioned the FBI or any problem involving the USC football team, except for another post-game article questioning Callahan's concentration after a miserable defeat.

The *Daily Cal* also had a blurb about a football day prank, apparently involving some Cal students who had spray painted large dollar signs on the side of the bus transporting the USC football team to and from the Claremont Hotel above the campus to Memorial Stadium.

Many of the students were feeling dejected, but not Kaitlin. She saw the exercise, even if not successful, as a potential career opportunity.

She waited until the other students left Professor Stewart's house. "Professor, I've got a favor to ask. Is that okay?"

"Sure," Stewart responded. "What is it?"

"Remember, professor, what you told us on the first day of class? You said that after the semester you'd help us find jobs."

She smiled broadly. "Well, here's your chance. After grad school I really want to get into television as a reporter or producer. I'd like to talk to Mr. Summerland about this and take a look at his studio. Would you object if I went to Sacramento and briefed Mr. Summerland about our activities? It'll give me a perfect excuse to drive up there."

The professor didn't hesitate. "Do you want me to call him?"

"No, that's okay," she responded. "I can handle it."

Later that evening she sent an e-mail to Summerland's home account.

> Mr. Summerland:
>
> My name is Kaitlin Brown. I am a member of Professor Stewart's Journalism 250 class that is helping you with research. I did my undergrad work at Princeton. Would it be possible for me to come up to Sacramento to brief you about our progress? We've come up with a plausible – but unsubstantiated – theory about Johnny Callahan. I'd also like to spend a little time with you talking about television journalism. My career goal is to be a broadcast reporter, and I'd certainly appreciate any advice you might have to offer. Thanks.

She knew she was taking a few liberties with the truth. Her

"plausible – but unsubstantiated – theory" couldn't be proved. Why, she thought, would an all-star quarterback from a well-to-do family conspire with another teammate to throw a football game when his multi-million dollar pro career hung in the balance? She figured Jack Summerland would dismiss this theory within seconds of hearing it. But she wanted the chance to enlist Summerland as a mentor who might help her land a job in broadcasting.

Within 30 minutes, Kaitlin had a reply in her e-mail inbox.

> Kaitlin: It doesn't look like you have any hard evidence I can use in a story, but why don't you come up Sunday afternoon around four o'clock to brief me on Callahan. I'm interested in your research. I have to work and get a story on the air, but I should have some time before the newscast to show you around the station.

Kaitlin smiled. "All right!" she exclaimed to herself triumphantly. She quickly hit the reply button and wrote, "Great. I'll see you then."

Thirty-Six

Sitting in his Sacramento hotel room, wearing shorts and no shirt to cover his ample belly, Terrence Burke muted the television and negotiated his laptop through Jack Summerland's e-mails. He smiled at the irony. Callahan once was a star quarterback for the USC Trojans and now Burke would be saving Callahan's limitless political future with an illegal Trojan Horse computer program. With only a second's hesitation, Burke scanned the exchange with Kaitlin Brown and immediately dialed his benefactor.

"Mr. Dreiser, I've gotten a hit from Summerland's computer. I intercepted an e-mail from a student at Berkeley. Evidently, Summerland has enlisted the help of some students to look into Johnny Callahan on his behalf. She has offered to brief Summerland at the TV station on Sunday.

"The e-mail doesn't sound like she really has anything. If she did, she wouldn't wait a couple of days to meet with Summerland. I'll keep an eye on it."

He paused for about 30 seconds. "Yes sir. Right away."

Burke didn't know it yet, but his Sacramento assignment was about to get more complicated. Burke was monitoring Jack Summerland's computer communications and figured, now with Carl Jansen dead, the only thing stopping Johnny Callahan's U.S. Senate appointment would be the meddling of that pesky television reporter and perhaps his friends from Berkeley.

But Gladstone Dreiser told him to forget about the student. He wanted Burke to take care of something more pressing. "Did Marty call you yet?"

"No."

Burke hung up the phone, and then on Dreiser's instructions dialed Marty Frank's cell phone.

"Marty, this is Terrence Burke. Mr. Dreiser told me to call you."

"I received another blackmail note," Frank said. "I didn't respond to the first one, but he still wants $200,000 in cash sent to a mail box in Sacramento. I had assumed the blackmailer was Carl Jansen, and once Jansen was killed, I expected never to hear from the bastard again."

Burke probed further. "Is there any hint in the e-mail message as to the identity of the sender?"

"No," responded Frank. "Wait a minute. Yes, there is, as a matter of fact."

"And?" Burke asked.

"It doesn't tell me who the blackmailer is, but it offers clues. The sender made reference to something involving Johnny and me a long time ago."

"I know all about it," Burke exclaimed.

"You what?" Frank's voice trembled.

"I said I know all about it. I took a little trip to Tucson and checked out Jansen's place. I found, shall we say, some very incriminating evidence stuffed in his freezer."

"What evidence?"

"A detailed accounting of one of your escapades with Callahan."

Burke outlined what Jansen knew.

"Needless to say," Burke continued, "if this gets into the wrong hands, both of you are finished. Who else knows about this?"

Marty paused, as if thinking. "I don't know how anyone else could know about this. We've…we've got to keep this under wraps."

"That's what I've been hired to do," Burke said. "Jansen could have nailed you, but that's been taken care of. We still have to worry about Summerland, and this blackmailer, whoever he is. By the way, I've discovered that some students at Berkeley are helping Summerland with research."

Burke thought for a moment, then asked Frank, "Where's the box located?"

"The what?" Frank responded.

"The box – the mail drop where you're supposed to send the money. Where is it located?"

"It's one of those private mailbox stores with hundreds of locked mail boxes," Frank said. "It's in a storefront on Tenth Street between J and K, a couple blocks from the Capitol. I know the place because that's where Johnny has set up a separate address for campaign donations. Sometimes I pick up the checks for him."

Burke pressed Marty for information. "Tell me about this place. Is it staffed by anyone? Do customers have 24-hour access?"

"There are two rooms. The mailboxes are in the outer room and inside is another room where they hold packages and other items for customers. The place is staffed Monday through Friday until 5 p.m., I think, and Saturday until 1:00 p.m. But customers have 24-hour access to their boxes in the outer room because they're given two keys – one that opens their mailbox and another that opens the front door."

"What does the neighborhood look like?" Burke asked.

"It's on Tenth Street. There are a lot of storefronts – a clothing store is across the street, a cookie place is next door, and there's a small restaurant nearby. It's close to J Street and Cesar Chavez Park. Across the street from the park is a parking garage, and…."

Burke interrupted. "A parking garage? Indoors? Outdoors? Describe the garage."

"It's just a parking garage – five or six stories, I think. The top story is open to the sky."

Burke thought a few seconds. "If I was on the top floor of the garage, could I see the front of the mailbox place?"

"Yeah, I think so. You'd have a clear line of sight."

"Okay," Burke said. "Here's the plan. Summerland has some students in Berkeley working for him, but I don't think they have anything concrete. Whoever is blackmailing you is much more dangerous. I know a way to draw this guy out."

Burke instructed Marty to send an e-mail to the blackmailer saying he overnighted $200,000 in cash for afternoon arrival the next day, Saturday. Then, Burke told Marty to fill a FedEx box with paper and send it to the designated mailbox for Saturday delivery.

"What's your plan?" Frank asked.

"It's simple," Burke explained. "Late tonight I'll use your key to get inside that mailbox drop, and I'll mount a miniature video camera high on the wall directed at your mailbox. What's the number?"

"It's 3546. Where are you going to get this miniature camera?" asked Frank.

"I've got a whole cache of cameras that come in handy during situations such as this. I brought a couple up with me from L.A."

As he spoke, he rifled through his briefcase and pulled out a tiny pouch, no larger than a dime. He removed what looked like a tiny pewter-colored screw.

"My favorite is something called a ScrewCam that operates in black and white with low light. As the name implies, it's about the size of a screw. I have one installed now at a construction site for one of my clients."

"That's amazing. Like something out of James Bond," Frank said.

"That's nothing," Burke responded. "I've got a couple of wireless pen cameras, a button camera, and an ear bud camera. I've stuck cameras in smoke detectors, teddy bears and sunglasses."

He again reached into his briefcase and picked up a small box. He reached inside the box and pulled out a tiny 30 millimeter color pinhole miniature camera no bigger than an olive.

"I have something here that is perfect for nailing your blackmailer," he said. "Cost me all of $140 each from a spy show on the Internet. It's got a 73 degree field of view. No one will see it, and I'll rig a transmitter that's hooked up to a nine-volt battery. Pretty simple, huh?"

"Oh, I see. And you'll watch the feed from the garage across the street."

"Yeah," Burke said. "I'll patch the receiver into my laptop and monitor the camera shot from the top of the garage and wait for this guy to pick up the package at box #3546. It'll be Saturday afternoon. It should be pretty quiet downtown and pretty empty at the mail drop. The camera angle will be wide enough for me to identify whoever picks up the package, and my vantage point from the garage roof will be perfect."

"And, then what?" Frank asked.

Burke smiled. "It'll be like picking off JFK from the Texas School Book Depository."

Thirty-Seven

Thirty-Seven

The bell atop the Church of the Blessed Sacrament told Terrence Burke it was one o'clock.

He reviewed everything in his mind. He had it all figured out. Just like D-Day, he thought.

The mystery blackmailer would arrive at Sacramento Mail Services sometime that afternoon, expecting to retrieve a package full of hundred dollar bills. The blackmailer quite likely would be the only one in the building on a Saturday afternoon, and Burke would be able to recognize him instantly – thanks to the miniature camera he mounted above the front door the night before. Using Marty Frank's key to gain entrance, it took Burke only minutes to install the spy device.

Burke had considered various scenarios. Should he follow the blackmailer? Should he scare him? No, he thought, this guy knew too much. Burke recalled his last conversation with his employer.

"Do what you have to do," Gladstone Dreiser told him.

It was clear to Burke what Dreiser meant.

Burke sat in his car by the garage railing overlooking Tenth Street, his eyes focused on the image being transmitted from mailbox #3546 to his computer. The screen clearly showed the mailbox with a wide enough angle to identify the owner of the box. He had seen one man, about 30 years old, he thought, walk into Sacramento Mail Services in the past 15 minutes, but the man hadn't approached box #3546.

About five feet away from Burke's perch, hidden in a dark corner of the stairwell and covered by a jacket, rested a loaded Springfield M21 tactical rifle with scope. It was one of Burke's favorite tools of the trade. He looked up from the computer screen to make sure he remained alone on the top floor of the parking garage. From his top floor vantage point across the street, he had a clear shot at the front of the mailbox store. For his getaway, he had parked a block away on Eleventh Street. He noticed two men, obviously homeless, sitting on the sidewalk just outside Sacramento Mail Services.

At one point, Burke thought he heard voices on top of the parking garage. He quickly grabbed a small digital camera out of his pocket and began clicking off shots of the city as if he were a tourist. In between shots, he peeked behind him. Nothing there. Shaking his head, he wondered if he was becoming uncharacteristically antsy in his old age.

His eyes fixed on one of the homeless men outside the mail drop. Even from nearly a block away, he could see the grizzled old man talking to every passerby, undoubtedly asking each one for money.

Then, in an instant, he saw a man unlock the front door to the mailboxes. The man took one step then held the door open for a woman, who walked in as well. Burke's eyes fixed on the computer screen. Burke seemed startled when he saw the woman, casually dressed in jeans, a dark blue T-shirt and a baseball cap, turn the key to open box #3546. Burke's heart started racing.

It's a woman! In an instant, Burke tried to re-think his plan. What if she's some sort of decoy? What if she's just a gofer for the real blackmailer? Then, again, what if she's the one who threatened to bring down a potential U.S. Senator?

Burke hurriedly snapped shut his laptop and laid it on the ground. He scanned the parking lot one more time, then lunged at the stairwell, opening the door and grabbing the rifle. He took a deep breath and aimed the weapon at the front of the mailbox store and waited for the woman in the dark blue T-shirt to exit. Ten seconds, fifteen seconds. What's taking her so long? Is she talking to the man inside? Did she open the package and see that it was filled with paper?

The man and woman emerged from the mailbox store nearly simultaneously. The man exited first, and the woman locked the door behind them. Burke saw she was carrying a box with the distinctive FedEx logo. Burke closed his left eye and took aim.

As the woman turned toward the street, Burke gently squeezed the trigger. The store's glass door shattered. He missed! The woman had bent down to give a quarter to a homeless man sitting on the sidewalk against the wall, and the bullet had whizzed past her head. Burke saw the man pointing in his general direction and heard him yell, "Up there, up there!"

Burke quickly broke down his rifle, grabbed his laptop and walked briskly toward a stairwell on the Eleventh Street side of the parking lot. Once on the ground floor, and a block away from the shooting scene, he walked out the parking structure and trotted to his dark green Ford F-150, breathing hard and sweating profusely.

Stunned that his shot missed, and angry at himself for botching the job, Burke cruised the downtown area for 20 minutes looking for the woman in the blue T-shirt. She had escaped.

Thirty-Eight

Julie Forsett had never been so scared in her life. When she heard the gunshot and saw the glass door behind her shatter, she knew she was in too deep. She sensed that her life might end within seconds.

A smallish, thin woman, now in her mid-40s, she had been a better-than-average high school cross country runner in Alamo, an East Bay bedroom community. She kept in shape and today it paid off. Instinctively, she sprinted down Tenth Street, towards the Capitol, with the package cradled in her right arm. She cut right through an alley, then left on Ninth Street, past K to L Street. Still at a full sprint, she ducked into an office building that mostly housed high-priced lobbyists. The lobby was empty. Of course, she thought. This is Saturday.

Gasping for breath, she took the elevator to the eighth floor and walked down a long hallway, where she sat on the carpet and caught her breath. It was a perfect place to hide for a while.

Julie Forsett had endured tough times before. In high school, her running ability had attracted some interest from four-year universities, but by graduation she had no scholarships in hand, a mediocre grade point average and no thoughts about her future. She enrolled in Diablo Valley College in nearby Walnut Creek but dropped out after one year to take care of her ailing mother. Years later she married a computer technician whose job required the family to relocate in Reno. They enjoyed a solid middle-class life and had two children before her husband ran out on her. She was left with little money and no job. Julie Forsett considered herself a survivor, but she was desperate. She now was a single mother of ten-year-old and eight-year-old boys, making peanuts as a sales clerk at a local convenience store.

As she sat on the floor against a hallway wall, Julie thought of her two children she left behind with friends in Reno. She had come to Sacramento on a mission – a mission to secure the future for herself and her two sons. She knew a secret about the governor's son and his best friend, a man the media called "the second most powerful politician in California." She buried her face in her hands and started sobbing. Only seconds later, almost as an afterthought, she realized she still clutched a large package. This could change everything, she thought.

She tugged at the sealed flap on the box and ripped it open, expecting to find neat piles of $100 bills. As she peered into the envelope, her heart skipped a beat. No money, only paper. She started crying again, trying to muffle the sobs in case someone was working during the weekend in one of the offices.

Julie tried to figure out what had gone wrong. She had made the two-hour drive to Sacramento and identified a downtown mail drop for her blackmail scheme. She had used what computer acumen she had picked up from her ex-husband to set up an untraceable e-mail account and taunted Marty Frank with the threat of reviving a decades-old dirty secret. She was convinced that Frank would do anything to make her go away. She didn't figure he'd try to kill her. She bungled the blackmail attempt and almost lost her life. She shuddered as she thought of her boys' futures without her.

Julie was fairly certain she had scampered into the office building unseen by her attacker. But she didn't know if he was wandering the streets near the Capitol, waiting for her to show herself. After nearly two hours waiting in the hallway, Julie walked down the stairs to the first floor lobby and gingerly poked her head out the front door, looking left, then right, then left again. Satisfied that she was alone, she took a zigzag path to her safe haven – a motel on Eleventh Street a few blocks away.

"Hi, baby," she said in the phone to her oldest child. "I'm doing great," she lied. "I'll be home in a couple of days, okay?"

Julie laid down the phone and switched on the television. She was curious to see if the evening news covered the incident on Tenth Street.

She opened her laptop, turned the power on and thought about her next e-mail to Marty Frank.

"Nice try, you bastard," she wrote. "I'll give you one more chance before I tell the world what you did. But this time..."

Before she could finish the sentence, the KBLT anchorman caught her attention.

Clay Harvey on camera

Topping our news tonight...a bizarre shooting incident in downtown Sacramento.

Video – Front of Sacramento Mail Services

Police say a sniper fired a single rifle shot through the glass front door of Sacramento Mail Services on Tenth Street early this afternoon.

Video – Close up of bullet hole through window

Apparently, the bullet narrowly missed a woman who was leaving the building at the time. Witnesses said she bolted quickly down the street after the shot was fired.

Video/Audio – Hector Lopez/Witness

"It was real scary. I heard the shot and then the sound of glass shattering. That lady was lucky she wasn't hit."

Video – Parking structure

Police tonight are telling us they have no suspects or apparent motive for the shooting. They said the shot was fired from the roof of a nearby parking structure.

Video/Audio – Elissa Bohannon/Sacramento P.D.

"From all indications, it looks like a professional was involved. We don't know who the target was but would like to talk to her."

Video – Shattered glass at Sacramento Mail Services

Police say a miniature camera had been planted inside the store's front door. They declined to say anything further.

Clay Harvey on camera

Anyone who might have information about the shooting is urged to call the Sacramento Police Department.

Julie stared at the television screen in disbelief. A miniature camera? A professional hit man? She shuddered at the thought that she was a sitting duck for one of Marty Frank's henchmen and knew that she was lucky to still be among the living.

Julie looked at the computer screen and quickly deleted her partial message to Frank. Instinctively, she got up and closed the drapes on the window. What now? she thought.

The news had been droning on. She wasn't paying attention, until the anchorman introduced an update on the Johnny Callahan Senate selection.

Clay Harvey on camera

Here in Sacramento, we're expecting a major political development any day now that promises to have nationwide ramifications. It's Governor Frank's appointment of a successor to fill the U.S. Senate seat of the late Bernie Edelstein. We're joined in studio now by our political reporter, Jack Summerland. Jack, what's the latest?

Summerland on camera

Well, Clay, our sources tell us that Governor Frank is about to name Assembly Speaker Johnny Callahan to fill the vacant Senate seat.

This shouldn't be too much of a surprise, of course, because it is no secret that the governor and Callahan are close personally and politically. Callahan played college football with the governor's son. We expect an announcement no later than mid-week.

Harvey on camera

But the path to the Senate hasn't been smooth, has it?

Summerland on camera

It has been a little rocky, but most of that has not been Callahan's doing. First, there was a false report in a tabloid publication that said Callahan had cavorted with a prostitute. Then, there was an apparent attempt to entrap the speaker in a bribery scheme. That backfired, as well.

Harvey on camera

Assuming Johnny Callahan does go to Washington, what are the political implications?

Summerland on camera

Earlier today I spoke to veteran political reporter Harrison Delmonte of the *Washington Post.* He said the nation's capital is abuzz about this announcement. Currently, Democrats have a razor-thin 50-49 advantage in the Senate. Callahan's presence would create a 50-50 tie, and Vice President Hollings then would be able to cast the tiebreaking vote if a bill is deadlocked. Republicans, therefore, would have working control of the Senate, making it easier for the president to get his agenda through Congress.

Second, everyone sees Callahan as a future political player. Maybe even president some day. He's young — not even 50 yet — personable and dynamic. And it certainly doesn't hurt to come from a state that has one-fifth the necessary electoral votes to elect a president.

Harvey on camera

Jack, thank you. You'll be back with us tomorrow?

Summerland on camera

Yes. We're putting together an in-depth video package on the upcoming Senate selection. I'll be back live with that report.

Clay Harvey on camera

Great. See you then. We'll be right back with a tragedy at the Sacramento Zoo.

Julie clicked off the television and stared blankly at the wall. What do I do now? she wondered. She knew she didn't dare try to arrange for another money drop, now that the police were saying she was dealing with a professional killer. A few hours ago, she was hoping to secure some degree of financial independence for herself and her two children. Now, she just wanted to stay alive. She also wanted to nail Johnny Callahan and Marty Frank.

Julie opened the desk drawer and withdrew a local phone book. She thumbed through the pages until she reached the "K" section. K-A Auto Glass, KB Car Repair, KBLT Television. The station was located less than a dozen blocks from her motel. That reporter, Jack Summerland, just said he'd be at the station on Sunday. Julie decided that seeking money from Frank was too dangerous. Now, she wanted revenge, and Jack was going to help her get it.

Thirty-Nine

Sunday dawned warm. Light streaming through cracks in the shutters awoke Jack Summerland early and he had trouble getting back to sleep. A little after nine o'clock he called the KBLT assignment desk and said he'd be at his desk by eleven. He wasn't going to his Capitol office today. There would be no hint of news on a Sunday, merely hundreds of tourists meandering through the rotunda, basement and first floor of the Capitol building, traipsing through the restored century-old offices of the governor, treasurer, attorney general and secretary of state, and gawking at the self-promoting wall displays from most of California's 58 counties.

The tour highlight would be the painstakingly restored rotunda, the centerpiece of the Capitol's nearly $70 million restoration in the early 1980s. Dominating the floor space in the center of the rotunda, a curious nine-ton larger-than-life-size sculpture by

Larkin Goldsmith Mead. The sculpture, titled Columbus' Last Appeal to Queen Isabella, had nothing to do with California history but occupied a place of honor nonetheless. Pioneer banker D.O. Mills bought the sculpture for $30,000, and in 1883 he donated it to the state.

Other tourists would be drawn to the portraits of California's former governors, all in traditional and formal pose except for Jerry Brown's abstract portrait – reinforcing his image as Governor Moonbeam. On the second floor of the rotunda, the history of California is depicted in a set of 12 murals commissioned for $10,000 through an act of the Legislature in 1913.

Jack also knew that at any time of day, even on a Sunday, a small knot of out-of-towners would stop outside the governor's office and wait for a chance to catch a glimpse of Colin Frank. It would be a long wait, for Frank was 400 miles away on the large yacht of one of his major campaign contributors.

Jack pulled into the long circular driveway in front of the KBLT studios. He inserted a key card that opened a sliding gate to the employee's parking lot.

Once inside the newsroom, he checked the newswires and a few political websites. Jack wore his Sunday news uniform – blue jeans and tennis shoes with a blue buttoned-down shirt, blue and gold tie and a Navy blue blazer. Reporters often dressed casually on the weekend, mindful that the camera only shot them from the waist up.

Jack pressed three buttons on his phone. Across the newsroom, 26-year-old Samantha Raleigh, the weekend assignment editor, picked up the phone.

"Hi Sam," Jack said. "I'm in today."

"I know," she said. "I got the word that you'd be gracing our presence."

Jack stood up, so his head could be seen over the top of his cubicle, and waved at Samantha. "I've got a *Today Show* piece to put together on the Callahan appointment. I'll put together a similar story for the five o'clock show."

Samantha, who spent three years on the assignment desk at a Santa Barbara television station, hated political stories. They were boring. She'd much rather have Jack cover a fire, or train wreck. But she didn't dare suggest it. Jack was a respected political broadcast reporter. He didn't cover fires. She was glad just to have him on the Sunday newscast.

"Whatever you think is best," she answered. "Will you need a cameraman?"

"No. There's no one in town to talk to. And no one is making news today. I'll just advance the Callahan announcement using footage I've gathered the past few days. I could use an editor by one o'clock."

"Okay. Oh," she suddenly remembered, "you got a call from some woman about an hour ago. She didn't want to leave her name or go into your voicemail. She said she'd call back."

"Whatever," Jack responded with distinct indifference.

Jack carried a stack of video discs into an edit booth and started viewing video of Johnny Callahan, Governor Frank and Senator Barnes. From the NBC affiliate in Los Angeles, he had received a satellite feed of old footage of Callahan playing football in college and sitting on the Orange County Board of Supervisors. He selected a seven-second clip of Callahan throwing a short pass during the 1985 USC-UCLA game and a brief shot of Callahan arguing a point at a board meeting.

Viewing time codes on every disc, Jack neatly logged every video snippet he wanted to use, down to the frame.

He wrote two versions of the story — a 4:25 piece for KBLT's evening news — after all, it was a slow news day and the station still had a lengthy show to fill — and a much shorter story to feed to New York for the Monday *Today Show.*

Over the years Jack had put together several stories for the network, mostly in his younger days when he was a general assignment reporter. His biggest national story was a raging forest fire in the mountains east of Sacramento one summer. New York didn't usually care for reports on California government, although he did get national play after a prominent state senator was convicted of corruption in federal court. He had written a tight 1:30 story. To his surprise, the network didn't change a word of it.

Years before, he had covered a story for the network's evening news. By the time it was edited by a producer in Burbank, and again by a producer in New York, he hardly recognized it. It felt good to get another political story on the network. He expected to get razzed by some of his press corps colleagues at the Capitol in the morning.

As Jack viewed the video in the edit bay, a phone on the wall outside the edit booth rang. Jack answered. "I'm transferring a call to you, Jack," Samantha said.

Jack waited a second, then heard a voice. "Mr. Summerland?"

"Yes."

"My name is Julie Forsett. I saw you on the news last night talking about Johnny Callahan."

"Yes. How can I help you?" Jack responded.

"I have information about Callahan and Marty Frank that must be released to the public. They're guilty of a terrible crime."

Jack thought about Carl Jansen's pitch about Callahan. He wondered if the woman was trying to plant another phony story. "What crime are you talking about?" he asked.

"I'm staying in a motel not far from the station. Can I come in and talk to you?"

"Look," he said, "I get calls like this all the time. I'm really busy here. How do I know this is real? Do you have any evidence?"

"I promise this will be worth your while," Julie said.

"Okay," Jack said, unconvinced.

Julie could read Jack's doubt in his voice.

"Look," she said. "I'm really scared. My life has been threatened."

She paused a few seconds. "You know that shooting at the downtown mailbox drop?"

"Yeah, I heard about it."

"I'm the one the sniper was trying to kill. It's all because of what I know about Marty Frank and Johnny Callahan."

Jack didn't really think he'd be handed such a sure-fire story, but there was something in the woman's voice that sounded legitimate.

"Okay," Jack said. "I'll meet with you. Where are you located?"

Julie calculated quickly in her mind. "Not here," she said. "This place might be watched."

The thought of Carl Jansen floating in the Sacramento River and now this mystery phone call seemed to be too coincidental to ignore. He said nothing for several seconds, waiting for the woman to continue.

"I'd feel safer at the TV station. Okay?"

"That'll work," Jack said. "I'm editing all afternoon, so I'll be in the office."

"I'll come by when you get off work," she said.

"I have a live report at five o'clock, so I'll be done here about 5:15. Why don't you come by then and we'll talk."

Jack then remembered that for security reasons, the front door to the station was locked all weekend and there was no receptionist on duty.

"There's no one at the lobby desk and the front door is locked," he continued, "but if you can find the security guard wandering around, he can call me so I can escort you back to the newsroom."

Jack hung up the phone and went back to viewing video, uncertain if he had received anything more than a crank phone call. He wondered how many of these calls the police get every day.

Jack and an editor finished the *Today Show* story and watched as it was fed to New York. The story played up the fact that Callahan would be a swing vote in the Senate and a likely national political figure for years to come. He reminded himself to set his Tivo in the morning so he could save it.

Shortly before four o'clock, as Jack reviewed his script for KBLT's five-clock newscast, Samantha yelled across the newsroom.

"Hey, Jack. You've got a guest. She says she's a student at Berkeley and that you are expecting her," Samantha said. "She's waiting outside in front."

Jack walked down a long hallway, past two studios and the sales department. He opened the front door and re-introduced himself to Kaitlin Brown. He closed the door without noticing the dark green Ford F-150 parked 150 feet away on D Street.

Jack gave Kaitlin a quick ten-minute tour of the news department – the maze of cubicles in the largely empty newsroom. He introduced her to the weekend crew of producers and writers.

Back at his desk, Jack explained that he had just finished sending a report to New York and had to put the finishing touches on his early evening report.

"Wow," she said. "This is a great opportunity for me. Thanks, again."

As Kaitlin watched and occasionally scanned the Associated Press wire on an unused computer, Jack finished reviewing his script.

Jack sent his script to the director about ten minutes before airtime. Before heading to the make-up room, Kaitlin brought him up-to-date on the students' research. The students found one weekend – in November 1985 – when Callahan and Carl Jansen might have crossed paths. Callahan was in Berkeley with his USC football team between Friday and Saturday night. Jansen was in Berkeley teaching and researching a book while on leave from the FBI.

The students' best guess, she told him, was that perhaps Callahan fixed the USC-Cal football game in 1985. "We don't have any proof," Kaitlin said, "but it's certainly plausible. He had the worst game of his career and admitted afterwards that he was distracted."

Jack exhaled deeply. Another likely dead end, he thought. "I'm sorry, Kaitlin. It's a nice theory, but there's no way I can go with guesswork like that. As I told you earlier, it doesn't look like you found out anything I can use."

Shortly after five o'clock, Kaitlin sat quietly in a corner of the studio as Jack delivered his story for Sacramento viewers live from the KBLT news set. The bust of a methamphetamine lab outside Modesto led the newscast, followed by a drowning in the American River.

Jack's story offered nothing new – no hint of scandal involving Callahan. He wanted to tell more, but he couldn't. All he had were several hunches that something might have happened in the Assembly speaker's past. He had no proof of anything and certainly couldn't go on the air and accuse Callahan of being involved in a plot to murder a former FBI agent.

Then there was the phone call from Julie Forsett. A crackpot? A jilted girlfriend who wants to accuse him of rape?

Jack knew the story he really wanted to pursue, but he didn't dare hint there might be some problem in Johnny Callahan's past. For the evening newscast, he strung together recent video clips to bring viewers up to date on the search for a replacement for the late Senator Edelstein. He also inserted a brief clip of a Sacramento political consultant discussing the ramifications for California should its Assembly speaker head for the Senate.

Jack walked Kaitlin down the long hallway leading to the station's lobby. He wanted her to leave quickly, in case Julie Forsett showed up. He couldn't work on a story and baby sit a college student at the same time. As they walked toward the lobby, he noticed Kaitlin's short blond hair and kewpie doll face. If I were 30 years younger, he thought.

He walked her out the front door and squinted into the late

afternoon sun. The two shook hands and Kaitlin headed for the visitors parking lot. The station was located in a mixed-use residential/commercial area, just north of the Capitol. A long circular driveway, with a fountain in the center, led to the entrance. There were two parking lots — a large one for employees, and a small lot around the side of the building about 50 feet from the entrance for visitors. Jack waited near the front door and scanned the area for a woman who might be his mystery caller.

Sitting in her car, in the back of the visitors lot, Julie Forsett saw the reporter and a young woman walk out of the station, shake hands and separate. She had slipped out of her motel through a back alley and arrived at the station more than two hours earlier, picking a parking spot offering the most cover. For much of her wait, she had pretended to read a newspaper as she continuously scanned the station grounds looking for anything suspicious.

While Julie waited, she had seen a dark green Ford F-150 slowly make its way around the driveway outside the station's front entrance. Instinctively, she slumped down in the driver's seat. Who'd be cruising around a TV station on a Sunday? She craned her neck to get a look at the driver, but the fountain in front of the station blocked her view.

Barely peering over the dashboard, Julie recognized the news reporter from his on-air report the previous night. He appeared to be waiting for someone at the front entrance of the station. Still wary of the dark green truck, she realized that she had to make her move. She inhaled deeply and pushed open the car door. She walked briskly towards the reporter, looking down and away, just in case her assailant was watching.

Simultaneously, Kaitlin pulled her car out of the lot and stopped to thank Jack again for the tour. The three of them converged near the fountain. Kaitlin rolled down the car window and extended her hand to the reporter.

Without warning, the unmistakable sound of a gunshot

pierced the quiet air. First one shot, then a second shot.

The first bullet missed its mark, whizzing only inches from Julie's left ear, smashing through the thick glass front door to the television station and lodging in a wall in the foyer.

Perhaps three seconds later, the second bullet whirled Julie a quarter turn in a clockwise direction. She let out a scream and fell to the ground in excruciating pain. As tears welled up in her eyes she could see blood flowing out of her right arm.

"Get down, get down, get down," Jack yelled at both Kaitlin and Julie. Kaitlin ducked her head below the dashboard, terrified and shaking wildly. Jack reached through the open window in Kaitlin's car and leaned on the horn for about five seconds, trying to scare away the assailant and attract the station's security guard. He heard the screeching of tires on pavement and saw the dark green pickup peeling out of the driveway in front of the station. It disappeared quickly.

In a matter of seconds, Jack ran through the options in his mind. Think and be logical, he told himself. His first thought told him to seek refuge inside the station and wait for an ambulance. But one look at Julie's blood-soaked shirt and the sound of her groaning in agony sent him in a different direction. He had to get her to a hospital as quickly as possible.

"Move over, move over," he commanded Kaitlin. "I'll drive."

Kaitlin, trembling and on the verge of tears, slid over to the passenger seat. Jack helped Julie into the back seat. She seemed dazed, in shock.

As Jack lifted Julie into the car, he felt her gushing blood running down his forearm. In the bloody mess he couldn't tell where she had been hit. Waiting for an ambulance could take several minutes. Jack probed Julie's right arm and shoulder with his finger and felt a hole about an inch above her bicep. He ripped off his tie and used it as a tourniquet. He had heard two shots. Was she hit a second time? Luckily, a small Sacramento County health center was only six blocks away on C Street. He drove past it every day on the way to work. But this is Sunday evening. Is it open?

The station's private security guard – where the hell had he been? – arrived at the station's front door, panting and gasping for air.

"Call the cops!" Jack yelled as he jumped in the driver's seat.

As he raced out of the station's driveway, heading east towards 12th street, Jack quickly glanced back at Julie, who was slumped in the back seat. She was as white as a fresh snowfall and moaning in a steady monotone. She looked like she was going to pass out.

"Don't worry," he said. "We're almost there." Despite all the blood, Jack thought she had only been hit in the arm. Then, almost without thinking, he glanced in the rear-view mirror. On his heels, not more than 10 feet behind him, he saw the dark green Ford F-150. In an instant, he saw that the ugly driver was gritting his teeth. "Stay down! Keep your head low!" he commanded to his passengers. Jack ran through the red light at 12th Street, dodging a vagrant who was crossing the street. A city-installed traffic calming barrier – designed to slow traffic speeds in Sacramento's mid-town area – forced Jack to turn left at 14th. The clinic is just a block away, he thought.

Jack turned right on C Street, then crossed 15th Street, his tires screeching, and saw the clinic on his right. With a sudden jolt, the dark green pick-up rammed into the rear of Kaitlin's cherry red Nissan Altima. Jack lurched forward, his chest slamming into the steering wheel. He felt a painful sting and realized he hadn't put on his seat belt. "Try to buckle up," he yelled at the two women. "We're in for a wild ride." Another groan from Julie.

"Damn," he said out loud. Jack knew he wouldn't have time to stop the car in front of the clinic. Quick, think – where can I go to get help for this girl? In an instant, it hit him. Sutter General Hospital, located across the street from historic Sutter's Fort,

Sacramento's earliest settlement. It was about a mile away.

Still on C Street, Jack swerved to avoid two cars on 16th and gunned the engine. In one block, C Street dead-ended at the Blue Diamond almond factory at 17th Street, forcing him south. At E Street, there was another dead-end. With a darting glance in his rear-view mirror, Jack pivoted the car eastward along E Street. Burke's Ford F-150 shadowed every move. Jack hit yet another dead end at 20th. "Goddam sonofabitch," he yelled in frustration.

"What's happening?" screamed Kaitlin.

Jack yelled, "This is ridiculous. I'm like a rat in a maze. And I can't lose this guy."

Jack made an instant decision. Burke was so close he could almost smell his bad breath. There was no way he could negotiate these downtown streets with this assassin on his tail. Of course! he thought. The Capitol. It would be crawling with armed security, even on a Sunday evening.

Jack knew instinctively that he, Julie and Kaitlin had a good chance of surviving if he could make it to the Capitol.

Jack gunned the engine as he negotiated a right turn onto G Street and raced toward the downtown area. He ran two red lights, then jammed his foot on the pedal, swerved onto 12th Street and headed due south towards the Capitol building. Eight blocks – a half-mile, he calculated, in less than 30 seconds. Jack gunned the engine again with the green pickup right behind him. E Street, F Street, G Street. Five more blocks. Luckily, Sunday afternoons in downtown Sacramento didn't draw much of a crowd. He and Terrence Burke just about had 12th Street all to themselves.

Jack knew his only hope was to make it to the Capitol basement where security guards always were on duty.

As Jack sped through a red light across J Street, now only two blocks from the Capitol, his mind raced. Can I beat this guy to the Capitol? He heard another shot that missed its mark. The Senator Hotel loomed in the foreground, blocking his view of the

Capitol building.

He was at K Street. One block to go. At L Street, the northern boundary of the Capitol grounds, Jack saw the unmanned kiosk guarding the entrance to the driveway leading to the basement. Just past the kiosk, the driveway makes a sharp turn.

"Hold on!" he yelled as he slammed on the breaks. With tires screeching, the car's left-rear panel careened into the sturdy, wooden kiosk. At an angle, the car plowed through the lowered wooden gate.

In an instant, a heavy metal barricade, buried beneath the concrete driveway, automatically surged to the surface. The car hit the barricade with such a force that Jack was certain that had it not have been for the deployment of the Altima's airbags, he would have been thrown completely through the front windshield.

Stunned, and bleeding from his forehead, Jack looked first at Kaitlin. She had been jolted and looked frightened, but otherwise seemed alright. The front of the Altima was twisted and crumpled. He unbuckled his seat belt and turned to look at Julie. Her eyes were closed tightly and she seemed to be shivering. Her blood had soaked the back seat. Dazed, Jack passed out.

Jack's hastily devised plan served its purpose. Terrence Burke, concerned about the potential swarm of highway patrol officers at the Capitol garage's entrance, wasn't about to follow Jack. Burke slammed on his brakes just after Jack careened into the barrier. He slipped down L Street and disappeared downtown out of harm's way.

Forty

At first, all he could sense were unfamiliar female voices. It was like he was trying to come out of a deep sleep but wasn't yet ready to wake up. He tried to open his eyelids but failed. He couldn't make out the words being spoken, but within seconds he recognized that unmistakable, antiseptic smell. Of course, he realized. I'm in a hospital.

"He looks different," one voice said. "I can't wait to tell my mom that we saw a real celebrity," another said.

Jack Summerland was slowly coming out of a drug-induced slumber. He gingerly moved his head and saw the early morning sun force its way through a crack in the window shade, casting a slight shadow in the room. Jack's head pounded and whenever he moved, he was aware of bruises and aches throughout his body.

"Good morning, Mr. Summerland. Do you know where you are?"

Jack tried to talk but his throat was terribly dry and nothing came out.

"You're at the UC Davis Medical Center," a pretty 30-ish nurse said as she pushed a straw into his mouth. "You were brought in late yesterday afternoon after a car crash at the Capitol building. Nothing's broken. You're probably going to be back to normal in a couple of days."

The nurse smiled. "You know, you're the second TV guy we've had in here in the past month. That weather guy, what's his name? Oh, yeah, Bernard something, he was in here for some tests a couple of weeks ago."

The nurse realized she was talking too much, so she quickly took the straw out of his mouth and placed the cup of water on a table next to his bed. She waited for her patient to say something.

Instead, Jack closed his eyes, exhaled and leaned back on his pillow.

Slowly, it came back to him. The meeting. The gunshots. The chase. The screeching tires. The crash.

He sat up with a start. "I've got to get out of here," he croaked. "I'm on deadline."

"Hold your horses, big guy," nurse number one said as she gently pressured his shoulders back onto the bed.

"Is any part of me broken?" he asked.

"No, you're going to be fine, Mr. Summerland. I think they just want to keep you here for the day for a few tests."

Groggily, Jack asked about Kaitlin and Julie.

"Miss Brown is okay. We released her earlier today."

"And the other woman, Miss Forsett?"

"She's okay, too. The doctors patched up a bullet wound in her right arm."

The nurse continued. "You know, you were on the news last night. That was some crash."

Just then, Karen walked in the room. Jack couldn't tell if she was sympathetic or angry.

"Jesus, Jack. You okay?" she asked.

Jack nodded but said nothing.

"The newspaper said you were shot at and followed by someone, and that two women were in the car with you. Is that true?"

Jack could tell Karen was both sympathetic *and* angry.

"Yes. I've been working with a journalism class at Cal and one of the students came up to tour the station. The other woman said she had some important information for me. Someone shot at us at the station, then followed us and fired some more shots."

"Again, who were these women?" Karen was needling Jack now.

"I told you. One is a student who wants to become a TV reporter. I'm working with her class on a project. It's Ed Stewart's class. I've mentioned him to you before. The other woman is a potential source. I just met her for the first time seconds before the shooting."

Karen forced a smile. "Well, the good news is, you're famous. You made page one with a photo of the wreck," she said. Karen handed Jack the morning's *Sacramento Bee.*

> Sacramento television reporter Jack Summerland and two women were injured Sunday night after crashing their vehicle into a metal barricade leading to the state Capitol's north entrance.
>
> Witnesses said Summerland, a veteran political reporter at KBLT, was driving and appeared to be eluding a second vehicle, which was following at a high rate of speed along 12th Street.
>
> California Highway Patrol spokesman Lawrence Knaur said one of Summerland's passengers, identified as 43-year-old Julie Forsett of Reno, had been shot once in the right arm. She was taken to UC Davis Medical Center. A hospital spokeswoman said Ms. Forsett was in stable condition.

> The other woman in the car, 22-year-old Kaitlin Brown, is a graduate student in journalism at the University of California, Berkeley. A hospital spokeswoman said she was treated for minor injuries and released.
>
> Summerland suffered a concussion and contusions. He was being held for observation and is expected to be released sometime tomorrow.
>
> Joanna Parsons, a visitor from Huntington Beach, said she was walking to the Hyatt Regency Hotel when she heard tires screeching along 12th Street.
>
> "I thought I heard a shot, maybe two," she said. "As I looked up, this dark green pickup truck was right on this guy's tail – maybe two feet away. Both were going real fast. Then the first car rammed through a parking guard rail outside the Capitol and kept going. I couldn't see anything, but I heard this awful crash."
>
> Parsons said she saw the trailing pickup speed down L Street.
>
> The CHP and the Sacramento Police Department are conducting a joint investigation of the incident. In a statement, they said they had uncovered no motive for the attack on Summerland. Police said they intended to question Summerland today.
>
> Police said a private security guard told them the chase began at the KBLT studios after shots had been fired. KBLT officials were unavailable for comment.

Karen watched Jack read the story. She took a deep breath. Jack looked around the room to make sure no one else was within earshot. "Remember how I told you that there was something fishy with your boss?"

He paused a second, then continued. "Well, it looks like someone is trying to take me out. First, I get a call from a former FBI agent. Before he can tell me anything, he's murdered and dumped into the Sacramento River. The woman in the car with me last night told me on the phone that she had been shot at by a sniper. Then, shots are fired at us at the station and someone follows us as we tried to go to the hospital. All this happened after I started looking into Callahan's background."

Karen stammered. "I, I, I still can't believe Johnny could be part of this. He's not that kind of guy. He's got too much to lose. You don't have proof."

"You're right. I don't have proof, but I'm convinced he's involved," Jack said. "Do the math."

Just then, Karen put her hand to her mouth. "Ohmigod," she murmured.

"What is it?"

She hesitated and started shaking. "I…I don't know how to put this, but I think I may have contributed to what happened."

"What are you talking about?"

"You see, Marty pumped me for information. He asked me – no, he told me – to keep him up-to-date on your activities. He said I had to remain loyal to the office and to Johnny. He said my future was at stake. I thought he was just…I don't know what I thought. I – Ohmigod – I told him about your phone call from Jansen. I told him you were meeting him at Christy's."

In an instant, Jack recognized that a key piece of the puzzle had been put in place. "So that's how someone found out about my meeting with Jansen."

"I didn't think it would come to this," Karen said, sobbing. "I'm so sorry. Are you going to tell the cops about this?"

"What can I tell them? Right now, it's all circumstantial. All I've got are suspicions."

Karen then fished in her purse and retrieved a single sheet of paper, a brief advisory for the news media. "You should see this," she said. "Governor Frank is announcing his appointment of Johnny to the U.S. Senate tomorrow morning."

Jack interjected, "Tomorrow?"

"Yes, the media advisory is going out late today. It won't mention Johnny's name, so as to keep what's left of the suspense going. But Johnny gets the job tomorrow and leaves for Washington on Wednesday. He'll be sworn in immediately and then will be available to vote on the big oil drilling bill pending in the Senate."

Jack thought for a minute. "Do you believe me?"

"I'm not sure, but you're pretty convincing," she said.

"Look, Karen, I'm stuck in this hospital bed for today. I am so frustrated. I should be at work. It looks like I won't be out until early tomorrow morning. Nothing, and I mean nothing, will stop me from being able to cover the announcement in the governor's office. I've got to figure out what to do and you've got to help me."

"How?" she asked.

"Find Julie Forsett. She's somewhere here in the hospital. She might be able to unravel all of this."

Forty-One

Forty-One

A junior member of Governor Frank's press staff leaned into the microphone on the lectern. "This is a test. This is a test. 1, 2, 3. This is a test."

The governor's council room filled up rapidly. KBLT sent two crews – Jack Summerland and Ron Middleton to shoot video for subsequent newscasts, and a separate video crew to feed the news conference to the studio for a live KBLT break-in. Two other local stations pre-empted regular programming, as well. The network monitored the video from New York so it could use a snippet on the evening news.

Jack had hoped Julie Forsett would be the key to the Callahan mystery. Karen had tracked down her hospital room but was told she was too sedated to have visitors. When Jack tried to talk to her, he was told she had checked out of the hospital. Two sources, Carl Jansen and Julie Forsett, had tantalized him with the political story of the decade. Jansen was dead; Julie was missing. Jack resigned himself to the fact that he likely would never get to the bottom of this story.

Ron set up his tripod and camera on the riser in the back of the room. Jack sat in his seat in the last row, directly in front of his photographer. He had a small bandage on his right temple. Otherwise, no one would have known he was in a car crash two nights earlier. One of his colleagues, radio reporter Millie Cofferman, walked over to Jack and gave him a hug.

"You okay?" she asked. "You know you're not supposed to *make* the news."

"It wasn't my idea. I'm fine, just a scratch."

Other reporters noticed Jack's presence. Soon Jack was holding court for a half-dozen reporters, careful not to say anything that might jeopardize a potential story.

Elsewhere in the governor's office, staff made last minute arrangements before the news conference – copying the governor's prepared remarks for the press, updating the credentialed media list, making last minute phone calls to key reporters, and putting the finishing touches on a news release that would be sent to news organizations from California to Washington, D.C.

"Governor Frank Appoints Assembly Speaker Johnny Callahan to the U.S. Senate," headlined the release.

Inside the governor's small private office, Callahan, Governor Frank and Marty Frank sat around the governor's desk.

Callahan looked again at his written remarks and looked up at Marty. "I know you can't make it back to Washington until next week. But I'll be looking forward to your arrival."

"Sounds great," Marty responded. "You know the old saying: 'All for one and one for all.'"

Barry Conroy, the governor's press secretary, knocked on the door and entered the office without waiting for permission. "Governor," he said, "we're going to have a huge crowd for this one. The *New York Times* has flown Harrison up from L.A. Even the *Chicago Sun-Times* is here. ABC and CBS aren't relying on their local affiliates. They're sending their own crews. NBC is monitoring Channel 4's coverage and will write their story from New York. We've got crews from San Francisco, L.A. and San Diego credentialed for this one. The California Channel is feeding the announcement live to all the other stations throughout the state."

The governor turned to Callahan and smiled. "So, Johnny, what's on tap the next few days?"

"Well," Callahan responded, "I thought about taking the red-eye tonight, but I don't sleep well on planes. Besides, my vote on the oil drilling legislation won't be needed until Thursday. The California Republican delegation is throwing me a party tomorrow night. Justice O'Malley will swear me in on Thursday morning. Then it's off to the Senate floor."

Frank sounded fatherly. "You know, we're expecting great things from you back in Washington. Stay out of trouble – no scandals – and stay true to your conservative beliefs without going overboard. I predict that in no time you'll be seen as presidential material. You're young, pragmatic but principled and photogenic."

"I'm not sure I can really think about that right now," Callahan said. "I have to prove myself in the Senate and then win election outright."

Frank scoffed. "The Senate is a piece of cake. You don't have to make really tough decisions. You can stake out your ground, debate your colleagues and pontificate on weekend talk shows. It's not like being governor. In the Senate you won't have to take heat for raising taxes, you won't have to cut the benefits of the blind and elderly or be accused of letting the highways go to pot. You've got a solid track record here in California. And it doesn't hurt, of course, that California is the 800-pound gorilla in presidential politics."

Conroy interrupted. "It's time to get going. With so many stations going live, we can't pull a Jerry Brown."

Governor Frank laughed. He was old enough to remember when Governor Brown arrived 14 minutes late for his annual State-of-the-State address in the 1970s. California television stations routinely interrupted programming to carry the address live. KBLT fed the broadcast statewide, using one of its reporters as anchor. The poor guy ran out of ad lib material while he waited for Brown to appear. He had an advance copy of the governor's speech and ended up reading it word-for-word. The station vowed never again to run a Brown speech live.

Conroy walked inside the news conference first. "Fifteen seconds," he said. Television reporters were winding up their live introductions. Holding a microphone in his right hand and some notes on a 3 x 5 card in his left, Jack looked over his shoulder at the podium, then turned to face the camera, telling his viewers, "Here now are Governor Frank and Assembly Speaker Johnny Callahan."

Still cameras clicked as Governor Frank and Callahan emerged from a door behind the podium. The lectern had been affixed with the official California seal.

The room was packed. Print reporters sat in the front rows, television reporters were in the rear. Staff members for the governor and the Assembly speaker stood off to the sides and occupied seats in the far rear, behind the television cameras.

Frank approached the lectern with Callahan standing five feet behind him and off to one side. The governor waited for the clicking of the still cameras to die down. In the back of the room, behind the rows of chairs, Callahan counted 14 television cameras. Many of the television reporters stood next to the cameras so they could communicate directly with their photographers.

Because the announcement was being fed live throughout California, Governor Frank waited until he received a hand signal from one of his aides.

"Ladies and Gentlemen," he began. "When U.S. Senator Bernie Edelstein passed away recently, I received mountains of advice about who I should appoint as his successor. Some people said I had to choose a Democrat, because Senator Edelstein was a Democrat. Others urged me to appoint a rock-ribbed Republican, or a person of color, or a woman.

"My staff gave me a list of 15 potential appointees. I trimmed the list to ten and interviewed each one personally. In the end, I looked for a person with integrity and an impeccable record. I looked for a person who has the courage of his or her convictions but is not afraid to compromise when necessary.

"I considered Democrats, Republicans and independents – even a few people who have never been involved in electoral politics. In the end, it came down to one question. Who is the best person for the job? Who would make the U.S. Senate and the American people proud?

"Ladies and Gentlemen, I am pleased to introduce California's newest U.S. Senator, Johnny Callahan."

Staffers standing behind the reporters applauded. Reporters, trained not to show any kind of favoritism, diligently took notes and offered no hint they accepted or rejected the governor's choice.

Johnny Callahan took five steps to the lectern, pulled a page of talking points from his coat pocket and began reading.

"I am deeply honored and humbled to be appointed to the United States Senate. And I want to thank my political mentor, Governor Colin Frank, for having faith in me and my abilities to uphold this office.

"I will be a forceful and dedicated advocate for California. Part of our ongoing budget problems has occurred because we Californians export more tax dollars to the federal government than we receive in services. I will add my voice to those who say we need to bring reason and fair play back into the equation.

"I intend to represent *all* Californians – Republicans, Democrats and independents. Over the years in Sacramento, I believe I have earned a reputation of being fair, honest and trustworthy.

Those characteristics will be the hallmark of my actions in Washington.

"I fully understand the political ramifications of my appointment, and I am aware of the heated debate that preceded my selection. With the vice president casting all tie-breaking votes, Republicans now will be in a position to exert renewed influence over the nation's public policy agenda.

"I know some of you in the media have speculated that I could become the swing vote in the Senate on sensitive, politically ideological issues. Let me say this: I am a proud member of the Republican party and I believe in what the party stands for – lower taxes and a smaller government. But I can promise you that before every vote — *every vote* — I will weigh all sides and arguments and vote on the merits of each bill before me.

"Thank you. I'd be glad to answer questions."

In unison, three voices shouted, "Mr. Speaker."

"Yes, John," Callahan said as he pointed to veteran Associated Press reporter John Coleman.

"Mr. Speaker, the first major issue you will deal with is the President's oil drilling legislation, carried by Senator Carpenter. Environmental groups say this bill could devastate wide expanses of wilderness in Alaska. Can you tell us your thoughts on this bill?"

Callahan carefully parsed his words. "At this time, I cannot. I expect to be briefed on the legislation on my flight to Washington. Speaking in general terms, I am torn. On the one hand, our country cannot be held hostage to Middle Eastern oil barons who threaten our economy every time they raise the price of a barrel of oil. We only have to see how the price of gasoline has spiked in recent years and how that has affected numerous sectors of our economy. On the other hand, I treasure our country's natural resources. You will recall that I opposed offshore oil drilling legislation a couple of years ago. I favor a balanced approach – resource development and conservation. Again, I haven't decided how I will vote on the oil drilling bill."

Callahan then called on Donna Capezio of the *Fresno Bee.*

"Mr. Speaker, there seems to have been an orchestrated effort to scuttle this appointment. First, there was an unflattering story in a tabloid publication. Then, there was an apparent attempt to entrap you into accepting a bribe. Can you comment on this, please? Who do you think was behind these efforts?"

Callahan smiled. "You know, the truth always wins out. I have no idea who was behind these scurrilous attacks on my character. But they didn't work, did they? That tabloid had to recant the story even before it was printed. The newspaper admitted its mistake and apologized. I accepted that apology. As for the entrapment, I don't know who was behind that, either. I'm trying to put those episodes behind me. I intend to move forward with my new life in the Senate."

Callahan answered questions for another 20 minutes on subjects ranging from gay marriage and abortion to aid to Israel and the war on terrorism.

"One more. Daniel?"

Daniel Terhune, a reporter for Callahan's hometown *Orange County Register*, asked the question that Callahan's supporters hoped would be asked.

"Mr. Speaker, could you comment on a blurb in this week's *Newsweek*, which describes you as a potential candidate for president down the road?"

Callahan's answer was well rehearsed.

"Oh my!" he said with a smile. "I'm flattered with all the attention. And, again, I hope to make all Americans proud of my actions in the Senate. But I've been appointed to do a job for California, and I'll need the votes of Californians when I stand for election next year. What happens in the future cannot be predicted. Thank you very much."

Governor Frank hurriedly returned to the lectern. "Wait a minute, everyone. There's someone else who wants to say something." He paused a second. "Go ahead, Mr. President."

A voice on the telephone line cleared his throat.

"Mr. Speaker, or should I say Senator Callahan. This is President Vernon. I just want to add my congratulations to your appointment to the United States Senate. You will be joining a select deliberative body that occupies a rare place of honor in our country. I look forward to working with you in the years ahead."

"Thank you, Mr. President," Callahan said. "I appreciate your kind words."

Jack had started for the door before the President was introduced. He quickly turned to his photographer. "You got it, right?" Ron Middleton smiled and said, "You think I'm a rookie at this?"

As the crowd mingled and Callahan received warm congratulations, Jack buttonholed Billy Galster.

"Jack, how you feeling?" Galster asked.

"I'm fine. Thanks for asking."

"Who in the world was chasing you?"

Jack gave away nothing. "I have no idea. I'm as surprised as everyone else. Hey, Billy, how about a live interview tonight with the speaker for our five o'clock? You owe me after I took the fall for that *Starlight* fiasco."

"Can't do it, Jack. Johnny is doing a CNN interview at five, MSNBC at 5:10 and Fox at 5:20."

Jack tried Plan B. "What about our six o'clock show, or even the eleven?"

"Six is out," Galster said. "Johnny's got a private dinner with friends over at River Bistro. But he'll back in the office tonight. I'll ask the boss. Why don't you check with me later."

As Jack headed out of the news conference, he spied Karen who had joined much of Callahan's staff at the announcement. Jack and Karen exchanged smiles from about 20 feet away. Making his way into the main hallway of the Capitol, Jack had to weave through dozens of groupies, mostly tourists, who wanted to be part of the action. Jack saw a knot of reporters surrounding a man who appeared in his mid-20s and was conservatively dressed in a blue suit.

"What's going on?" he whispered to a newspaper photographer."

"Oh, it's some guy from a conservative group urging Callahan to support an anti-gay marriage constitutional amendment." Jack shrugged. "And that lady over there," the photographer said as he pointed to another impromptu hallway interview session, "she's from Planned Parenthood. Guess what she wants from Callahan."

Jack decided to grab a few seconds of footage of each advocate to help round out his story. "This will be good flavor," he told Middleton. Jack figured he had a little more than an hour to put his story together for the noon show.

Forty-Two

Forty-Two

Jack and Ron wrapped up their noon show story on Callahan's announcement. They decided to skip lunch so they could work on developing a fresh version of the story for the early evening newscast.

Jack interviewed a few of the speaker's colleagues in the Assembly and, once back at the station, scanned the newswires and websites for other tidbits. The Associated Press scooped everyone with an interview with Ruth Edelstein, the late senator's widow, who said she was disappointed Governor Frank didn't appoint someone more in line politically with her husband.

Jack placed a call to the San Francisco office of Colleen Fitzpatrick, California's other U.S. Senator, a Democrat, and received a brief statement saying she looks forward to working with Callahan on a number of mutual problems. She singled out the need to pass disaster relief legislation that included significant funding to fight California wildfires and flooding.

Then, Jack called Billy Galster to check on his earlier interview request. Galster told Jack that Callahan would be working late that evening and reluctantly had agreed to a live interview on the eleven o'clock news, as long as the interview took place in the speaker's office.

"I'm not sure why, but at first Johnny didn't want to do this interview," Galster said. "It took some doing, but I convinced him that next year's election campaign begins tonight."

At 2:25, Jack started writing his script for the five o'clock newscast. He had been living this story for so long, it felt like it almost wrote itself. Middleton, meanwhile, started making a list of video that likely would be used in the story and he scanned the day's footage, noting the exact time codes of every scene and potential sound bite.

In mid-story, Jack left his cubicle to receive a fax at the newsroom secretary's desk when he noticed his mail slot was crammed with fresh material. Most of it was junk. He hadn't cleaned it out in days. Then, he noticed a FedEx envelope addressed to him resting on an adjacent file cabinet. He took one look at the return address and gasped. It was from the law office of Towne, Roberts & Simpson of Houston, Texas. He ripped open the package and read the contents.

"Jansen!" he said.

He turned to the secretary and loudly asked, "When did this FedEx come in? How long has it been here?"

The secretary shrugged. "I think it came in yesterday. You weren't here."

Jack grabbed the package and marched into the news director's office, closing the door behind him. The secretary, concerned she had made a mistake, anxiously waited outside the door looking for a clue. Peering through the large glass window separating Jimmy Johnson's office from the newsroom, she could see that the conversation was animated. Jack paced the floor and pointed to some papers he had removed from the FedEx envelope. At one point, Johnson made a phone call and the two listened on a speaker phone. Every once in awhile she made out a few words from behind the closed door. "It's just a piece of paper," she thought she heard the voice on the speaker say, followed by, "You have no proof; legally you're at risk here."

The conversation continued with Jack doing most of the talking. When Jack emerged from the office, the secretary felt relieved that she wasn't summoned to Johnson's office. But Jack appeared quite agitated. He walked briskly to his desk and sat down staring blankly at his computer screen. A minute later, he got up and walked out the back door to the parking lot and paced about 150 yards while Ron finished editing their story for the early evening newscast.

Twenty minutes before airtime, Jack and Ron made the nine-block drive to the Capitol's west steps.

Bystanders couldn't help but gawk at the sight. Here, with microphones at the ready, stood eight television reporters nearly shoulder to shoulder in front of tripods and cameras – each tethered to giant satellite trucks queued along Tenth Street. Usually such spectacles were reserved for celebrity crime trials, mass murders and natural calamities. Even politics has its day once in awhile.

Ever since most of the television industry replaced film with videotape and enhanced live capabilities in the mid-1970s, television news directors had been told by media consultants that audiences liked the idea of seeing news reports live. You never know when something might break, and they'd like to be comforted to know their favorite reporter was on the scene — just in case. So it was that a pack of television reporters detailed the Senate appointment of Johnny Callahan – live in front of the Capitol, a full seven hours after the appointment was announced.

The lineup included stations from Sacramento, San Francisco, Los Angeles, San Diego and Fresno – among them three Spanish language stations. Most newscasts started at five o'clock but the Callahan story wasn't the lead everywhere. In San Diego, the lead story was a continuing scandal involving a city councilman; in San Francisco, one station led with a pit bull attack of a girl in the Mission District; two Los Angeles stations led their newscasts with a robbery at the home of a Hollywood starlet that only *People* magazine readers would recognize.

The rest of the stations thought the Callahan story was the most important news item of the day. A few seconds after five o'clock, and almost in unison, the reporters started their chatter.

Conrad Dalton on camera

The big story today in Sacramento was the worst kept secret at the state Capitol. Governor Colin Frank appointed Assembly Speaker Johnny Callahan to the U.S. Senate, succeeding the late Bernie Edelstein.

Jack Summerland, live at the Capitol, says the appointment has significant implications in Washington. Jack?

Jack Summerland on camera

Speaker Callahan will be sworn into office on Thursday, creating a 50-50 deadlock and breaking the Democratic hold on the U.S. Senate. Republican Vice President Clifford Hollings will break any tie votes on the Senate floor. Governor Frank had been under pressure to appoint a Democrat to the seat that had been occupied by Democrats since 1968. But party loyalty was too much to overcome.

Video — Frank and Callahan at news conference

In Johnny Callahan, the Senate gets a moderate conservative with movie-star good looks who some say is destined for stardom. As Assembly speaker, Callahan was a deal maker. He truly believes that politics is the art of compromise and building consensus.

Governor Frank made the announcement at a jammed news conference in the Capitol.

Video/Audio – Governor Frank

"My staff gave me a list of 15 potential appointees. I trimmed the list to ten and interviewed each one personally. In the end, I looked for a person with integrity and an impeccable record. I looked for a person who has the courage of his or her convictions but is not afraid to compromise when necessary."

Video – Callahan playing football

Johnny Callahan first caught the public's eye when he was a star quarterback at USC in the early 1980s.

Video – Callahan on Board of Supervisors

After a stint with the Orange County District Attorney's office and private practice, Callahan entered politics, winning seats on the Newport Beach City Council followed by the Orange County Board of Supervisors.

Video – Callahan on Assembly floor

After election to the state Assembly, Callahan rose to the top quickly, becoming speaker. He worked closely with Governor Frank and was the early favorite to be named to the Senate post.

Video – News conference

Looking forward to the Senate, Callahan said he wouldn't be pigeonholed politically.

Video/Audio – Callahan

"I intend to represent *all* Californians – Republicans, Democrats and independents. Over the years in Sacramento, I believe I have earned a reputation of being fair, honest and trustworthy. Those characteristics will be the hallmark of my actions in Washington."

Video – News conference

An unexpected congratulatory message – via phone from the White House – came from President Vernon.

Audio – President Vernon/Video – Callahan smiling

"I look forward to working with you in the years ahead."

Video – Sen. Edelstein campaigning

One person who did not approve of the Callahan appointment was Senator Edelstein's widow, Ruth. She criticized the governor for not appointing someone more in line with her late husband's philosophical agenda.

Video – Assembly footage

In the Assembly, Callahan's colleagues offered mixed reactions. Republicans were exuberant. Democrats circumspect.

Video/Audio – Assemblyman Calvin Donotea (R-Riverside)

"He'll be a great senator. He's just what this nation needs, a straight-talking, common sense leader."

Video/Audio – Assemblyman Carlos Hermosa (D-Los Angeles)

"I have always thought that Johnny Callahan is out of step with mainstream California. But I have no problem with his integrity, so I'll reserve judgment until I see how he performs in office."

Video – Sen. Fitzpatrick

Colleen Fitzpatrick, now the senior senator from California, issued a brief statement urging Callahan to join her in vigorously supporting the disaster relief bill pending in the Senate.

Video – Callahan leaving news conference

After decades as a local and state elected official, the senator will have to learn about an entirely new set of issues – the war on terror, foreign aid and Social Security.

Video – Hallway news conferences

Outside the governor's office, advocates for both Planned Parenthood and the National Defense of Marriage Alliance sought airtime on various public policy issues — an example of the new pressures Johnny Callahan will now face.

Summerland on camera

> As California's new senator heads east, the Assembly Republicans have a decision to make. Because they are the majority party, they're entitled to select the next speaker. A caucus is scheduled for tomorrow morning to pick a new leader. Conrad?

Summerland prayed that Dalton wouldn't ask him about the weather. "Jack, so when does Callahan actually take his seat in the Senate?"

If Dalton had been paying attention during Jack's report, he would have remembered Callahan's Washington timetable. Jack wondered if Dalton was combing his hair during his story, or perhaps he was flirting with his co-anchor.

Jack resisted the urge to say, "Well, you stupid idiot, as I mentioned during my report, Callahan flies out to Washington tomorrow and will be sworn in on Thursday." Once, just once, Jack wished he could say something like that. Instead, he played it straight.

"That'll be Thursday, Conrad. Just in time to vote on important oil drilling legislation."

Dalton glanced at his script. "And tonight at 11 you'll have more?"

"That's right, Conrad. At 11 we'll have an exclusive interview with the new senator, live from his office at the Capitol."

Jack ripped the earpiece out of his right ear and helped Ron pack the gear.

As the last of the equipment was being loaded into the truck, a woman walked across Tenth Street from the stately Library and Courts Building and approached Jack. She wore dark sunglasses, a baseball cap covering her short-cropped blond hair and a jacket that obscured the fact that her right arm was in a sling. Her eyes darted left and right.

"I wanted to thank you for saving my life the other night," she said. "I'm in real trouble. My name has been in the papers, so I've got no choice but to go public. This story will make you famous from coast to coast."

Forty-Three

The scotch and wine flowed in the private room upstairs at the River Bistro along the banks of the Sacramento River. It was a Who's Who of California Republican politics. Assembly Speaker Johnny Callahan, of course, was the guest of honor. Governor Colin Frank was the official host.

Also seated around a large dining table celebrating Callahan's rise to national prominence, were the Assembly majority and Senate minority leaders, Marty Frank, three powerful lobbyists, a prominent Washington columnist and several of the state's business leaders – among them, Herman Peterson and Dr. Henry Culbertson, two of the funders of a statewide ad campaign promoting Callahan's appointment to the U.S. Senate.

All laughed as the bearded, barrel-chested man sitting next to the governor regaled the celebrants with heretofore secret stories of some of Hollywood's biggest stars. "He was so nervous, he vomited all over Stonewall Jackson's uniform," Gladstone Dreiser said amid the laughter.

A waiter passed out champagne. Everyone took a glass except for Johnny Callahan. "I'm still working tonight," he told the waiter.

"Working?" asked Dreiser. "Tonight?"

"I'm cleaning out my office," Callahan said, "plus I've got a couple of interviews."

Governor Frank offered a toast. "Here's to our rising California star – the future President Callahan. After a round of cheers, the new senator stood before the group, half-smiling. He raised his arms and held out both hands as if to say, "Back off. No more of this talk about the presidency."

Truth be told, Callahan couldn't help but think about a future in the White House. He had solid conservative credentials, but he wasn't as polarizing as most Republicans in Congress. He was young and good looking, and he had experience at the local, state and now federal levels of government. He was a good fundraiser and had a stable of friends ready to move.

Callahan also was a student of history. He knew that only a handful of U.S. Senators ascended to the White House directly from the Senate. Next to being vice president, being a governor seemed to be the best path to the White House – a la Carter, Reagan, Clinton and Bush. Callahan's original game plan was to run for governor when Colin Frank's term expired, but grabbing a seat in the Senate – without even having to campaign for it – was an opportunity he couldn't pass up.

After the toast, Callahan buttonholed Marty and eased him into a corner where no one could overhear them.

"Do you know anything about that incident with Summerland the other night?" he asked.

"No," Marty lied.

"He's still snooping around, right?"

"I've got it handled. Stop worrying."

Callahan continued. "From everything I've seen, I just can't trust that guy anymore. I can't believe Billy roped me into giving him an exclusive."

"I told you," Marty said. "Stop worrying. This should be the best night of your life. Bite the bullet. Summerland's been a pest, but you need all the exposure you can get."

Marty excused himself, glass in hand, and walked outside to the restaurant's veranda.

"Heard anything?" he asked the man seated alone at the table for two.

"Naw," the man said.

"You know, you really blew it. The cops are crawling all over this thing. How did you know this Forsett woman was going to be at the TV station?"

Terrence Burke scowled. "I didn't. She just showed up while I was keeping tabs on the student. I had to act quickly. But now, I don't think she's our real problem. She's scared to death. If she was going to do anything, we'd know it by now. Besides, she's a blackmailer. She can't go to the cops. I'll bet she was just working you for some easy money. Jansen was our real worry, but not anymore. Besides, Johnny's in."

"You better be right," Marty said.

Back at KBLT, Jack gave Ron editing instructions for the story recap at eleven o'clock. This video version would be much shorter than the early evening story – only a minute in length – allowing four minutes for an exclusive and live interview with Johnny Callahan.

While Ron worked his magic in the edit booth, Jack poured two cups of coffee and walked into the conference room.

"You're safe in here," Jack told the woman. "Can you tell me what you know?"

Julie tensed up and spoke barely above a whisper.

"I've met Johnny Callahan and Marty Frank before," she began. "It was years ago. I was a freshman at Diablo Valley College and they were football players at USC visiting the Bay Area for a game at Cal. I'm living in Reno with my two boys now, and I have tried to put this incident out of my mind. But a couple of weeks ago, mid-April, I think, I read a story in the *Reno Gazette-Journal* about how Callahan was being considered for the U.S. Senate. Ever since, I tracked the story on the web."

"Okay, so you met them years ago."

"Back in the '80s."

"What happened?"

Julie instinctively reached for her cup of coffee with her right hand and winced in pain. She put down the cup and sighed deeply, her hands revealing a slight tremble. "On the night before the game, I went to Berkeley with a couple of friends and ended up at a fraternity party. I got pretty drunk. And we scored some coke. I was pretty stupid back then. I remember leaving the party and walking along Channing Way on the south side of campus. I remember falling and all of a sudden these two guys drove up and offered me a ride. It was stupid, I know, but I got in their car. I was so out of it I didn't know what I was doing."

"You're saying Callahan and Frank picked you up?"

"Yes. They were the ones."

"That doesn't make sense," Jack said. "They had a football game the next day and the entire team had a curfew that night."

"It was them, I'm telling you. I didn't really follow football so I didn't know who they were at first. I got in the back seat and Marty Frank got in with me. Johnny Callahan was driving. I felt terrible and my head was spinning. Frank was all over me. At one point I slapped him in the face and shoved my knee in his crotch. He got real angry and said, 'Do you know who we are?' I didn't, of course. Then he said, 'That's Moses, the famous quarterback.' I remember Callahan turning his head and saying, 'Damn it, Marty, shut up.'

"I remember they drove into the Berkeley hills. I thought I

was going to be raped. Then I passed out and…."

Jack interrupted. "Is that it? They broke curfew on the night before a game?"

"No, let me finish."

Julie told Jack the rest of her incredible story – what she witnessed *after* awaking from her stupor and what she had kept a secret since 1985.

"My God," he said. "You didn't go to the police?"

"No…I couldn't."

"Why not?"

"At the time I didn't know who these guys were. I couldn't identify them and I had absolutely no credibility. I had been so drunk I passed out, and…and…I had drugs in my system. I also was pretty scared."

"Then a couple of weeks ago, it all came back to me when I read that Callahan was nicknamed Moses and that he was going to be a U.S. Senator. I decided to, you know, get them to help me out financially."

"You were blackmailing them?"

"Look, I'm not proud of what I did, but I'm desperate. My job is crap and I've had two kids to take care of by myself ever since I split with my husband. I need the money, so I asked them for $200,000. Even after some guy shot at me at the mail drop I couldn't go to the cops and tell them I was trying to extort $200,000."

It was nearly ten o'clock. Jack had to get to the Capitol soon for his live interview with Callahan. He picked up the phone and started to dial Jimmy Johnson at home. He wanted to tell the news director about Julie's story, how all the pieces were fitting together. Before he finished dialing, he stopped, paused for a second, then hung up. No, he thought to himself. I've been down this road before.

Ron popped his head in the door of the conference room. "We've gotta go," he said. "Give me a minute, will you?" Jack responded. "I'll be right there."

Jack looked at Julie but said nothing, staring at her for several seconds. He grabbed the phone and called Karen who was working late at the office packing Callahan's records and mementos. "Karen, it's Jack. I need your help."

Forty-Four

KBLT, like most television stations, tended to put its youngest and least seasoned reporters and photographers on the night shift. In most cases, management didn't like to pay four hours of overtime to a higher-paid dayside staffer. But Jack had talked the eleven o'clock news producer into letting Ron Middleton finish the story the two of them had been working on for weeks.

Jack had cringed at the thought of a rookie photographer — one he barely knew — handling an assignment that would take nuance and courage. This wasn't going to be a run-of-the-mill interview. He was glad to have his trusty sidekick with him.

Shortly after nine o'clock, an engineer had been dispatched to the Capitol to set up the microwave link to the station from the Assembly speaker's office. The signal would be sent from the camera in the speaker's office, out a west-facing window to the live truck, which would be parked on Tenth Street. The transmitter on the truck would beam the signal due north to a receiver fixed to the station's transmitting tower behind the studios. The signal then would be downlinked to enable a live picture from the Capitol.

Middleton wanted to leave for the speaker's office by ten o'clock to set up the camera and lights and to test the signal. About ten minutes before Middleton was set to leave, Jack grabbed the photographer by the arm and escorted him into an empty edit booth. He closed the door so no one could hear.

"Ron," he said, "after tonight we'll either be heroes or we'll be looking for new jobs. You're the only one I trust to help me pull this off."

Forty-Five

A few minutes after ten, Jack and Ron pulled up on Tenth Street immediately behind the live truck. A station engineer, sitting in the driver's seat, gave Jack a quick thumbs up, telling him that they had a clear signal for the live interview. Jack looked up to the second floor of the Capitol and noticed that lights were on in the Assembly speaker's suite of offices. Jack carried a lightweight metal tripod, while Ron toted a camera and light kit. A slight woman, dressed in jeans, a tee shirt and a baseball cap, carried a utility bag. They hiked to the north entrance of the building, rang a buzzer and waited for a California Highway Patrol officer to let them in.

"Hiya, Jack," the officer said. "We got word you're heading up to Speaker Callahan's office."

"Yeah, Charlie," Jack replied. Jack had spent so much time at the Capitol, he was on a first-name basis with much of the security force. "We should be out of there by 11:20 or so."

The door to the speaker's office was propped open and a dozen cardboard boxes of papers and books were piled in the hallway. A few members of Callahan's staff were working late and cleaning out the office.

With Middleton trailing behind, Jack walked past the receptionist's desk and waited for someone to escort him into the speaker's inner office. He exchanged greetings with Billy Galster and the three of them started to lug the camera gear into the office. Just then, about 20 feet away, Jack saw Karen walking to the hallway carrying a cardboard box to add to the pile. The two exchanged glances but said nothing. Imperceptibly, Karen nodded at Jack and slipped into a back office. Julie Forsett followed her. Karen then dialed Marty's cell phone.

Jack had arranged two chairs for the interview, purposely having Callahan sitting in front of a shelf full of law books. The rich blue book covers made a perfect background.

At 10:58, Callahan walked into the room, tightening his dark blue tie against a crisp white shirt. The speaker knew his way around a television studio and had shaved after dinner. A thin layer of powder took the shine off his forehead.

Jack thought Callahan appeared relaxed and without stress, despite the events of the past several days. He wondered how much Callahan knew of his investigation. He couldn't read anything from Callahan's demeanor.

"Hello, Jack," Callahan said as he sat down in the chair and fitted a small lapel microphone on his suit jacket. "Nice to see you." Jack felt relieved. At least he didn't call me an asshole, he thought.

In fact, Callahan seethed when he thought of Summerland's betrayal, and he had to be talked into sitting down for this interview. Still, he didn't let his feelings show.

"Sam tells me you told him you were turning down the job offer," Callahan said. "I'm sorry it didn't work out. I think you would have been a great asset to my staff."

"It was a generous offer, but I just felt it wasn't right for me at this time," Jack said, offering no hint that he continued to investigate the mysterious events of recent days.

Jack fumbled with his lapel microphone and had difficulty looking directly at Callahan. He wondered if Callahan noticed. Does he suspect something?

"Mr. Speaker…uh, Senator, I guess I should say. Thanks for doing this interview with us. We appreciate it."

"My pleasure. Will you be sending this to your NBC affiliates throughout California?" Callahan asked. Already, he was thinking ahead to the following year when he'd have to stand for election.

"I'm sure we will," Jack responded, taking a quick peek at a small television monitor that had been placed in front of him. "We're on the air now with a couple of unrelated stories, then they'll introduce a pre-packaged story I edited this evening. It wraps up the day's events. Then, we'll be coming here live."

"Got it," Callahan said.

Through his earpiece, Jack heard himself narrating the one-minute lead-in to the interview – a cut-down story that included coverage of Callahan's background, the news conference and comments from Governor Frank and President Vernon. Ten seconds before the end of the story, the eleven o'clock news producer whispered in his ear, "Stand by."

Jack took a deep breath, and glanced one more time at his notes. He quickly looked around the room. It was just Jack, Ron Middleton, the speaker and Galster.

Jack swiveled his chair to look directly at the camera. "Go," said the producer into Jack's right ear.

The camera was focused on a two-shot, showing both Jack and Callahan sitting a few feet apart. "We're live now with Assembly Speaker Callahan at his Capitol office."

Middleton tightened the camera angle, zooming into Callahan and excluding the reporter.

"First of all, congratulations on your appointment. Tell us about your legislative agenda in the Senate, and particularly your first order of business."

"Well, Jack," Callahan began, "at the outset I want to thank Governor Frank for showing enough faith in me to make this appointment. My first order of business is to figure out where they've put the men's room." Callahan chuckled.

"I'm kidding, of course, but I know those who govern best are those who understand the process. I suppose I could tell you that I'm going to charge into Washington and push a tax cut proposal my first day on the job. But that would be foolish. I've got to learn the ropes and study mounds of briefing papers – on Social Security, for example, the war on terror, our relationship with North Korea, and all sorts of other issues. And I don't know yet what committees I'll be assigned to. Remember, this isn't a job for which I prepared and prepped. It's all rather sudden."

Jack tried to pin down Callahan on one of the most divisive issues before the Senate. "As you know, a number of Senate Democrats, including Senator Fitzpatrick here in California and at least one Republican, have announced their opposition to President Vernon's nomination of Oklahoma Judge Rupert Zellerbach to the U.S. Supreme Court. A Senate vote is scheduled in about a week. How are you leaning on this issue?"

"Again," Callahan warned, "I can honestly say I'm not prepared to answer that question because my appointment is so sudden. I will say that from what I've read, Judge Zellerbach will bring the integrity, judicial temperament and intellect that are required for membership on the Supreme Court."

Callahan played dodgeball with a few other questions before Jack wrapped up the interview with a familiar, "Back to you, Conrad." Galster left the room, and Jack thanked Callahan again for the interview, then hurriedly scanned the room. He was waiting for someone and thought perhaps his grand plan was falling apart.

Middleton glanced at Jack briefly, arching his eyebrows as if he, too, was waiting for something to happen. He unclipped Callahan's microphone, wrapped up a couple of cables and disconnected one of the portable light standards. Nonchalantly, he flipped a small switch in back of the camera that turned off the red tally light on top of the camera. By doing so, the camera could be operated without anyone realizing it. Unlike old film cameras, live cameras made no perceptible noise when operating. He left the camera on its tripod and hit the button widening the camera angle to include a view of the entire office. Then he flipped a small switch that activated the shotgun microphone affixed to the top of the camera.

"I'm going to the truck," Middleton told Jack, loud enough for Callahan to overhear. "I'll be back in a minute and tear down the rest of this stuff." The camera was now on autopilot. Without a cameraman, it was sending audio and video directly to the truck. A video tape recorder in the truck recorded everything.

For about two minutes, Callahan and Jack made small talk and discussed the speaker's upcoming trip to Washington.

Almost on cue, Marty Frank and Terrence Burke burst into the office. Karen had done her job perfectly, Jack thought. Marty used her as a spy; Jack made her a double agent.

Jack had told Karen to call Marty and tell him that Jack had a witness to what he and Callahan had done in the Berkeley hills years ago. Sure enough, Marty took the bait. And look who he brought with him – that scarred, ugly son-of-a-bitch who shot Julie Forsett outside the studio and chased him into the Capitol parking garage.

Callahan was startled. "What's going on here," he said directly to Frank. He turned to Burke, "And who the hell are you?"

"I'm protecting your career, Senator Callahan," Burke said.

Callahan was confused. "What are you talking about?" He turned to Marty. "Marty, what is this?"

Marty Frank said nothing and stared directly at Jack. Karen, listening at the door entrance, her heart pounding wildly, slowly backed out of the sight.

"I think I can explain everything," Jack said, purposely turning slightly to face the camera and shotgun microphone.

Jack continued. "Do you remember November 9, 1985? You and Marty Frank were in Berkeley that day for a football game against Cal. The night before the game, you and Marty broke curfew, drank a few beers and drove around the Berkeley hills with your sister's car."

Callahan admitted nothing. "What are you talking about?"

"You got drunk, broke curfew, then the two of you played the worst games of your lives the next day."

"Every football player has a bad day sometimes."

Jack turned toward the door. "Julie?"

From the other side of the door, Karen escorted Julie Forsett into the office. Julie had an angry look on her face. She took off her cap and stared intently at Johnny Callahan.

"Who are you?" Callahan asked.

"My name is Julie Forsett. I was in your car that night. You thought I had passed out in your back seat. You thought I slept through the whole thing."

Recognition swiftly swept over Callahan. She knows. "Ohmigod," Callahan said in a low voice. "Ohmigod." The shotgun microphone picked up everything he said.

"You were driving," Julie continued, her voice quivering, "and I was in the back seat with your buddy. I had passed out for awhile, but when I awoke, the car was parked on the side of the road. I was dazed at first but I remember you and Marty Frank arguing, then Frank getting out the car. I quietly lifted my head enough to see Frank drag a woman into the bushes. You ran her down and your buddy hid the body. I was so scared I put my head down again and pretended I was still unconscious, but I saw it all, you bastard."

Jack interjected. "Her name was Elizabeth Antonia Cohen. She was a student at Cal. Her friends called her Toni."

Callahan and Frank were stunned and speechless, but Terrence Burke took action. He reached into his inside coat pocket and pulled out his nine millimeter Beretta, pointing it alternately at Jack and Julie. Karen stood at the doorway shaking and frightened.

Jack planned on this convergence of characters. That's the trap he set with Karen's help. He didn't figure on the gun. Metal detectors on the first floor guarded against outsiders bringing weapons into the Capitol, a response to the 9/11 terrorist attacks. Then he remembered. Burke must have come in with Marty through the basement entrance bypassing metal detectors. Besides, Frank was the governor's son who also happened to be a well-known friend of the speaker.

Frank probably drove up to the kiosk in the driveway leading to the Capitol basement, waved his access card to raise the guardrail. Once close to the basement, the metal garage door would open automatically. Jack figured the cops probably gave Marty – and Burke, his passenger – swift access to the basement. He figured they'd use a mirror to inspect the bottom of Marty's car, but they might not have checked his passenger for weapons.

Burke continued to wave his gun, unsure what to do next. The camera continued to record everything.

While events unfolded in the second-floor speaker's office, Middleton made his way out of the Capitol to the live truck parked on the street. He watched the stunning developments on a small monitor in the truck and told the operator to keep the antenna upright. Middleton called the station and got the eleven o'clock news producer on the line. "Cassie, are you watching your monitors? Look what's going on in the speaker's office. You need to punch this up live. Now."

The newscast was in a commercial break. The owner of a Folsom car dealership hawked Hummers. Cassie squinted at the bank of small black and white monitors. She instantly recognized Jack Summerland and focused on the Capitol confrontation.

"Tom, quick," she barked, "give me audio on number three – the live cam." Within seconds, she knew Middleton was right. Instead of trying to explain through an earpiece to her anchor team what was happening, Cassie Bateman ran out of the control room, through a heavy metal door and into the studio.

"Something's going on in the speaker's office involving Jack, Johnny Callahan and a few other people. We have a live feed. One person has a gun," she said breathlessly. "That's all I know. Conrad, we're going live with it out of the break. Ad lib something. Then we'll take the feed live. Stand by."

"We're going now to breaking news at the Capitol," Dalton told viewers after the break. "We don't have information as to exactly what is happening, but we do know that our reporter Jack Summerland and Assembly Speaker Johnny Callahan are involved in some sort of disturbance. What you are about to see is a live feed from Callahan's Capitol office."

The first words that viewers heard were from Callahan. "Okay, okay," he said, not realizing his words were being fed live throughout Northern California. "I… I… I… we did break curfew," he stammered.

"Shut up!" Marty yelled. "Shut up!"

Callahan exhaled deeply. "It's out now. I want to get this off my chest. I borrowed my sister's car to go driving up in the hills. I was behind the wheel and I hit the girl. I swear it wasn't my fault. She was running across the road. She came from out of nowhere." He turned to Marty. "Marty, you tell him. It wasn't my fault."

"What happened next?" Jack asked.

"I… I was very upset," Callahan continued.

"I had a few beers and shouldn't have been driving. Marty told me to stay in the car while he looked at the girl. He came back a few minutes later to say he couldn't save her with CPR. He said she had died."

Marty still said nothing as an ashen Callahan, his lips trembling, related how he panicked that night in the Berkeley hills. "I was scared. I didn't know what to do. Look, I had planned to play a few years of pro ball then become a lawyer. We knew that if this ever came out we could end up in prison and our careers would be over. After Marty got back into the car, I looked around and saw no one, so I just gassed the car and we drove on."

Callahan now seemed to be in shock. "I, I killed this girl and was more worried about myself. I was young and foolish. I'm so sorry. I'm so sorry."

Jack turned to Marty. "Why don't you tell us what really happened?"

Marty's jaw dropped. He exhaled deeply. "Well, I suppose this vulture reporter has the whole story, so I might as well tell you. The girl did run across the road and you smacked right into her. But you didn't kill her."

"What?" said an astonished Callahan.

"You were such a weenie. You started freaking out. While you were in the car, I went to look her over. She was groggy, but alive. She accused us of being drunk and running her over. I knew we couldn't let her identify us. We'd be ruined if she lived to talk. So, while you had your head buried in your hands in the car, I made sure she'd never be a problem for us."

Jack had backed to the edge of the office, so that he wouldn't block the camera shot of Callahan and Frank revealing their crime.

Marty continued. "I put my hands around her throat and I squeezed, gently at first, then with more pressure. After she died, I dragged her body to the side of the road, pushed her down a small hill and covered her up with some dead leaves."

Callahan looked directly at Marty. "You mean… you mean I didn't kill that girl? You mean ever since then you've let me believe that I killed that girl? I was taking care of you, giving you jobs all these years, protecting you because I thought you were protecting me. Now you tell me that *you* killed the girl and I helped you cover it up?"

"The question now is what are we going to do about it?" Marty said. "Apparently, there were two witnesses – an FBI agent who was banging this girl and our drunk friend over here."

Marty smiled and looked in Burke's direction. "We know one witness can't testify against us because he's dead. I took care of that myself."

As the camera continued to roll silently, Jack tried to get Marty on the record.

"What do you mean?" he asked.

"Thanks to your girlfriend I knew you had set up a meeting with this guy at a bar. While you were stuck covering the vice president, I went to the bar ahead of time and convinced this guy I was with you. I told him you wanted to meet him at the station. When I held a knife to his throat he told me everything. Do I need to draw you a picture as to why this guy ended up like swiss cheese dumped in the Sacramento River?"

"You should know I have a statement from the agent explaining everything he saw back in '85," Jack said.

"Sorry, but that won't work," Marty shot back. "He certainly can't be cross examined in court, so his statement isn't worth the paper it's written on. And the only other witness was a junkie trying to blackmail a U.S. Senator. Some witness she'll be."

Jack wanted to tell everyone that the entire confession was being recorded, but he didn't want to force Burke to take any action.

Looking directly at Callahan, Marty said, "I know I can keep my mouth shut, and I trust Mr. Burke to keep quiet. If you can, too, then we're home free. What do you suggest we do about our reporter friend and the junkie?"

An astonished Conrad Dalton watched everything unfold on a monitor attached to the anchor desk. "You are watching a live feed from Assembly Speaker Johnny Callahan's office," he told a hundred thousand stunned late-night Northern California viewers.

Unseen in the anteroom adjacent to the speaker's office,

Karen gingerly slipped off her shoes and tip-toed backwards as quietly as possible. She made her way to her desk and reached under the middle drawer, fumbling for the silent panic button. Every legislator and key staff had panic buttons at their desks in case of intruders. It usually took only seconds for armed officers to swarm the office.

"Mr. Burke," Marty said, "you are paid handsomely for your work. May I suggest you do your job and make sure our reporter friend has covered his last story, and take care of the junkie, too."

"With pleasure," said Burke, grinning.

"No," yelled Callahan. He grabbed a paperweight from his desk and flung it at Burke. A bullet discharged from the gun missing its mark. The bullet lodged in the wall. Julie dropped to the floor and crawled for cover against a bookcase. Instinctively, Burke pivoted slightly to his right and fired the gun again in the direction of the thrown object.

Callahan fell to the floor, his left thigh bleeding profusely. Burke raised the gun and started to aim it at Jack when three state police officers and two Assembly sergeants-at-arms burst through the office responding to Karen's silent alarm. The first officer through the door shouted, "Drop the gun, drop the gun, drop the gun!" A second officer rushed to Burke, forced him to spread-eagle against the wall and had him handcuffed in a matter of seconds. The third officer, not knowing what exactly was happening, told both Jack and Marty to raise their hands while Callahan writhed in pain on the floor.

Back at the studio, Conrad Dalton came back on the air. "Ladies and gentlemen, you are watching an extended Action 4 newscast – a live broadcast from Assembly Speaker Johnny Callahan's office. To recap, Callahan – who was appointed to the U.S. Senate earlier today – has admitted he was driving a car involved in a hit and run accident decades ago when he was a student. Governor Frank's son, Marty, on camera admitted to a murder. It appears Speaker Callahan has been shot in the leg by an unknown assailant, who also tried to kill our political reporter, Jack Summerland. That's all we know right now. We'll have updates as available and complete details during our early morning broadcast tomorrow and on KBLT.com. For the time being, we join the *Tonight Show* in progress."

Forty-Six

Forty-Six

Jack splashed cold water on his face. It was 3:50 a.m. He stifled a yawn, then turned on the hot water and pulled a razor and shaving cream from a small locker in KBLT's "Green Room" a few feet from the entrance to Studio B. After a quick shave, Jack applied a coat of TV9 makeup.

"Ten minutes," yelled the morning news producer. "Ten minutes."

Jack hadn't slept all night. After the fracas at Speaker Callahan's office the night before, he edited a webcast story and news updates that aired periodically throughout the night and early morning hours. The station's news director, Jimmy Johnson, had seen the bizarre events unfold live on the eleven o'clock news and rushed to the station to supervise overnight and morning coverage.

Jack was beginning to get one of those headaches you get

when you drink too much coffee and don't get enough sleep. It felt like a giant tumor behind his left ear. Jack popped a few more aspirins in his mouth. Just a few more hours, he figured. "Just get me through this day," he said to himself as he knotted his tie and smoothed his trusty blue blazer.

A camera had been set up in the middle of the newsroom. Master Control had established connections with NBC in New York. Jack was about to hit the big time – a live report for the *Today Show*, which aired at seven o'clock eastern time, four o'clock in California.

Standing in the middle of a well-lighted but nearly empty newsroom, Jack affixed what reporters affectionately called a "peanut" in his right ear, allowing him to hear audio from the studio. An oversized KBLT banner could be seen over his left shoulder. He clipped a microphone on his lapel and waited for his cue.

The large clock on the newsroom wall read 4:05. The *Today Show* anchor had teased Jack's story with a 30-second version during its news roundup at the top of the hour. The network gave him five minutes for his in-depth wrap-up, convinced that the story was too bizarre and visual to cut.

"As we reported earlier, a story of murder and political intrigue in California with U.S. Senate-designate Johnny Callahan implicated in a decades-old homicide. Jack Summerland of our Sacramento affiliate KBLT broke this story and has an exclusive live report. Jack?"

Summerland on camera

California Assembly Speaker Johnny Callahan had everything going for him. He had just been appointed to the U.S. Senate to fill the seat vacated by the late Bernie Edelstein.

But this morning, Callahan is in police custody after a KBLT investigation found that Callahan was involved in the 1985 death of a young University of California, Berkeley, student. That investigation culminated in gunfire and several arrests late last night at the state Capitol.

Video – Callahan/Frank argument

This was the scene last night in Callahan's Capitol office. With our camera feeding live images to shocked viewers, Callahan and Marty Frank — the son of Governor Colin Frank and a long-time Callahan friend — started arguing about a 1985 drunken joyride in the Berkeley hills in which a 22-year-old student was hit while Callahan was driving.

Video/Audio – Marty Frank

"You started freaking out. While you were in the car, I went to look her over. She was groggy, but alive...I knew we couldn't let her identify us. We'd be ruined if she lived to talk. So, while you had your head buried in your hands in the car, I made sure she'd never be a problem for us...I put my hands around her throat and I squeezed, gently at first, then with more pressure. After she died, I dragged her body to the side of the road, pushed her down a small hill and covered her up with some dead leaves."

Video/Audio – Burke firing gun twice, hitting Callahan with the second bullet

Video/Audio – State police officer

"Drop the gun, drop the gun, drop the gun!"

Video — Callahan being taken into custody

Callahan was wounded in the left thigh during the Capitol melee. He was taken into custody. Police say he will be charged with complicity in the decades-old murder.

Video — Frank being placed in police car

Police say Frank will be charged with the murders of the student — Elizabeth Antonia Cohen — and former FBI Agent Carl Jansen, a witness to the Berkeley crime.

Video — Burke being placed in police car

Police also took into custody a man identified as Terrence Burke. Police have charged Burke with the attempted murder of a second witness to the Berkeley killing, identified as Julie Forsett, a former Californian now living in Reno.

Video — Julie Forsett

Ms. Forsett was a young college student back in 1985. She witnessed Frank dispose of the body.

Video — Jansen document

According to a statement by Jansen — released to KBLT after Jansen's death — Jansen was an FBI agent on leave in Berkeley to research a book and teach criminology.

Video — Picture of Cohen from Cal yearbook

Jansen said he and Ms. Cohen — one of his students —

were having an affair and argued one night at his rented home in the Berkeley hills.

Video – Close-up of Jansen document

According to Jansen's statement, Ms. Cohen ran into the street where she was struck by a car driven by Callahan.

Both Callahan and Frank were in Berkeley as members of the USC football team, which played the University of California the following day. They had broken curfew and drove a car belonging to Callahan's sister's into the Berkeley hills.

Video – Callahan and Frank

Jansen said in his statement that he witnessed the accident but couldn't identify the two football players at the time because he had fallen down and hit his head on a rock. Jansen said he called Berkeley police but only was able to provide a vague description of the hit and run driver.

Video – Photos of Callahan in USC football uniform

Only recently, Jansen said, did he recognize Callahan as the driver of the car. He had seen old photos of the former football star accompany news reports of his likely appointment to the Senate. One headline referred to Callahan as "Moses."

Video – 1985 USC/UCLA football game footage

Jansen said he suddenly remembered that after the accident, the car's passenger used the same unique nickname.

Julie Forsett said she also heard a reference to "Moses" that night but didn't make the connection to Callahan until she read a recent article about his playing days at USC.

Video – Jansen photo

Jansen acknowledged that once he realized that Callahan was involved in Ms. Cohen's murder he tried to ruin the Assembly speaker's political career.

Video – *Starlight* front page

Jansen admitted he planted a phony story in a tabloid newspaper…and tried to entice Callahan to take a bribe. Both efforts failed.

Video – Jansen murder scene

Moments before a scheduled meeting with KBLT, Jansen was stabbed to death. His body was found in the Sacramento River.

Video – Photos of Callahan and Frank

The Callahan secret had been kept under wraps as the fast-rising politician — with Marty Frank at his side — became a national figure with a future that political analysts said was limitless.

Summerland on camera

There had been a vague hint that Callahan and Frank were involved in something that Friday night in 1985.

The following day their USC football team lost to Cal 14-6 in what one sports columnist called the "upset of the cen-

> tury." Callahan and Frank had the worst days of their football careers.
>
> After the game — and only 17 hours after Ms. Cohen's death — Callahan told reporters he was distracted during the game. In his words..."I had a lot on my mind besides football."
>
> Reporting live from Sacramento, this is Jack Summerland. Back to you in New York.

Jack pulled off his lapel microphone. He was drained. From the other side of the newsroom he heard applause from the handful of news employees who work the early morning shift. Jimmy Johnson, smiling broadly, led the way.

"Hey Jack," someone yelled from the assignment bullpen. "You've got AP on line one."

"Put them on hold, will you?" Jack said.

Jack walked into a conference room off the newsroom floor. Waiting to interview him were two police officers. Karen sat in the corner.

Karen smiled broadly, a look of relief on her face. "You were wonderful, absolutely wonderful," she told Jack.

Jack turned to the officers. "Give me a minute, okay?"

Jack then grabbed Karen's hand and led her to his desk in the newsroom. "I couldn't have done it without your help. You made it happen."

"I'm so sorry I ever doubted you," Karen answered. "Can you ever forgive me?" Jack didn't hesitate. "Why don't we go out for breakfast. We have a lot of catching up to do."